THE [ ]
WITH[ ]

Elizabeth shivered in the darkness, deeply aware of Justin standing beside her. He smelled of woodsmoke and rainwater and pine. And his heart was pounding as fiercely as her own.

"It's overwhelming, isn't it?" Justin murmured, referring to the vast dark forest surrounding them. He put his arm around her.

"Hmm, yes," Elizabeth agreed, not thinking of the woods at all. Invisible currents danced in the air, and she sighed aloud.

Justin turned to gaze questioningly at her in the dim light. "Elizabeth?" Then, as if reading the desire in her eyes, he enfolded her in the warmth of his embrace....

ABOUT THE AUTHOR

Gail Hamilton grew up in a small rural community in southern Ontario and later attended university in Toronto. Armed with an Honours B.A., Gail taught high school English for one year. Realizing that she wanted to rewrite all her students' essays, she soon decided a career change was in order. Seven published romances later, it's obvious that Gail's taken the right path!

Gail Hamilton
WHAT COMES NATURALLY

Harlequin Books

TORONTO • NEW YORK • LONDON
AMSTERDAM • PARIS • SYDNEY • HAMBURG
STOCKHOLM • ATHENS • TOKYO • MILAN

Published May 1987

First printing March 1987

ISBN 0-373-70260-4

Printed in Canada

CHAPTER ONE

"GO FOR IT, Trudy! Now!"

Elizabeth Wright's cinnamon-colored Rolls, purring toward a high-profile charity benefit at Roy Thomson Hall, dropped its stately pace, jumped two lanes and halted precipitously. A smoke-windowed Cadillac was forced into the rift created ahead. When the Cadillac tried to fall back, the Rolls did the same, weaving a skillful duel that finally forced the Cadillac to pull up first in front of the Hall, a piece of modern architecture near Toronto's waterfront that resembled nothing so much as an overturned cut-glass salad bowl, in Elizabeth's view.

Inside the Rolls, Elizabeth laughed softly and complimented her chauffeur, who was an old hand at this. Elizabeth's companion for the evening, Kevin Longfield III, frowned.

"What'd you do that for? We could have beaten Archer easily."

In Kevin's more simple world, getting there first was the name of the game. Elizabeth socked him with her devilish grin, so different from the sweet public smile that was pasted on a million cosmetics labels.

"Strategy, my boy. You'll see."

Kevin was one of the most desirable—not to mention solvent—escorts in the city. He had a long, elegant demeanor and an eye for the main chance—a family trait that had kept the Longfields awash in money for three generations. This Longfield had felt somewhat cut off out at the Great Lakes, where he'd been working in the family's shipping business, and had been overjoyed at the chance to grab the spotlight on the arm of a sizzling entrepreneur in the cosmetics world. Now he wondered what he was in for.

Baffled, he took in the famous mass of honey-colored hair, the keen profile and the forest of stiffened gold tulle, which clung, by some unimaginable feat of engineering, to the lithe, scrupulously exercised body. Though she appeared relaxed, spots of color reinforced the blusher on Elizabeth's cheeks. Her every scrap of attention was fixed on the Cadillac until, emptied of its passenger, it pulled away. As always, the presence of Justin Archer roused her the way a whiff of gunpowder stirred a warhorse. Kevin was likely to be forgotten until she had won the first skirmish of the evening.

Her timing was exact. Elizabeth emerged grandly, pausing with Kevin just long enough to let the rumor of her presence travel ahead of her. Then she swept in through the doors, a moving sunburst of gold sequins and glittering tulle that caused all gazes to swivel from previous arrivals to her direction, as if by telekinetic force. Justin Archer's appearance just ahead of her had conveniently gathered photographers and officials into a knot by the door. Imposing as he was in his black tuxedo and white ruffled shirt, he could not compete with Elizabeth's dramatic entrance.

"Wonderful," breathed Kevin, smiling with all his might for the photographs that were certain to be in the newspaper the following day. He couldn't wait to visit his father's office, where the executives would survey him with newly speculative stares.

Elizabeth favored the waiting spectators with the same lovely smile that adorned her products. She had a way of looking casual that made one think of a queen moving among equals. No hint of the energetic scramble for entry position betrayed itself in the languid grace with which she flowed forward in her majestic gown. She had accomplished exactly what she had set out to do. She had, for the moment, stolen the show.

Justin Archer and Elizabeth Wright detested each other—and the whole world knew it. Strong feelings between them had begun the moment Elizabeth had walked into Archer Beauty Enterprises as an eager-eyed young chemist, and they'd intensified when, a mere eight months later, she had stormed out, declaring that the arrogant crown prince could stuff his job because she intended to show them all.

Further details of the altercation had never been unearthed despite the relentless digging of the gossip columnists. However, Elizabeth kept her promise. She successfully developed her own line of beauty products in just six years and defiantly stamped her face and name on every label. Now her company was big enough to rival Justin's own, and the ensuing battle was followed with the same relish the initial one had been.

Elizabeth and Justin were regularly invited to the same gala events, gallery openings and charity junkets, partly because publicity-hungry hosts hoped that the silken control would someday slip and they would go for each other's throats. Such expectations were always disappointed. Elizabeth and Justin hid their animosity behind a thick veil of courtesy. The knock-down, drag-out fights were assigned to their advertising agencies, the subtle innuendo, gleeful put-downs and outright scorn heaped upon each other's products limited only by the shrieks of their respective legal counsel.

"And tell me, Ms Wright, how do you feel about your chances of winning the Albright Award tonight? Sources say your name is neck and neck with that of Mr. Archer?"

A young reporter, still learning her trade on the society circuit, had elbowed her way to Elizabeth, notebook in hand.

Elizabeth had smiled to herself for hours, imagining the climax of the evening. For outstanding business achievement, the Albright had to be hers. How delightful to publicly stomp on the instep of Justin Archer without even twitching her toes!

Conversation dropped perceptibly within a five-yard radius. Elizabeth's lids lowered slightly and her smile grew even sweeter. The earnest reporter was obviously hoping for an indiscreet jab at Justin or a betraying statement of how much Elizabeth wanted the Albright.

"I trust the wisdom of the judges in placing the award where it is most deserved," Elizabeth replied with a bland and proper modesty completely belied by the sparkle in her eyes. "My heartfelt congratulations will go out to the winner, whoever he or she may be."

Inside, she was grinning. By the consensus of her peers, the Albright would stamp her company the up-and-comer of the year. Contracts, financing, high-flying distribution deals—all would soon be hers for the snap of her fingers. To win would mean Elizabeth had finally made it. Her rising star would outshine Justin's at long last!

She began her progress across the pearl-colored carpet of the lobby under the immense curving glass roof. The reporter scurried after her.

"But how will you feel, Ms Wright, should the Albright go to Mr. Archer?"

Like ripping his jugular out!

Elizabeth smiled even wider, full of empathy for the young woman who was trying so hard. She almost wished she could spill the beans but proprieties had to be observed.

"Why, I shall congratulate Mr. Archer on his good fortune," she replied dryly. "It's not every day he manages such a piece of luck."

Only then did she fling back a glance, cementing her small victory. As usual, Justin stood immovable amidst the spectators, regarding her with that insufferable quirk of the brow that seemed to say, "Now that you've made your splash, we'll get back to normal here."

She knew that Justin was used to being the eye of the hurricane. It pleased her that she'd taken some attention away from him—if only for a few moments. He lounged as if he expected the Albright to leap gratefully by itself into his lap.

Arrogant wretch! ranted the inevitable small voice at the back of her mind. *Born with a silver spoon, everything easy. Damned ego bigger than a weather balloon!*

Down, girl! He's hardly worth getting hot under the collar!

Not that she wore a collar...or sleeves or even straps. Her dress began deep under her right arm and rose in a dramatic asymmetrical slant to a flamelike point atop her breasts. The back of the dress had a similar effect. A sweep of bare white shoulder separated the two points, which ought to have continued into a connection but didn't. This maddening defiance of gravity drew constant attention.

She had chosen the gown deliberately and circulated in it to very good effect with Kevin at her side. Kevin, in his bony way, was quite handsome, especially when swelled to his full height. He was obviously proud to be Elizabeth's escort and was behaving with the polished manners the Longfields were known for. Elizabeth flicked him periodic glances of amusement. How long would his assurance have held up, she wondered, had he encountered her a dozen years ago, rough as a burr and clawing her way out of back-street urban poverty?

Massive contributions for tickets had entitled them to front-row-orchestra seats for the celebrity-studded show, the profits from which were to go to charity. Elizabeth was famous for her support of certain causes, though no one guessed it was because she knew firsthand how it was to be empty of stomach and desperate to scrape up the rent for a freezing, roach-ridden room. The moment she had acquired her first job at Justin Archer's, she had sealed away her past. It had never pursued her. She was another person now, and as far as she was concerned, no one in her present glittering world had to know whence she had come. She settled in to enjoy the entertainment, but she had no sooner slipped her evening bag down beside her than an usher stopped in front of her, tickets in his hand.

"Right here, sir."

Drat! Justin had been seated right next to her. Some wag at the box office, no doubt!

"Good evening, Elizabeth," intoned the all-too-familiar voice. "We seem to be sharing the row."

She accorded Justin a faintly bored look but did not deign to rise to the smugness in his voice. The years had not blotted out the memory of that mouth inches from her own, the hard body trapping hers against the white laboratory wall. Nor would she forget that furious voice saying, "Elizabeth, you'll keep working for me or I'll see you work for no one in this business, ever!"

Oh, yes, the memory lived. And with each day of her success, each dollar of profit, she shoved that memory back down his throat, savoring every minute.

A lazy smile curled along her lips.

"Hello, Justin. I see you've brought Maria again."

Her tone implied that it was too bad the poor fellow had to press his employees into extracurricular service. Never mind that Maria was his top cosmetics model and dizzyingly beautiful in a mauve silk-mousseline creation with tulips at the hem. Justin had been seen with Maria a number of times lately, causing Elizabeth to wonder just how far things had gone. Poor Maria. Didn't she know Justin had absolutely no scruples about getting maximum use from his staff?

Justin smiled back, accenting the slashing cheekbones mentioned admiringly in every fluff piece about the cosmetics tycoons. He was supposed to have a smattering of native blood—a load of hogwash, if Elizabeth had ever heard any.

"Maria honors me," he returned with enough veiled irony to indicate a high opinion of his own attractive-

ness. "And who is your fortunate companion tonight?"

Kevin stood up, ever ready to fight in this old war he
didn't understand. He did Elizabeth proud, holding
his own in the matter of bearing. That and a respect-
able bank account were all Elizabeth asked of any date
brought near Justin.

The bare amenities taken care of, they all sat down,
Maria in the hot seat between Elizabeth and Justin.
Elizabeth turned her attention back to the stage,
though her peripheral vision allowed her to see long
legs stretching on the other side of Maria's seat, and
lean hands, brown from the Caribbean sun or the
tanning studio, resting inches from Maria's arm.

Gamely retaining her grace, Maria leafed through
her program until her hand stilled. The wag in the office had been at it again. The large advertisement that
Elizabeth had placed in the program had been posi-
tioned next to Justin's on the opposing page. Justin's
featured Maria using Justin's product to rinse away
pollen-filled grime from the day—a clear reference to
Elizabeth Wright's Petal Pollen for the skin. Elizabeth's ad showed a woman who looked just enough
like Maria to point out the connection, struggling out
of a chemical spill to the safety of a flowery island
sprinkled with bottles of Wright's Natural Cucumber
Cleanser. She might as well have proclaimed in the
headline that Archer Inc. turned your face into a
chemical mess.

Elizabeth swallowed back glee. She had to give Ag-
gie at the ad agency a bonus. Too bad Maria's head
was blocking whatever discomfiture Justin was showing. Elizabeth relaxed in her seat. She could enjoy the

show even with Justin so near. The Albright was as good as on her mantel.

"Here we go," exclaimed Kevin as the lights dimmed. He slipped his hand over Elizabeth's on the arm of the seat—the part Justin could see. As each performer came and went, the hand grew warmer and damper. But it lost its grip altogether as the emcee announced the unexpected climax of the show.

"Ladies and gentlemen," the man cried with great excitement, "a surprise appearance, a wonderful last-moment addition to our program. Direct from California, Toronto's own success story, Miss Diana Daniels!"

There was a moment of startled silence, then wild applause. Diana Daniels was Toronto's pride, a hometown girl whose prodigious talents had sprung her to the peak of stardust and glitter. Yet she'd never forgotten her roots, and she twisted the busiest schedule to perform at home whenever she could.

Elizabeth was as dazzled as everyone else. Diana was big time, a great actress and, tonight, a singer crooning a smoky torch song that melted the audience into their seats. Elizabeth melted, too, but she also watched closely, fascinated by the almost palpable aura of energy and heated sensuality radiating from the small, single figure in the spotlight, a figure swathed in mystery and glamour. She easily dominated the big stage and held the audience in thrall.

Elizabeth's business was to figure out the elements of glamour and pass them on to her customers. Diana had a personal impact that could never be put in a bottle. She was simply glamorous in the ancient meaning of the word—able to draw power, to draw magic about herself. She was not tall, but she looked tall. Her body swayed sinuously with the music. Her voice evoked such a rich mosaic of emotion that something caught involuntarily in Elizabeth's throat. When Diana finished and began to smile and bow, wave after wave of applause swept the house, and the audience sprang to its feet.

"Thank you, Diana," said the emcee warmly. "The people out there love you. They really do. Listen to that applause!"

Diana nodded, light glancing off the elaborate beading of her dress. She lifted her head under her wild mass of hair while the emcee stated that, at her request, some of the proceeds of the show were to go to her own favorite cause: the Great Lakes Basin NatureWatch Association, which battled the greatest threat to the region, acid rain. It was partly on behalf of this watchdog organization, the emcee explained, that Diana had made the arduous journey just to appear here tonight. She retired to the wings while Mr. Sanger, head of the chamber of commerce, took the microphone.

"And now, the Albright Award," he boomed sonorously, "in recognition of outstanding performance in business, in community support and in innovative and forward-looking leadership. The winner will be somebody to watch in the eighties, folks; a genuine first-class show."

Kevin's hand tightened. Elizabeth felt a smothering excitement in her breast. Her moment in the limelight was coming.

Everyone around them had gone silent, too. Normally, there would be only polite interest in a rather boring business award, but since Elizabeth and Justin were at loggerheads on this one, the audience's attention was riveted.

"Here goes," whispered Kevin, who appreciated the importance of ritual recognition. He puffed up in anticipation of reflected glory at the reception afterward.

Mr. Sanger, having watched too many Academy Award shows, made a small production of pulling the envelope from his pocket, sliding on his bifocals and clearing his throat.

"And the winner is—" he paused, squeezing the utmost drama out of the moment "—Justin Archer of Archer Beauty Enterprises!"

Elizabeth stared, certain she'd heard wrong. Her breath vacated her lungs while Kevin's fingers stiffened over hers.

She could not mistake the truth when Justin rose to his feet and strode to the platform. His thick sweep of burnt-sienna hair, perfectly cut, right down to the wayward tendril escaping at his forehead, gleamed under the lights. Triumphant pleasure was written all over his face.

"And now," cried Mr. Sanger, glowing even more with importance, "our own Diana Daniels has kindly consented to do the honors in presenting this award."

Amidst a renewed frenzy, Diana stepped out and moved to where Mr. Sanger handed her the impressive bronze-and-mahogany plaque. Her throaty voice congratulated Justin, and she placed the plaque in his hands. Justin promptly tucked it under his arm and stepped to the microphone—as if he owned the stage, Elizabeth thought spitefully.

"I can't express my surprise and delight at the honor just accorded me. And the greatest pleasure—" his smile flashed white in the tan of his face ''—is receiving the honor from the hands of so lovely a lady as Diana Daniels, a model of beauty all of our patrons can strive toward. Thank you, Ms Daniels.''

He kissed Diana's fingers with a flourish. Applause swelled as he straightened, still holding Diana's hand. Elizabeth barely managed to find her breath and quell a galloping tide of blood before it reached her cheeks and gave her away to the myriad avid eyes she could feel fixed on her from behind.

Yeccch! she thought wrathfully. *Just look at him soaking it up. Look at him showing off his perfect teeth and his perfect mane. He's as phony as a three-dollar bill. You still need a lesson, Justin Archer, and I'll beat you yet, I will!*

Justin shook hands with Mr. Sanger and bowed again to the lively approbation. Confidence—or pure ego, depending on whom one was asking—exuded from him. To Elizabeth, he looked like a man who had had himself carved to order from a six-foot block of oak, added King Tut's swagger and worked on his smile until it could drop a cheerleading squad at five hundred yards. One brow was always lifted as if he was keeping a private joke from the world, and no item of clothing had ever suffered lint or a wrinkle. She knew he deliberately used his striking gunmetal eyes to dispense blessings of pleasure, or to strike terror into the hearts of those who managed to cross him. It was a certain bet that the last person he smiled at every night was himself.

Elizabeth straightened her spine. Shaking her hair slightly to cover any residual red spots, she fixed her public smile on her face and clapped politely. To her left, Maria was torn between overt enthusiasm and decent restraint. Kevin applauded reluctantly, following Elizabeth's lead.

"Elizabeth, I'm—"

"Don't say a word, Kevin," Elizabeth hissed through her teeth. "Just don't say a word!"

Startled, Kevin subsided while Maria looked straight ahead. Cameras flashed, and to her left, Elizabeth spotted the young reporter scribbling furiously, her face rapt, her pen obviously spewing forth worshipful prose. Justin's smug face would appear in business monthlies coast to coast and south of the border. And he would grow even more smug, Elizabeth thought glumly, when he spotted the bulge in accounts receivable.

As Justin arrived to collect Maria, the audience rose to its feet, murmuring. More aware than ever of the eyes focused on her, Elizabeth turned nonchalantly.

"Well, well, the fellows have finally gotten together to recognize your existence. My congratulations. I know how you like collecting trophies for your wall."

Driven by circumstance, she actually went so far as to extend her fingers. Justin reciprocated by taking her hand. His voice dripped irony.

"Why, thank you, Elizabeth. It's so nice to be recognized by such an active colleague as yourself."

Elizabeth hadn't touched him in six years, so it was a shock to feel her palm suddenly sweating and burning. She pulled away at once and dropped her hand into the extravagant folds of her dress. It wouldn't do to break out in spots in full view of this crowd.

Uncharacteristically, Justin paused, glancing sharply at Elizabeth as something deep in his eyes flared and died away. Then he was surrounded by other people congratulating him, and Elizabeth took Kevin through the doors to where the reception was set up. She held her head high, satisfied her armor hadn't cracked in public.

"I hope that wasn't too big a disappointment," Kevin said anxiously.

Thank heaven she hadn't gloated to him in the car.

"Oh, no," Elizabeth smiled. "These little awards are tossed about all the time. I've had my share."

But they both knew it wasn't just any little award. It was the stamp of approval by the establishment. It got the recipient looked at where it counted.

Her throat closed for just one second. She had worked so hard. She had struggled, she had starved, she had mixed her first preparations in her bachelor-ette kitchen and had peddled them from a carryall on weary shoulders. So many nights, and the only thing that had kept her going was her refusal to be beaten by Justin Archer's animosity.

Oh, well, let Justin have his moment. Next year I'll show him. Next year...

"Oh, look, Elizabeth. There's Diana Daniels. She's actually going to circulate!"

Kevin had forgotten his dignity and was staring goggle-eyed at the elegant apparition momentarily visible among a horde of admirers. Elizabeth was surprised. Diana rarely mixed with the public—her way, Elizabeth suspected, of preserving the aura of mystery that drove fan magazines crazy with specula-tion about her.

Though Diana vanished in the crowd, Elizabeth could feel her presence taking over the room. She sighed, thinking of the heights that were given to only a few to scale. She was well aware that much of her own personal impact was simply a combination of chutzpah, determination and a certain amount of clever illusion. Diana was real fireworks. Born to glamour. She had Elizabeth's genuine admiration.

"Let's try to get a look at her."

Kevin was now hauling Elizabeth along by the wrist, as star struck as any sixteen-year-old. Elizabeth ended up jammed in a mass of tuxedos and silk in the attempt to get close to the star.

Thanks to Kevin's elbows, the crowd broke. Elizabeth found herself face-to-face with Diana, who was turning away from her bedazzled escort, Mr. Sanger. Again, Elizabeth confronted that electric sensuality that filled the air with invisible sparks. For once in her life, she was speechless as she took in Diana's gleaming dress, which seemed to make the air shimmer around her. She saw pointed, expressive features, emphatically alive in a frame of thick, tawny hair, wild as a lion's mane; she saw a body carried with grace, and deep, caramel eyes that were absorbing and recording the surroundings with a keenness and an interest that were clearly the key to the singer's prodigious personal charm. To Elizabeth's astonishment, the caramel eyes stopped halfway around the circle of admirers and fixed on her.

"Elizabeth Wright," said the inimitable voice, conveying pleasant surprise.

"Ah . . . yes. How do you do, Ms Daniels."

Diana nodded graciously and continued to eye Elizabeth intently.

"I recognize you from your labels, Ms Wright. It's fascinating to see you in real life. I make a study of faces, you know."

"Really. I'm flattered. I—"

A thin, rapidly breathing man wriggled between them.

"Ms Daniels, oh, Ms Daniels, I saw you in *Far Winds* and I simply adored you in it. How exciting to be an actress. My mother is dying to meet you...."

The tide washed in again, jostling in front of Elizabeth and taking Diana Daniels with it, like a treasure momentarily tossed up by the sea and swept away again. Elizabeth and Kevin didn't stand another chance of getting close, so they moved back into the crowd, already feeling their brief sprinkle of stardust fading. Elizabeth's sense of disappointment returned, though her princesslike bearing would never have shown it. She turned on Kevin's arms as a robust, paunchy older man moved into view.

"Oh, there's Mr. Carston. I wonder..."

Mr. Carston, failing to see her, rolled right on by to where Archer was standing.

"Well, Archer, old buddy, you got the big one tonight, didn't you? Great stuff!"

He thumped Justin on the shoulder with boisterous force.

"Guess so," Justin replied, smiling as though he had planned the whole thing. "Thanks."

"Listen, I've been thinking," Carston boomed, "about that distribution deal you asked for. I can swing it. Slap that Concerto line of yours into just about all my stores!"

Elizabeth sucked in a scandalized breath. Carston was head of Carston Pharmacies—with about nine hundred stores across the country. She had been maneuvering to get that shelf space for months, and now Justin was snatching it from under her nose! The old boys' network was at it again. So much for the award being meaningless!

Carston rumbled on for a few more moments before lumbering off in another direction. Kevin headed to the bar to get drinks. Justin turned around to Elizabeth, a glinty-eyed smile illuminating his face.

"From your expression, I'd say you overheard that," he said in a low voice.

"A fluke, Justin. That garish new packaging of yours and that award. We'll see how long it lasts."

"Oh, it'll last, Elizabeth. Trends are changing. The novelty of your mushed-cucumber-and-avocado paste is wearing off. You'll have to open a vegetable stand yet."

She forced her gaze to meet his unwaveringly. His expression was as insufferable as ever, and his eyes narrowed, revealing, Elizabeth thought, all of his wolfish determination to ruin her. And for what? A rich man's pique, that's all. Her blood boiled up briefly under her skin before she quelled her anger.

"Do you imagine that I couldn't make a splendid success of a vegetable stand?" she inquired musically.

"Some things I can imagine, some I can't. For instance—" his eyes traveled insolently from her clever coiffure to her sparkly gold sandals and back up again "—how does that dress stay up?"

Elizabeth had felt every centimeter of his inspection hotly, though one would never have guessed it. She smiled a smile as insolent as Justin's own.

"Force of will!" she tossed back just as Kevin stepped up, bearing two glasses of fine champagne.

The invisible forces clashing in the air between them receded. Elizabeth accepted her drink. Justin turned away with a small private smile that nettled her.

Halfway across the room, Elizabeth ran smack into Mr. Carston. He could not ignore her this time.

"Oh, hello, Elizabeth. How are you?"

"Why, just fine, Charlie. I see you've been congratulating Justin, too."

Her smile only added to the slightly accusing tone of her words. She might as well have declared aloud that she'd overheard everything. Carston fidgeted slightly.

"Oh, uh, yes. That new Concerto packaging of his really hits the eye. Guess I'll take it on. I'll get space for you as soon as I can, Elizabeth. Now if you had a gimmick..."

"Charlie, Charlie Carston. Well, how the hell are you, fella? Long time no see."

A hardware magnate zeroed in. Elizabeth and Kevin, left standing once again, retreated to the buffet. Elizabeth refused to budge from this post and consumed twice her normal ration of anchovy canapés. She made fiercely cheery small talk with Kevin and anyone else who drifted over to see how she was taking her lumps. Finally, the guests began gravitating to the door.

Elizabeth did not encounter Justin directly again. She didn't need to. She was acutely aware of his progress through the room, as well as the pretty tilt of Maria's head toward him and the tiny giggles of women as, one by one, they fell victim to his legendary charm. His life, Elizabeth thought acidly, consisted of a number of poses: Mr. Macho Tycoon, who could keep his employees jumping with a single thunderous glance; Mr. Smooth and Cool, up on the stage, collecting his award; Mr. Charisma, over there now, oiling up his many admirers; and underneath all those layers, Mr. Ruthless. Let down your guard once and he'd serve you bankruptcy papers for breakfast. Not that Mr. Ruthless wanted to do this to everyone. Just to her.

And, on top of all this, most unfairly, a seductive, dizzying maleness always surrounded Justin. And not even Elizabeth—especially not Elizabeth—could deny its power.

She leaned more heavily on Kevin's arm, laughing delightedly at his remarks. Kevin glowed and preened, his head bent in pleased intimacy. He steered her importantly toward the door, his lanky legs keeping step beside her. Justin, too, was taking his leave. With a small breath, Elizabeth realized he had been watching her.

At functions such as these, they usually said a civil goodbye to each other. Justin nodded slightly, his neck unbending. If there was anything Elizabeth remembered about him, it was the rigidity of his spine underneath all that sinuous ease.

"Good night," she said distinctly, half-expecting Justin to flaunt his bronze plaque under her nose.

Justin's gaze slid to Kevin and then back to her. A tiny muscle flickered at the corner of his jaw. Only Elizabeth noticed—but then, she knew exactly where to look.

"Good night, Elizabeth. And by the way," he added just as they were turning away, "happy birthday."

Elizabeth looked at him in astonishment. Ten past midnight. His greeting was technically true, though it was about the last thing she had expected to hear out of him. She half swung around, ready to bristle, but for once the quirked eyebrow was level, and his mouth was clean of that infuriating little smile.

"Why, thank you, Justin. How kind of you to remember."

She spoke with the pleasant archness that usually goaded him into his smirk. But his mouth remained serious, his expression closed. Was she crazy, or were there lines at the corners of his lids that she hadn't seen before? On this of all nights there should be no hint of weariness tingeing his relentless vitality.

At her side, her hand throbbed as if he had touched it again. Something clanged and thudded inside her. For no reason at all, she recalled a linen-covered café table years ago in Yorkville. There had been just that expression on Justin's face before....

Oh, Justin, if only you had an honest bone in your body!

The moment the thought broke surface, Elizabeth hammered it back down. She would have no regrets. No, siree! No matter how much champagne she had swallowed. Six years had passed; of course he had lines. And if he got tired, well, she got tired, too. Cripes, did he have to be given an award to actually look sincere?

"There's Trudy now."

She bore Kevin off to her waiting Rolls. When the car pulled up before the luxury waterfront condominium where Kevin resided, Kevin leaned toward her in the seat. Elizabeth happily provided Kevin with the kiss he apparently felt his due, taking care not to stab him with her tulle.

"Happy birthday," he said, nuzzling her ear with surprising skill, "even if it was that Archer fellow who happened to remember."

Elizabeth knew that Justin never "happened" to remember anything. By now, she was sure he had done it to point out her advancing age in the fickle cosmetics world. She hated to think he could still cause a flutter in her breast.

"Mmm," she murmured noncommittally.

Kevin nuzzled her ear again and then casually asked, "What was your dustup with the fellow all about, anyway?"

Elizabeth, however, was never taken off guard on this subject. Suddenly, Kevin's expensive lips lost their appeal. She untangled herself.

"A private disagreement, Kevin, best forgotten by all."

As if she would ever forget!

Kevin hovered; then, judging his chances, he lunged at her. "Oh, Elizabeth, you're delicious! Kiss me!"

His breathing became heavy, adolescent. He attacked Elizabeth's throat, abandoning himself, though the spiky tulle fought back. Elizabeth closed her eyes tightly, but against laughter. She knew she could take Kevin home with her like some tasty consoling dessert after an evening of disappointments. Intently, she listened to her own body rhythms and then gently, kindly, pushed Kevin away. To continue with him would have only increased the feelings of disappointment—feelings that were not entirely Kevin's fault.

CHAPTER TWO

WITHOUT KEVIN it was empty in the back seat. On the way home, Elizabeth impulsively diverted Trudy into the old Cabbagetown section of Toronto.

"Stop for a minute. I want to look around."

They pulled off Ontario Street into a side street that was all narrow brick gables, carriage lamps and artistically curving walks. A silence invaded the car, bringing Elizabeth back to another time, when she was a child living on this street. Before the renovators. When Cabbagetown was the most notorious slum in the city instead of the address now so much in demand.

She was here because she needed reassurance.

"You've come a long way, dearie," she whispered softly to herself.

And she had. She'd come out of a two-room third-floor flat where she and her mother had gotten along on welfare or on a waitress's wages; she'd gotten away from the unhealthy diet of cheap pasta, the smells in the staircase and a fuzzy future that loomed over each day's struggle to survive.

And certainly the same struggle was going on that very moment in cramped, dark apartments where whining children didn't have room to play. That was why Elizabeth gave so generously to charities and attended so willingly all those gala events.

Encased in the gold embrace of her dress, her own Rolls Royce gleaming under the street lamps, she was reassured. She, Elizabeth Wright, had máde her own luck, fought her way out, almost clear to the top—and she meant to stay there, Justin or no Justin.

"Home, then, Trudy," she called out, her voice light again. "I imagine you'd like to get to bed as much as I would."

She lived just north, across Bloor Street, in Rosedale, an enclave of massive old mansions adorned with Gothic tracery, mullioned windows and splendid grounds behind stone walls. Elizabeth had renovated one to suit her taste, not touching the parquet or the inlaid paneling or the baronial fireplaces but installing the latest electronic gadgetry and letting her rather oddball decorator run loose.

Trudy dispatched, she rustled up the curved staircase to her private suite, shed the sensational dress and settled contentedly to her dressing table. Here she faced the secret known only to herself and her mirror: Elizabeth Wright, dewy ideal on a million tempting labels, was not beautiful.

Oh, she wasn't ugly, either; just ordinary, just a little bit uninteresting. What emerged when the sculpted cheekbones and clever eye shadow had been wiped away was a moon-shaped, rather contourless face with lashes too pale to show off their thickness and lips that lost their definition without the carefully applied color that turned them luscious as fresh fruit. Her hair, which ought to have been wild with natural curl to compliment her round face, was poker straight and had been the despair of her teen years, when it had clung about her head like undernourished seaweed, despite every tortuous attempt to make it sweep back like the pictures in the magazines.

Later, of course, she had discovered the body wave. Now her hair was grand just on the strength of the new mousse she had been personally testing for the last four months. She intended to sweep the market with it in the spring.

After cleansing and toning, Elizabeth selected her special almond-milk moisturizer and worked it upward with feathery strokes until her face was a map of creamy circles. Far from being distressed with her looks, Elizabeth was pleased. Tickled, in fact. Her daily loveliness, accepted everywhere without question, was a personal triumph, a living testimonial to her own skill and the honest effectiveness of Elizabeth Wright products. If *she* could look this way, so could every woman—and that was the foundation of conviction upon which her growing empire rested. Every woman deserved all the advantages she could get!

When the moisturizer had been allowed to soak the ritual ten minutes and had then been wiped smooth, Elizabeth stood up and began her stretching exercises. Her body was one of the best cared for in the city. She reached for the ceiling, then touched her toes in her private sitting room, which was decorated with nutmeg carpeting, an old fireplace, a corner jungle of benjamina plants and broadleaf philodendrons and a trompe l'oeil painting of a swan on a blue lake that was so real the bird seemed alive in the room. Behind her, double French doors opened to her bedroom, and through the bedroom, more French doors opened to a private deck installed above the old conservatory.

The doors were flanked by pairs of horses' heads carved from pink quartz.

The phone rang as Elizabeth slipped into her second yoga position, causing her to start. She knew who it was and picked up the receiver with a sigh.

"Hello, Momma. How are you?"

"Just fine, Bess. I knew I wouldn't get you tomorrow, so I'm phoning now to wish you happy birthday."

Elizabeth half opened her mouth to ask her mom to stop calling her Bess, but she knew it was hopeless. She had been Bessie as a youngster and she'd hated it. The name always made her think of a cow.

"Thank you, Mom."

"I saw your picture in the paper Saturday at the boat race. That Kevin Longfield is a fine-looking fellow. Been going out with him long?"

Little elastic bands tightened in Elizabeth's midriff despite her best intentions. Why did her mom always act as if her daughter were sixteen and had just found a new boyfriend?

"I'm not 'going out' with him, Mother. He's just a suitable escort for these kinds of occasions."

There was the inevitable silence while her mother sorted this out and then the inevitable second try.

"Well, he looks nice. Maybe he's the one for you, Bess. You're thirty-one, you know. Most girls your age have settled down already."

"Mother, they're not girls, they're women."

"Okay, women. Now, Kevin Longfield..."

"Mom, you haven't even asked how the business is."

"How is the business?"

"My profits just broke a jillion dollars, and Princess Di is doing a makeover demo at the mall next Saturday."

Mrs. Wright laughed indulgently. "Glad to see you're getting a sense of humor about it. That business takes up far too much of your time, if you ask me. Now, I'm not saying you haven't been a wonderful success, dear, but a girl who's thirty-one is pretty darn close to being left on the shelf and she should—"

Red lava bubbled inside Elizabeth's stomach. She struggled to contain herself.

"I'm not a package of overaged spinach!"

"I didn't mean—"

"I know you didn't. Oh, Mom, let's not talk about it. How're Morty and Tong?"

The conversation, deflected onto Mrs. Wright's cats, ended amicably. Yet when Elizabeth hung up, cords were standing out on her neck, and her lips were compressed to invisibility.

"Crap!" she exploded so suddenly her cantankerous tabby started up from his pillow. A former alley cat, Orange-O was ever paranoid about eviction from all this fabulous luxury.

Elizabeth took five deep breaths and the cords disappeared. *Why is it,* she wondered, *that the ones we love most can exasperate us so?* She ought to be used to it by now: that lack of comprehension about where her money had come from, the money that had purchased the fine town house Mrs. Wright now inhabited. Elizabeth's mother still subscribed to the myth poor women used to comfort themselves—that somehow, Mr. Right would come along and rescue them all.

If Elizabeth had listened to her mother, she knew, she might well have been a single mother on welfare herself right now. She might have been trapped in so many underpaid futureless jobs that she may have ceased to believe personal effort could make any difference to her life at all. She, too, might still have been waiting for Mr. Right.

Settling down again on the rug, legs crossed, Elizabeth straightened her spine, vertebra by vertebra.

I remember your swollen feet, Mom, from the waitressing jobs, and that's why I'll never get angry. But, oh, you nearly ruined my entire life with all that boyfriend stuff!

She closed her eyes, involuntarily remembering her early years in school, sometimes going without breakfast, sometimes without lunch. She had been bright, a quick learner, eager to please. But Mom had wanted her to be popular and had spent precious money on impractical blouses and dime-store jewelry. When she'd started high school, her friends were already quitting all around her. She didn't see any point in breaking her neck to study when everyone else was hanging out and having fun. Besides, her hormones had started to percolate. All the girls were boy crazy. At sixteen, with Mom's full encouragement, Elizabeth became boy crazy, too.

"Get yourself somebody real nice. Like that Donny Clenman. You know what I mean!"

The dream glowed in Mrs. Wright's eyes, even though her own husband was a shadowy figure to Elizabeth, having hightailed west, never to be seen again, when Elizabeth was five.

Well, "nice" Donny Clenman had bolted when Elizabeth told him she was three weeks overdue on her period. Vividly, that night was burned into her mind. Choked with panic, she had stumbled out into a dark park, all the veils of romance torn from the terrifying face of reality. A life of drudgery, crowded rooms and cheap food lay ahead. Mr. Right would not save her. Her mother had been wrong.

How cold she had been, how scared. She had felt the slats of the park bench pressing into her spine, had seen the bits of paper scraped along the asphalt by the breeze and had noticed the tulips some vandal had torn apart. In her mind, she'd begun to think about not only her mother but all the other women she knew. Timid Mrs. Borman, whose husband beat her every Saturday night after his drink with the boys. Jenny Watts, whose desperate search for love had resulted in three children by three different fathers, none of the men interested in their offspring. Alice the Whale, who ate to compensate for being put down every minute of the day by her mean-spirited live-in boyfriend. Pete and Mildred Kline, who tried hard but were slowly getting crushed under the burden of retarded twins and a lack of money; Pete's job as a watchman did not pay well. At worst, she saw abandonment and abuse; at best, hard work, struggle and too many children hanging around street corners. Mr. Right had not saved anybody and never would, despite the continuing myth that someday he was sure to gallop out of the mist.

Nor could the government be relied on. Social-assistance money was shrinking, and programs were being cut. Elizabeth had seen the homeless kids, the teenage prostitutes without job skills shivering at the curb—some runaways, some there because they themselves had babies they had no other way to support. What those poor creatures were forced to do for money caused Elizabeth's innards to heave.

A terrible pit had yawned before Elizabeth that night. Hidden in the shrubbery, she had slumped down, thin arms hugging her legs, forehead jammed against the hard bones of her knees. All night she had sat there, huddled, tears leaking silently from her lids, thinking only that Daddy was gone and Donny was gone and Momma was working so hard she couldn't do any more than she was already doing.

At dawn, cramps, then a sharp pain had racked her abdomen. The hot gush had struck her speechless. Not caring whether it was her period or a miscarriage, she had stood up shaking, dizzy with disbelieving joy. She wasn't pregnant! By some miracle, she'd been given a second chance!

If she had come to the park as a frightened child, she returned home a woman with a stark new view of the world. She thought about the smart ladies on Bay Street with nice clothes and briefcases. They would never fall into the pregnancy trap. They would think her a fool for allowing such dangerous nonsense. They would tell her that to wait for Mr. Right was laziness and irresponsibility tantamount to suicide. Mr. Right was not the answer. Money and education were.

Elizabeth never told anybody about her close call, but everyone remarked on her sudden lack of interest in boys and on the way she started hitting the books. After high school, she trained as a beautician, working until she had earned enough to go to university. After finishing a chemistry degree, it was only natural for her to be hired on at Justin's in the beauty business.

Expanding her lungs slowly from the abdomen up to the space under her collarbone, Elizabeth stretched toward the seventeenth-century andirons flanking the mahogany mantelpiece. This was all hers now. She had earned it herself. She was secure. So why did she let her mother irritate her so much? Why did she never get inured to it?

Because you're thirty-one, my sweet. Thirty-one!

Could it be that tonight her mother had struck a genuine nerve?

Elizabeth strode back to the mirror and examined her face in detail. Her smooth, carefully tended skin was reflected back at her, but she finally had to admit there were two tiny lines arrowing out from the corners of her eyes, and there was definitely a mark between her brows from all those years of intense concentration. Almost imperceptibly, but surely, she was aging.

Thirty-one!

Thirty had been a triumph. A milestone reached, a section of life successfully accomplished. But thirty-one. Ah, yes, that's when it truly hit. *You're in that decade, pumpkin. You're an over-thirty. Never can you reclaim your past!*

Impatiently, Elizabeth began to pace the carpet. She detested the North American cultural mind-set that said a woman was only as good as her youth. Wright cosmetics were for everyone. Weren't they? A little doubt began to gnaw. Had she been guilty of propagating the myth? Had she contributed, too? She forced those thoughts away and turned her mind to business.

The face of Justin Archer floated before her once more, and her mouth tightened as she remembered his smugness as he'd collected that award, and his easy success with Carston. Trends were changing, he had said. People were bored with the Elizabeth Wright label. Carston himself had hinted that she needed something new.

Most of all, Justin's triumph, premature to be sure, stung her where she lived. He thought he had won. My God, he thought he had won! Why, the very next thing might be an insulting takeover offer. Or the ultimate nightmare—Justin behind her own desk, firing her with glee! She had to find a way to show him. She had to find a way to cap their feud once and for all!

Hey, hey, calm down, kiddo. It's not as if there's a dent in your balance sheets.

But her heart was pounding. Another legacy from her childhood—the secret fear that everything could be taken from underneath her if she took her eyes off the store but once. She imagined each tiny setback as a new pulled thread that would unravel the fabric of her hard-won success. Wherever would she get another job? She couldn't even type properly.

Elizabeth went back to pacing the rug, determined to be realistic. Much as she hated to admit it, there might be some substance to Justin's words. His company had the money and the clout hers had not yet attained—not to mention the old boys' network, Carston and the Albright Award!

As she circled back, she passed her huge makeup mirror with its double row of lights embedded in the gleaming gold border. Her apricot satin pajamas glowed in the light. She seemed a very apparition of grace, yet an expression came over her face that would have startled Kevin: the wily, never-say-die look of the born street fighter, which, under all the silk and perfume, was the true essence of Elizabeth. Justin had roused her. The endless feud with him was expensive and tiresome and she was sick of it—but if she stopped now, Justin would stomp her down. And she was damned if she was going to let him beat her!

Her own products stood in a proud row under the lights, on a shelf specially built to display them like small works of art. The ones she used every night sat nearest—the cleanser, the toner, the moisturizer—all with her own face smiling optimistically back to her from the mint-green labels. There were also a few flowers on her labels—just enough to enhance the refreshing feeling she wanted to achieve.

Justin's new packaging was a deep ruby red vividly embossed in gold at all the edges, with his name in slashing script—in his own handwriting. His handwriting conveyed his personality as much as the bold, slightly one-sided smile that could make a stranger drop her fork in a restaurant. From hard experience, Elizabeth knew not to trifle with the force and appeal of such a personality.

Drawn in spite of herself, Elizabeth leaned closer to the mirror, and again caught sight of the tiny age lines. Was Carston right? Was the same label year after year, stamped with her own slowly changing face, boring? Where she had hoped to create stability and a loyal following in the midst of so much hype and constant change, was she merely turning stale?

She had adamantly refused to betray her customers by airbrushing her own face or resorting to any other photographic skulduggery, but could she really age on her own labels and keep up her sales? Even as part of her protested violently against the fact that women were judged by their appearances, the practical part of her warned against too much defiance of the powerful age taboo. She could not, after all, change society all by herself.

Drat Justin! Drat his craggy face, his peacock strut and his infuriating male assumption that he knew what women wanted. How dare he dictate to them. He didn't have the least idea what it was like to struggle with stringy hair or grow up in terror that your teeth wouldn't be straight or your nose appealing. He just mixed up whatever he felt like at his plant, poured huge sums into advertising and assumed women would then rush to slap his products on their faces—which they did.

Elizabeth's gaze flew back to her labels. She made simple, natural products, using herbs and vegetables. She had always been against the high-tech flashiness that Justin promoted. Her genius, she knew was marketing. She had come so far. She just needed one more brilliant coup to put Justin permanently in his place!

Simple, natural products! She knew Justin's company called her the Kitchen Witch and the Vegetable Woman, but there had been a time when Justin had wanted those very same products. Oh, yes, when she'd worked in his lab, he'd wanted them badly. Badly enough to turn that sensual smile on her and stroke her hair while whispering wonder at her ingenious mind. She had responded with parted, trembling lips.

Oh, such monumental stupidity!

Elizabeth pressed her hand to her mouth and turned from the mirror so quickly that a pair of rare *famille rose* Chinese jars tottered on their shelf. Talk about not having learned a single thing from Donny Clenman. Even now, as she thought about it, a hot wave of embarrassment caught her under the solar plexus.

Drunk from Justin's caresses, she had worked with inspired fury, streams of ideas pouring forth from her. Giddy with love, she had at last dared to stretch herself to her full capacity.

How genuine Justin's interest had seemed. Scarcely able to believe that the dashing heir to the establishment was fixing on her, Elizabeth had fallen for his impulsive gifts, his adoring words and the dizzying whirl of concerts and expensive restaurants. But the dream had crumbled one day when Justin's office manager had come back from vacation. At once, he had spotted the dreamy change in Elizabeth, and a crooked smile had curled across his lips.

"Well, well," he had purred, "I see Justin's getting the most out of you for his money. I wondered how long it would take him."

Flushing fiery red, Elizabeth had demanded to know what he meant, but Harvey, hoarding his nasty little grin, would say no more. Much as she'd tried to shuck off the comment, it had lodged under her skin and stuck there, reviving all her old distrust for men. A small, suspicious part of herself kept asking why someone as magnetic as Justin would be involved with her.

Even as she'd tried to push her suspicions away, they'd pursued her. She'd thought of /her origins, about how she did not belong in Justin's league. The night she came in late and found him removing all her notes from the lab without so much as a by-your-leave, she had blown up, demanding just what the hell he thought he was doing.

Had he tried to apologize, she thought, had he had one ounce of psychological smarts and offered honey, she might have been placated. Elizabeth was still capable of breaking into a cold sweat over just how easily she might have been placated. How easily her future could have been ruined.

However, Justin had simply stood there, glowering like a cornered wolf. The hot flare in him, out of all proportion to the situation, had alarmed Elizabeth. She saw only the arrogance of a spoiled, determined man accustomed to getting his own way. She had been unable to choke the shrillness from her voice.

"Anything you come up with while in my employ belongs to me, Elizabeth," he had informed her tightly. "You know that. I have a right to do anything I please with it—with or without your knowledge or permission."

Elizabeth knew this meant he would start new production with her work. Another, less intelligent woman might have been overjoyed. Instead, sudden comprehension of the true value of her ideas had blazed in Elizabeth's mind.

He's getting the most out of you for his money!

Justin would take the products she had conceived, develop them into a highly salable commodity and make a fortune while she, like a fool, continued to work on salary, just one more tool to make Justin rich!

Used! Just as Donny had used her. And now that Justin had got what he wanted, he would take his kisses to the next likely candidate who would be only too happy to strew her valuable ideas at his feet! Oh, what an idiot she had been!

Through a mist of red rage, Elizabeth had seen Justin talking but had not heard his words. She'd wanted to fly at his eyes, but too many scraps had taught her to keep her wits about her. She'd spoken coldly, through her teeth.

"Justin, your so-called exclusive claims are worthless. Take a close look at what I've written down. I haven't invented anything new. The formulas are hundreds of years old; they've been passed down from mother to daughter for centuries. Anybody can make them in the kitchen. All I did was go to the library and look them up!"

Justin had jerked as if she'd struck him. His jaws had worked but no sound had come out. In fury, he had slammed the sheaf of papers down on the long metal desk beside her.

"Oh, so now you tell me you were cheating all along, trying to pass off old-hat material as original stuff. Was it to cover your own incompetence, Elizabeth, or does it give you a big kick to sabotage the people who trust you?"

Elizabeth's body had gone numb, and then she was infuriated. She had sprung forward, gathering the notes against her ribs.

"All right," she had hissed. "Since you don't want my notes, I'll just take them. I'll show you just how worthless they are!"

Grasping at once her intention to leave, Justin had sprung, too, pinning her to the wall as she tried to ram by. A heavy pulse beat at his throat.

"If you walk out, I'll see that you're finished in the beauty business permanently! Is that clear? You'll never work for anybody again!"

His face had been stark, his eyes wilder than anything she had ever seen. Tearing herself from his grip, Elizabeth had raced down the long empty corridor and had slammed the door shut, never to return again.

She knew he meant his threats about blackballing her in the business, so she didn't job hunt. Typically, the one thing Justin hadn't envisioned was that she'd have the daring to go it alone and start her own company, facing down the terror and inexperience and a lack of money.

The merry tinkling of wind chimes on the deck brought Elizabeth back to the present—a present full of luxury and recognition. It would not be snatched from her. No, it would not. Let Justin keep his Albright. One more slam-bang marketing coup would show him where he stood.

To put herself in the mood, Elizabeth crossed to a tiny concealed refrigerator and extracted a bottle of champagne, her hands cool on the dew beading its green label. Skillfully extracting the cork, she splashed some of the liquid into a tulip glass and carried it out into the warm June night. Soft air scented with freshly mown grass surrounded her. She tilted her head up toward the tops of the vast dark maples.

"Come on, Elizabeth, think of something brilliant!"

The first taste of champagne brought a pleasant fizz to her palate. The second evoked Diana Daniels, whose magnetism could be measured in kilowatt power. *Far Winds*, that miniseries she had starred in two months ago, had drawn one of the largest audiences in the history of television viewing. Having died heroically to save her children from marauding soldiers, Diana would not reappear in the sequel scheduled six months down the line. Too bad. The audience promised to be almost as large. The story was so popular that stores were rumored to be setting up *Far Winds* boutiques to capitalize on the theme in their merchandizing. The series was a gold mine. If one could only grab a commercial spot on that . . .

Elizabeth all but crashed into an urn full of geraniums. A small company such as hers hadn't a hope of booking one of those juicy spots—unless, say, Diana herself were endorsing Elizabeth Wright products! And after all, hadn't Diana recognized her from her labels just now at the reception?

Heavens, maybe she even used the stuff!

The idea was so crazily audacious that Elizabeth just stood there, feeling as if she had swallowed all the champagne in one gulp. Just as quickly, the excitement evaporated. Elizabeth sank onto a cedar bench.

Ha! Sure. Get Diana Daniels to do commercial endorsements! You and how many multinationals would like to get your paws on that!

More money and more fame Diana did not need. What possible inducement could lure her into making a commercial parade of herself?

The impossible idea tantalized Elizabeth. Her products would acquire glitter. Diana wouldn't have to worry about appearing out of character during commercial breaks, since she wouldn't be in the sequel to *Far Winds*. Carston would fall all over himself to give Elizabeth space. Before she knew it, she could crack the tough international-distribution systems and go worldwide. Justin would choke behind his handcrafted silk tie every time he saw her label!

Elizabeth bristled and snapped with energy the way she always did when one of her inspirations hit her. She plucked leaves from the geraniums, lost one slipper and glowered at the Big Dipper in her attempt to dredge up every possible fact she could about Diana Daniels. The more she racked her brain, the more hopeless the concept seemed.

Cripes, you'd almost think I was trying to find something to blackmail her with!

A night bird winged past, dipping toward Lake Ontario. The lake, something about saving the lake. Elizabeth's eyes widened and she knew she had it. Much, much better than blackmail. Diana had taken all the trouble to appear tonight to help that—what was it?—NatureWatch cause. A known do-gooder, she. If Elizabeth promised to donate a percentage of the increased profits, might that not be a lure even Diana couldn't resist?

Lightning calculations danced through her head. She could afford it! Yes, she could, though just barely. She stood motionless, grinning into the darkness. Then she picked up her glass and lifted it to the moon.

"Happy birthday, Elizabeth," she toasted herself. "Many happy returns!"

CHAPTER THREE

"IT'S LEAKED! Archer's onto our scheme!"

Elsie, Elizabeth's executive assistant, flung a newspaper onto Elizabeth's desk, a paragraph slashingly circled.

> Rumor has it that Elizabeth Wright and Justin Archer are vying for the services of a certain Big Name to endorse their wares—the lure being a juicy percentage to Diana Daniel's pet cause. She could boot one of our favorite rivals way past the winning post in the old sales game! Let's see who's willing to bleed profit at the seams for Ms Daniel's lucrative nod!

Elizabeth's eyes blazed. "How dare he!"

He dared easily. Justin would grab a money-making idea anywhere he could get it. All the better if it wasn't his own!

Springing up, Elizabeth began to pace the office with an energetic fury quite at odds with her rosebud silk day dress. Loyal Elsie, who had been with Elizabeth since they had worked out of a converted garage, involuntarily took one step back. Sometimes just the mention of Justin Archer's name around Elizabeth was like tossing lit matches into a gasoline spill. That newspaper had started a conflagration. Whatever Justin had done to Elizabeth, Elsie hoped he fried.

"I knew something like this would happen. Oh, why is Diana Daniels so slow?"

Company secrets were impossible to keep. This one had probably been done in a copying machine somewhere between Elizabeth, the word-processing pool, her lawyers, the couriers, Diana's agents and maybe even the coffee boy. Justin and Elizabeth kept constant watch on each other through a sham of indifference. The result was mostly frustration, periodically relieved by a yummy tidbit snatched from the other side.

As always at times like these, Elizabeth saw only Justin's eyes the way they'd been that last shattering night in the lab: gray and cold as chrome in a face bunched up with the fury of being caught. Propriety and charm had been ripped aside, revealing the core of the man, the Justin who would use any weapon, even love, to win.

She shivered slightly, turning away from Elsie. No one in this world would ever find out that Elizabeth had been all set to toss her heart away.

"Well, don't you worry," Elsie muttered. "He won't get to Diana, either. She's as tough to crack as a member of the royal family!"

Elsie could be counted on for comfort as often as necessary. Elizabeth had rescued her from behind the grill of the Happy Howdy Restaurant, and Elsie had been infinitely grateful.

"You can say that again!"

Elizabeth halted before the window of her corner suite, which overlooked a grassy square with a fountain in the middle. The fountain, a happy legacy of some burst of civic improvement, was a scalloped circle around a bronze arch of leaping fishes, with water streaming forth from their mouths. She had felt, she remembered, such bursting excitement at moving into the ornate old building she had bought and renovated to house her business. Her office with its attached private lab occupied the top floor, along with the offices of her executives. Marketing was the next floor down, and then there were three floors devoted to the actual manufacturing and packaging of Elizabeth Wright products. The bottom, sealed behind the impressive entry foyer, was devoted to shipping and handling. Trucks came and went from the loading bays at the back, but in the front there were only the quiet square and the glistening backs of the fishes. A metaphor for the entire business, Elizabeth often thought: the serene elegant front pretending it knew nothing of the frantic constant scramble for survival behind.

Elizabeth seethed all morning, then seethed through lunch, two marketing think tanks and a feasibility report on a new source of wheat-germ oil. Finally, she seethed her way home and prepared to take out her frustration on her personal mail. She had the cream-colored envelope ripped to the seams before she noticed the California postmark and the fine, slanting handwriting.

Her seething burbled to a halt. Surprise and anticipation began to beat in her upper chest as she pulled out the sheet of expensive rag-edged paper. Like the address on the envelope, it was written in longhand. The first words Elizabeth took in were the two in Diana Daniel's signature.

"Whoopee!" Elizabeth shrieked. "I bet she's gonna take me on!"

The letter turned out to be not an acceptance but a rather strange request to go on a holiday. With warm courtesy, it inquired whether it could be possible for Elizabeth to be Diana's guest for a week, preferably two.

"Ah-ha! I told you, didn't I!" Elizabeth crowed to the hall clock.

The clock chimed the half hour, causing Elizabeth, unable to contain her delight, to kiss its antique filigreed face. Shedding her daily dignity, she jogged up the stairs, letting loose the spontaneous part of her that she kept so carefully hidden from everyone, save those few she took inside her circle of confidence: Elsie, her mother, Nora Welch, who was her housekeeper, Natalie at the spa and Pearl, who was in charge of her hair. Those were the people who truly knew the warm heart and the generous laughter that lurked inside Elizabeth and saw her brief releases of zany clowning.

They also saw flashes of her volatile temper and her grimness at business catastrophes. Still more rarely, they glimpsed the vulnerable Elizabeth, the one with the dark fear in her eyes, a fear that, no matter how successful she became, some hidden trapdoor would fly open and drop her back into the poverty from which she had so laboriously emerged.

Once, Elsie told her husband that Elizabeth reminded her of that queen in *Alice in Wonderland* who felt she had to keep running as fast as she could just to stay where she was.

But now Elizabeth was running for joy. In the privacy of her study, she dialed the California number as instructed. Since big bucks were involved here, she knew Diana's real purpose was to look her over carefully—and Elizabeth didn't blame her. The important thing was that Elizabeth had gotten her foot in the door. Once in, she knew she could make an excellent impression. That the letter gave no indication of what sort of holiday, or where, troubled Elizabeth not in the least. Diana was known to have a Big Sur hideaway and a secluded French villa, as well as a large summer place somewhere in the wilds of Ontario. Any one would do just fine.

After three intermediaries, Diana herself came on the phone.

"I can take the time off, Ms Daniels. Just name the place."

Diana's throaty laugh slid over the line. Elizabeth heard it issuing forth from a million TV speakers during a commercial break and imagined Justin's look of chagrin. Her hand tightened on the receiver with mounting excitement.

"Well, I hope you'll permit me the luxury of being mysterious," Diana said. "I like to give surprises. I'll inform you of the meeting place a day or so before you leave. And, oh—" the rich voice paused dramatically "—pack the barest minimum. One suitcase only. Everything will be provided, even down to clothes."

Elizabeth was taken aback.

"My goodness, Ms Daniels, I . . ."

Diana cut her off gently but firmly, allowing no more inquiries. Elizabeth hung up agog with speculation.

"Eat your heart out, Justin Archer," she said to the wall. Her life felt secure underneath her again. She hadn't had so much fun in years.

She put a lot of planning into the suitcase. A *big* suitcase. Her complete skin-and-makeup routine, along with exquisitely packaged gift samples for Diana. Her blow dryer plus attachments, curling iron and, of course, the miracle mousse with which she expected to take the market by storm. Her nightgown and negligee with the handmade French lace to wear for breakfast in bed. Sea Island cottons for cutting a silhouette above the blue Pacific. A dress with a formal jacket designed to intimidate lawyers. One evening gown, surely. Shoes and sandals to go with them all. Oh, how was she ever going to squeeze everything in?

Being Elizabeth, she managed. She left the office in Elsie's capable hands, it being the August slow time. She gave Nora holidays and arranged for a security firm to care for the house. Even as she transferred Orange-O to the comfortable town house where he had a temporary-residency agreement with Morty and Tong, she convinced her disappointed mom that she wasn't dashing off to meet a man. By Friday, everything was secured for a Saturday departure. By Friday evening, Elizabeth was pacing. It was nine o'clock and Diana still hadn't phoned.

At 9:05 the phone rang. Elizabeth leaped for it and was greeted by Diana's lilting tones, her crisp Canadian accent overlaid by California casual.

"All ready, Elizabeth?"

"Naturally, Ms Daniels."

"Okay. Tomorrow, go down to Harbourfront and turn west along Queen's Quay. You will be met."

"Here? In Toronto?" Elizabeth smothered her consternation.

"Yes, in Toronto. You'd better go to bed right away. You're expected at seven o'clock."

Nothing save a few more directions could be gotten from Diana, who hung up chuckling. It had been a long time since anyone had dared give Elizabeth the runaround, even someone with as much clout as Diana Daniels. Elizabeth stood with her lips pursed for a moment, then pulled open her suitcase. A yachting holiday. Not what she'd expected, but still okay. She'd better cram in her deck shoes and that lavender Lucy Amero anorak that looked so fetching. At least the boat explained the single suitcase. Yet what sort of yacht would not have room for at least two or three?

Trudy showed up with the Rolls at a quarter after six despite gusting winds and gray clouds spattering rain. Unsure what to expect, Elizabeth had donned an oyster-colored raw-silk pantsuit that could hold its own in a boardroom but had a jaunty semicasual cut well suited to the lounge of a luxury yacht. Her gold good-luck pin clung to the lapel. Cut-shell earrings adorned her lobes. A cunning shell-and-gold necklace brushed the place where her cleavage would have shown, had the suit been at all that way inclined. More shell patterns made delicate whorls on the toes of her textured pumps. Today, Elizabeth would be onstage, and she looked every bit the way she wanted to look: the head of a thriving, go-ahead organization. The only part of her appearance she was unaware of was the fresh pink flush giving away her anticipation at an adventure into the unknown.

Soon they were driving along Queen's Quay, the giant CN Tower soaring above them, on their right the mix of refurbished buildings, bobbing sloops, marine stores and entertainment centers of Toronto's revitalized waterfront. Trudy picked her way carefully, avoiding railway tracks and road barriers. They counted until they reached the proper opening in the fence. To Elizabeth's puzzlement, there wasn't a yacht in sight; only a square trailer and a knot of shaggy-looking people in sweat shirts and ragged shorts hanging around the door.

"This can't be it."

Trudy rechecked her references. "Has to be. You can see the number on the side of the trailer."

"Drive over. We'll ask."

The Rolls lurched incongruously across the now soaking lot while the people at the trailer door, oblivious to the raindrops, looked up curiously. Elizabeth was about to tell Trudy to drive on. Then she stiffened in her seat. There, turning in at exactly the same gate, was Justin Archer's Cadillac.

"If he's been following me I'll kill him! I really will."

Yet even she couldn't imagine him sinking so low to get to Diana Daniels. Justin might be a lurking predator, but in public, at least, he always tried to keep up a classy image.

The Cadillac pulled up beside the Rolls. One of the smoked windows rolled down. Justin's face appeared, as furious and surprised as her own.

"What are you doing here?" he demanded shortly.

"I might ask the same of you, Justin."

He glowered. A retort was forming on his lips when a compact young woman stepped out of the crowd at the trailer. Damp tendrils lay on her forehead from the rain, and her baggy green sweat shirt was frayed where the sleeves had been chopped off above the elbow.

Raindrops beaded her glasses as she splashed uncon-
cernedly through the puddles in torn sneakers.

"Aha! We've been waiting for you. You're the two
sent by Diana Daniels. I'm Suzy."

Two had been asked!

In comic unison, Justin and Elizabeth registered
shock and simultaneously tried to smooth their faces.

"*I* have been invited by Ms Daniels," Elizabeth said
pointedly. "I supposed she might keep a yacht down
here."

Suzy grinned, an expression that momentarily ban-
ished the impression of myopia caused by her thick
lenses. It was hard to tell whether she was twenty or
thirty. She'd remain agile and wiry as a mountain goat
right into old age.

"Sorry. No yacht. You're coming with us. This way,
please."

Oblivious to the weather, Suzy waved them toward
her. Elizabeth gritted her teeth, opened the car door
and made a bulletlike dash for the trailer, using only
the tips of her shoes for balance. Nevertheless, she got
mud on her left trouser cuff and cursed silently.

Inside, she was confronted by a desk jumbled with
paper, a stack of marine objects and more people
crammed against two windows looking over the
harbor. She turned to find Justin right behind her,
filling the whole door, cutting off escape. The brief-
est of rolling sensations struck Elizabeth's stomach
before she swallowed it back.

Today he was dressed in tan summer slacks, a
chocolate-colored sports jacket, an Oxford-cloth shirt
and a plain silk tie. Elizabeth noted that a few stray
raindrops had dared settle themselves upon his care-

fully smoothed hair. His Italian loafers remained un-scathed.

Suzy poked her head around from behind him. She had longish brown hair that had been caught casually in an elastic band. She was completely without make-up. Her jaw was very firm and square.

"Not in here. The bus, around back."

Neither Elizabeth nor Justin budged.

"Are you sure we're talking about Diana Daniels, the actress?" Justin asked with cultured incredulity. Elizabeth was sure he had never been on a bus in his life.

Suzy nodded. More drops fell from her hair onto her glasses.

"Oh, yes. I almost forgot." She fished about in the back pocket of her shorts and produced two envel-opes. "She sent a message for both of you."

Despite the wrinkles, Elizabeth recognized Diana's classy stationery. She tore open the missive, expecting it to say something like "April Fool's!"

Only it wasn't April. It was the second week of Au-gust.

"As promised," the handwriting read, "I have ar-ranged something unusual. Please do whatever Suzy says. And enjoy!"

There was no mistaking the slanting signature, identical to that on Justin's note.

"Okay, now come on, please. We can't waste any more time."

Ignoring her, Elizabeth and Justin eyed each other. Had they been alley cats, they would have been cir-cling each other, hair on end, ears flat against their skulls. Since they were people, they could signal their dislike only by narrowing their eyes sharply.

They both knew that this was not going to be a pleasant holiday, but a sweaty struggle for Diana's favor. Despite her charm, Diana was deliberately pitting them against each other. She was playing hardball here.

Breaking contact, Elizabeth was the first to brave the weather, but the sight that met her around the back made her forget the rain completely.

An ancient former school bus sat dripping, its back and front door agape. A number of seats had been removed from the rear to make room for a vast heap of backpacks. Beside the packs was a jumble of orange, which Elizabeth incredulously recognized as a pile of life jackets. The bus was hitched to a large trailer sporting three tiers of tightly lashed fiberglass canoes.

"This!" she croaked before she could prevent herself.

Suzy cast her a sideways look.

"Of course. Do get in. You'll get wet out here."

Only the knowledge of Justin behind her made her climb the grimy steps. The inside was as dismaying as the outside. The seats were battered. Some of the windows didn't close. Crude drop tables had been installed here and there so, presumably, bored passengers could play cards.

Before the back door was closed, more backpacks were piled in. The last entries were Elizabeth's fawn leather case and Justin's pigskin weekender, which sat like two bewildered aristocrats tossed to the mob.

Apparently all the people who had been hanging around the trailer were going, too. They crowded in behind Justin and Elizabeth, forcing the two far to the back. Laughing and chattering familiarly, they scattered themselves around, sprawling in seats along the entire length of the bus until the only option for Justin and Elizabeth was to take the two opposite seats right directly in front of the packs. Suzy herself got behind the wheel and tried the starter, which made a grinding, defeated noise against the drumming of the steadily increasing rain. A chorus of good-natured razzing rose from the passengers.

"Hey, Suzy, give it a kick!"

"Naw, put some gas in it. Betcha it's dry as a bone."

"Uh-uh," replied Suzy, unfazed, "it's just wet. How about you guys getting out and giving me a push?"

Cheerfully, the entire crew hoisted themselves up again and clomped out into the rain. At the back and sides of the bus they leaned into it, joking and teasing. The decrepit vehicle began to move, inching forward, then plunging lickety-split across the pitted lot with Suzy at the helm. The same moment she seemed about to crash into the chain-link fence, she lifted her foot from the clutch. The bus jerked, coughed and sputtered to life.

The passengers tramped back on, their hair slick, their shoulders and backs darkened with large rain stains. They began to settle into their seats again. But before they did, their banter died just for a moment, as each of them in turn took notice that Justin and Elizabeth had not budged from their places.

Elizabeth dismissed their looks. It was impossible, surely, that these characters had expected her, much less Justin, to push a bus in the rain....

CHAPTER FOUR

I DON'T BELIEVE THIS!

The refrain bounced around and around in Elizabeth's brain as the school bus rattled northward. Two hours had passed, and Elizabeth refused to ask how many more might be ahead. Besides keeping her suit away from the sticky-looking wall and ignoring Justin, she had little else to do but examine the other passengers. There were ten of them, including Suzy; not so many as she had first imagined. They were youngish. Twenties to thirties, she would guess, and about equally divided between the sexes. Beyond that, she couldn't identify them. They didn't look poor—she could always tell that by the betraying puffy look of malnutrition—but their utter disregard for personal appearance was appalling.

There seemed to be some sort of competition as to who could be the raggediest. Shorts had to be frayed. Most of the T-shirts had had the sleeves torn off and were faded and stained. Running shoes, festooned with holes, stuck out into the aisle. The odd sweater had been flung over the back of a seat, invariably elbowless and baggy from sheer old age. None of the females seemed to know about makeup. Elizabeth could have recommended a good barber for all of the men.

Some of the people seemed to know each other, for they laughed familiarly together as they played cards and Trivial Pursuit on the battered tables. Above them, homemade plywood luggage racks utilized elastics and hooks to hold the wild assortment of paraphernalia the passengers had jammed up above. The interior of the bus smelled like wet sheep because of the rain. Water seeped in through the stuck windows. Periodically, an amateurishly installed stereo system blared country-and-western music.

Justin remained silent, but the pulse at the side of his temple indicated that he, too, was entertaining less than charitable thoughts. He sat carefully in the center of the seat, royally upright as only Justin could sit.

That's right, Elizabeth thought caustically. *Don't let Diana catch you with your trouser creases ruined!*

Against the swaying of the bus, Elizabeth maintained her confident demeanor, though the presence of Justin throbbed continually through her consciousness—much like a toothache, she supposed. She could almost feel his weight shift with every jolt, sense the heat from his body under his pricey jacket. Since the moment she had discovered that Diana had invited them both, Elizabeth had been gathering herself like an athlete before the contest. Justin made her determined to think faster, deal harder, charm more sweetly and, above all, never let Justin glimpse a crack in her custom-built, fortified shell.

I'll break my neck to come out on top. That's probably exactly why Diana invited him along.

Which gave Elizabeth a half dozen second thoughts about Diana.

Elizabeth tried very hard to associate the glamorous actress with this rattletrap bus heading to an unknown destination, but she couldn't. She accepted it because she wanted Diana's endorsement so badly and because she was used to all sorts of promotional hijinks. Perhaps this was Diana's idea of a joke. Very well, she would be allowed her sense of humor. Elizabeth would start smiling when Diana herself appeared to end the charade.

One more hour passed, and yet another, with only a single stop at a tiny roadside café. Elizabeth, who did not drink pop, and very rarely tea or coffee, was hard put to find some bottled juice. Justin took nothing but remained standing apart, arms folded, face closed—probably trying for saturnine, Elizabeth supposed. Justin had been raised in the image business. Drop him on the moon and he'd square his shoulders for the camera.

The rest of the crowd jammed themselves in front of the tiny counter, shouting orders over each other's shoulders and then spilling out to sit on the steps, their hands full of hot dogs, potato chips, ice-cream bars and every other horror specifically designed to wreck health and skin. By now, Elizabeth could see there were newcomers in the group, whom the others had taken in, bombarding them with queries, sharing food. No one tried to introduce himself to Justin and Elizabeth or ask friendly questions. The two got curious looks and nothing more. Elizabeth wasn't used to such unsubtle exclusion. Like Justin, she was usually center stage.

"Clannish lot," she muttered under her breath.

Justin smoothed his tie.

"If you wanted to be one of the crowd, you ought to have pushed the bus."

So he hadn't missed that, either.

"I didn't exactly see you hopping out to lend a hand."

"No, you didn't. But then, I never wanted to be one of a crowd."

His gray eyes fixed on Elizabeth, satisfied with a dart well flung. Elizabeth wished she could tighten his tie knot until his self-satisfied expression was gone.

"Don't worry," she replied in a sweet voice dripping double entendre, "you couldn't ever be one of a crowd."

She was saved from his answer by the signal to get back on the bus. She climbed up behind the only silent member of the troop she had seen so far, a massive, taciturn fellow who had to be six foot five and was so broad in the shoulders he could barely fit in the door.

Not far north of Toronto, the rocky gray stones of the Canadian Shield had begun to poke up through the farmland. Now farms vanished altogether in favor of pines, marshy patches and bush. Lakes were glimpsed through trees. Crude advertisements appeared for campgrounds, boat rentals and fishing camps. They passed signs saying Go Home Lake, Reptile Farm and Trading Post, Live Bait and Jim's Taxidermy. At a highway cut, the names Frank and Helene were touchingly spray painted inside a heart on the rock.

Since the bus had left the tiny restaurant, Elizabeth had become aware that Justin's mood had tightened. Good. In some obscure way she had scored, and who was she to question an advantage? She kept her attention carefully focused on the landscape and suddenly realized she had never been north of Toronto before. She looked out the windows with livening interest. A completely urban creature, the legendary Canadian wilderness had meant nothing in her mind. Now she found herself a little disconcerted to find it was so close to her back door.

Finally, after five hours of highway, the bus veered off onto a dirt road and bumped precariously across the backs of rocky ridges, up and down like a funhouse ride. Suzy wrestled the wheel while the riders held on, and the tongue of the trailer gouged a trench when the humps were too much for the hitch to accommodate. Weathered ruins of a shack flew by. Then, nothing but deep bush and clutching branches pushed in on both sides. Elizabeth clung to the back of a seat and even Justin reached out a hand to steady himself.

At last, just when human habitation seemed a remote memory, they pulled into a bay, which sported a shed with a dock and a gravel patch big enough to park two or three cars. Elizabeth's spirits rose immediately. Diana would have sent a boat for her—for them—here. Most likely she had a luxurious hideaway secreted among the pines.

She stole a glance at Justin and saw by his increased attentiveness that the same thought had occurred to him. Girding herself, Elizabeth smoothed her hair and straightened her jacket. She did not intend to come out trailing in the upcoming battle of first impressions.

The bus crept down the precipitous entry to this speck of civilization and, through a series of contortions, turned itself so that the trailer backed on the water. Whooping, the passengers jumped out, pulling open the back doors and heaving the packs into a pile on the rock. Justin and Elizabeth descended gingerly and scanned the scene around them. Save for the shed and dock, nothing human confronted them; only a broad expanse of what looked to be a river. A river crammed with islands and twisting out of sight among trees, trees and more trees. Elizabeth could tell that Justin shared her simple heartfelt plea: *Diana, please, please come and rescue us.*

"Behind the shed is the last flush toilet before the North Pole. Don't miss it!"

No one seemed interested. They were too busy unlashing the yellow nylon rope from the canoes and carrying them, one by one, down to the floating dock. Some hauled their packs toward the dock, too, while Suzy darted about, keeping an eye on everything. From a heap of battered-looking paddles she selected two, measured them with her eye and walked over to where Justin and Elizabeth stood.

"Here, these look about the right size for you. Pick up a life jacket from that pile over there."

"But—"

Suzy was already speeding elsewhere. For all her seeming myopia, she was clearly in charge. The people, apparently familiar with this routine, had begun pairing up, slipping their packs into canoes and climbing in. Soon a small flotilla was bobbing about in open water and only two canoes were left. Suzy commandeered the taciturn man mountain and they carried two new packs down to the dock. From there she waved her arm beckoningly at Justin and Elizabeth.

"This is your canoe down here."

"I beg your pardon?"

Justin looked at the canoes with both brows pulled sharply together. Elizabeth recognized his "I'm-reaching-my-limit" expression.

"Your canoe. I'll help you load it, then we can all get going."

"Surely Ms Daniels will have sent a boat."

Suzy laughed.

"She has sent a boat. This is it."

Elizabeth and Justin exchanged looks mirroring equal disbelief. Elizabeth half opened her mouth when she remembered the words of Diana's note: *Do whatever Suzy says.* To protest might be a tactical error. Her face smoothed.

"I know," she said, brightening. "They're going to drop us off the way. I bet Diana's place is hidden up one of these channels."

She had not, so far, inquired as to where all the people and all the packs were heading. The less she knew about the others, the less she would have to interact with them.

Taking a deep breath, Elizabeth marched down the dock. However unconventional her mode of arrival was, she was darned if she was going to mess things up by an unsporting refusal.

The canoe was a red one. Two brand-new backpacks sat in the middle, stuffed tight and bulging. The sight reminded her. Elizabeth stopped short.

"My purse!" she exclaimed, involuntarily patting her hip, where it generally rode.

"You left it on the seat. It's with your luggage and all taken care of," Suzy assured her. "Have either of you had any experience with a canoe?"

Elizabeth mumbled noncommittally, loath to expose ignorance of what might well be Diana's favorite pastime. Justin, whom Elizabeth discovered right behind her after all, favored Suzy with one of his famous "how-can-you-even-ask" glances that implied he spent fun weekends running Niagara Falls in a barrel.

"I know my way around boats, miss."

"He certainly does. He's spent hours watching them from the yacht-club terrace," Elizabeth added sweetly.

A muscle displayed itself on one side of Justin's jaw and a brow hooked upward. Clearly he would rather drown them both than admit he wasn't a Hiawatha of the waters.

Okay, then, thought Elizabeth. *This ought to be interesting.*

Before either of them made a move, Suzy made them buckle on their flotation vests. The orange bulk ruined the lines of Elizabeth's chic outfit, but she was compensated by seeing Justin's sports jacket bunched tight under the bulky device. It was almost worth a giggle, and Justin knew it. He stepped angrily toward the edge of the dock, where Suzy stopped him.

"Elizabeth, you take the bow and get in first. I'll hand you your paddles. Since Justin has experience, he can handle the stern."

Elizabeth edged toward the frail-looking craft that bobbed and shivered at the lightest touch. Squatting on the worn wood, she cautiously extended a foot. The moment her toe touched, the canoe skittered away, almost dragging her off the edge of the dock. She heard a low croak of amusement behind her, but by the time she wheeled, Justin had a straight face again. He had gotten even for the life jacket.

Suzy grasped the gunwale of the wayward boat and held it firm against the dock.

"Just step in the middle and sit down on the thwart there. Don't be nervous."

Gamely, Elizabeth stretched out her foot again, centered it on the fiberglass bottom and heaved the rest of her body after it. As if on roller bearings, the canoe rocked wildly from side to side, nearly pitching her headfirst into the river. Before she could stop herself, Elizabeth squealed, then dropped ignominiously to the bottom of the craft until it steadied. Too late, she realized she had ruined both raw-silk knees of her trousers. Cursing silently, she followed instructions in edging herself over the forward thwart and settling her bottom onto the tiny little square that passed for a seat.

"Now you, Justin."

Unable to see behind her, Elizabeth was nearly tossed out a second time as the canoe bucked and sloshed. She had guessed right. Justin knew as little about this as she! Waiting till they steadied, Suzy handed them their paddles.

"Off we go."

Leaving them to manage, she hopped with agility into the yellow canoe with the human hulk in the rear and set off to join the others. As Justin and Elizabeth's canoe floated out, stern first, both of them picked up their paddles and stuck them into the water. The canoe careened forward, half-jamming the nose under the dock. The impact caused Elizabeth to drop her paddle. As she grabbed for it, her sleeve got soaked to the elbow and the canoe rocked dangerously. She got a disconcerting glimpse of waterweeds waving thickly below her like so many arms waiting to pull her down.

"I suspect," muttered Elizabeth, righting herself, "we're supposed to paddle on opposite sides to make it go straight. I thought you said you knew about boats.''

"Then why didn't you push us away from the dock?'' Justin tossed back, instantly putting himself in the right. He sounded as if he was talking through his back teeth to keep control.

The people in the other canoes, in a fit of high spirits, were racing off around the first bend. Only Suzy and her partner lagged, waiting for Justin and Elizabeth.

With much splashing, the two backed the canoe out and pointed it toward the center of the water. Paddling now on opposite sides, they got it moving. Elizabeth, who had previously only seen canoes gliding ethereally through the occasional old movie, was shocked at how much muscle it took to propel one. As the dock receded behind them, she experienced a clutching in her stomach. The river was wide and deep, and there was nothing between her and the bottom save the seemingly rickety canoe, which quivered and shuddered every time she twitched her nose. Sitting rigidly, she wielded the paddle with care while Justin propelled the canoe along with great splashing strokes that wasted all kinds of energy. How like him to show off the first minute he tried something, she fumed silently.

The canoe moved at a satisfactory clip but showed no sign of joining Suzy. In fact, it was curving away toward the opposite shore. Elizabeth panicked until she twigged onto a basic law of physics. If a bug had a slow leg on one side and a fast leg on the other...

"Justin, we have to switch sides. You're driving us around in a circle.''

He waited until the canoe was completely turned around, with Suzy to its stern, before he acknowledged Elizabeth's logic. They flipped their paddles to the other side, dripping all over themselves. The canoe obligingly began to seek the other canoeists. When it began to veer toward the dock, they switched again and finally arrived in Suzy's general vicinity.

"You'll never get anywhere fast that way," Suzy said. "Here, let me show you the J stroke."

She demonstrated an arcane motion that had the paddle turning sideways halfway through its motion. It was supposed to steer the canoe. Justin and Elizabeth tried it with absolutely no effect save to nearly ram Suzy.

"Well," she said a little disparagingly, "you'll have to practice when you can. We better catch up with the rest now or we'll lose them."

She regarded them steadily for a moment through her glasses, giving Elizabeth the uneasy impression that she was being closely examined and that Justin's pretense of skill had been exposed completely. When Suzy left them to follow as best they could, Elizabeth thought she heard a low curse exit with Justin's breath, but it could have been just the slapping of the water.

After failing at the J stroke, they discovered that by switching frequently, they could keep the canoe on a zigzag course that eventually got them to where the other canoeists were assembled—at an island, waiting for Suzy to lead the way.

Suzy's canoe glided forward out of sight, and the others, bubbling with energy, dipped quickly along behind, leaving Elizabeth and Justin in their wake. As their voices faded, Elizabeth felt a kind of panic seize her breast. What was she doing out here, anyway, bobbing about in a canoe with, of all people, Justin Archer? Yesterday, she would not have imagined anyone on earth being able to pull off such a feat. Was Diana Daniels a magician?

The panic increased as the last canoe shrank in the distance. Elizabeth clutched her paddle, feeling its hard grain against the palms of her hands. There was too much space around her. She was an indoor person, really, who took comfort in good solid walls. The sky here was a giant gray blanket over a river that didn't seem to have any banks. Their canoe seemed too treacherous a lifeboat on the surface of enough water to drown the population of Toronto. Elizabeth's nerves twanged with a sharpened desire to speed back to the dock. Surely she could reach Diana some easier way.

She half turned, intending to look back the way they had come. Her eyes met Justin's, and for a split second, she read there exactly the same impulse to flee. It was as clear as if they had said, "Let's do it!" aloud in the air. Had not their combined pride been a bigger obstacle than the river, they would have turned around in a minute. However, they were competing for Diana's endorsement. On they would go!

Besides, it was too late to turn back. All Elizabeth could see over her shoulder were two or three rocky headlands, with no clear indication of the way they had come. The prospect ahead was equally intimidating. What looked like solid land from one angle turned out to be surrounded by water from another angle. The river had broken into dozens of rocky islands covered in evergreens. Between the islands, labyrinthine channels led not only east and west but also north and south. It was total confusion—through which only Suzy seemed to know the way.

Well, thought Elizabeth bravely, *if this is what it takes to get to Diana Daniels, then this is what I'll do. But after she signs the contract, I'll give her a piece of my mind.*

They set out after the chattering group and kept Suzy carefully in sight as they picked their way through the wild waterscape. They brought up the rear, more than once paddling frantically to keep from losing sight of the pack. Elizabeth's arms had ached after the first fifteen minutes out, but she'd refused to slow. She blessed her exercise classes. Without them, she'd be draped across the bow now like a wet noodle, and she was darned if she was going to let Justin see her weaken. Where on earth was Diana's hideaway, anyway?

They paddled on, lost completely in the watery jigsaw puzzle. The landscape was a crazy jumble of pink-and-gray cliffs topped with evergreens and birches. Whole rock faces were seamed with cracks. Large chunks had fallen from the ends of loaf-shaped islands, like slices from a cake. The majesty was lost on Elizabeth, who only scanned the scene for a roof of glass, a sweep of cedar decking, the dock where Diana's motorboats would be tied up. The sun was already slanting low in the August sky. Something had to happen soon.

CHAPTER FIVE

WHERE IS DIANA'S HIDEAWAY? Elizabeth wondered in growing anxiety. She could feel Justin mulling over the same question.

It seemed as if they had been paddling laboriously forever, though her watch told her it had been scarcely more than an hour. Their canoe had wobbled drunkenly the whole time, and they'd almost got stuck in a waterlogged deadfall. If it hadn't been for Suzy hanging back to watch them, they'd have been lost ages ago.

Finally, just when the sun disappeared behind the pines, Suzy took a sharp right and beached her canoe on a long, smooth spit of rock.

"Campsite!" she called gaily. "This is where we spend the night."

The rock belonged to a large island covered, like all the others, with trees, brush and deadfalls. Four other canoes swung inward, bows grounded on the rock, sterns swaying while their occupants leaped out, lifted packs, hauled the canoes above the waterline and turned them upside down. Only Elizabeth and Justin remained, bobbing out on the river, staring at the island. What they were really looking for was a terrace, a rooftop, a dock, any sign that the place was inhabited—and inhabited by Diana Daniels. The only home they spotted was a hole high in a dead pine tree, a woodpecker popping in and out of it.

"She can't be serious!" Elizabeth was exhausted. Only her determination to put on a good show in front of Justin had kept her back rigid and her head nonchalant.

Justin shifted sharply in his seat. "You bet she can't! I'm going to straighten this silliness out this minute!"

"Oho! So Justin the king has finally reached his royal limits. This should be interesting."

He answered with a stroke that brought the bow up onto the shore.

"You get out first."

Elizabeth was only too glad to oblige. The craft swayed precariously back and forth as she sidled forward. Shakily, she stood up clutching the gunwales, leaned forward and put a foot over the side.

Relieved of her weight, the canoe slipped backward, leaving Elizabeth up to her calves in water. Uttering an indignant squawk, she staggered to dry ground. Both feet were soaked, and her pant legs were pasted to her legs.

After much splashing with his paddle blade, Justin pushed the canoe back up, looking much cheered by her mishap. "Hey, hold the thing steady."

"Hold it yourself!"

With a grunt, he used his paddle as a pole to shove the canoe savagely until it was almost halfway up on the rock. As he started to stand up, Suzy hurried over and pushed the craft free again, tipping her nose forward over the cargo.

"Too much weight out of the water. You'll put a hole in the bottom crawling around inside it like that."

She steadied the quivering bow while Justin tried to leap from the canoe straight to the curve of dry shore. He landed neatly, but the soles of his loafers betrayed him. He slid backward, wetting himself to the ankles.

"Bloody hell!"

Scrambling back up, he stood shaking one foot, then the other, resembling a large disgruntled dog. Elizabeth clapped a hand over her mouth as she shrugged off her life vest. Justin's killing look had no effect. She was relieved to see that from the waist up, at least, she still looked presentable.

Suzy had unloaded the canoe, hauled it single-handedly from the water and tossed the paddles in the pile with the others. She pointed to two packs.

"These are yours. Gifts from Diana. Your sleeping bag is strapped to the bottom, covered in plastic, and your tent is at the top. You'd best get it up before dinner because it gets dark fast at sundown."

Justin and Elizabeth stiffened in the midst of straightening their disheveled selves.

"I beg your pardon," said Justin in his calmest, most steely voice, "but shouldn't Ms Daniels make an appearance soon? We thought we were being taken to her Canadian vacation home."

Suzy glanced at them in some astonishment.

"Well, I don't know how you got that idea. Absolutely nobody lives along this river. I've heard Ms Daniels has a place on the other side of Algonquin Park."

"Then what are we doing here?" His towering dignity overcame even his squelching shoes.

"Why, you're members of the camping trip. Ms Daniels paid the shot and left you packs to boot. Some luck, I'd say."

"What, ah, camping trip?" Elizabeth inquired, the wet part of her legs going cold.

"This one. Two weeks in a circle down to Georgian Bay and back to where we started. Everything supplied. Should be a ball!"

In the ensuing silence, the woodpecker drilled into its tree, and the river made rude chuckling noises. Elizabeth and Justin forgot themselves so far as to exchange a glance of identical horror. Simultaneously, their patience snapped like two twigs in an angry fist. Without even knowing it, they shifted into their customary commanding stance. Movie star or no movie star, neither of them had time for nonsense such as this.

"I don't know about Elizabeth, but I've had enough," Justin declared in a voice that had caused many an underling to blanch. "Please direct me to the nearest civilized area. I'll get back to the city and speak to Ms Daniels from there."

When he turned, Elizabeth saw he had perspired clear through the back of his Bill Blass sports jacket—for Justin, an unthinkable thing to do. She suffered a vision of him stalking off and leaving her there.

"That goes ditto for me," she added hurriedly. "I'd like to leave at once."

A high-pitched whine surprised Elizabeth, and she slapped the back of her hand abruptly, then stood looking down at the tiny corpse. It took some moments before it registered that it was a mosquito. She hadn't seen a mosquito in years. Her precious skin was being attacked. She began to panic. Already, she'd suffered the humiliation of ruined shoes and paddle blisters.

Suzy's calm look turned to one of mild exasperation.

"I just told you that there *is* no nearby civilization,
so get yourself set up for the night. Molly and I have
to get supper on the move."

Someone called Suzy. Justin stepped up to block her
way, an angry flush climbing his neck. Too stunned to
take her eyes away, Elizabeth stared.

"Look, didn't Diana Daniels tell you about us . . . I
mean me? I was asked to a business meeting, not a . . . a
kiddie camp-out. Something is terribly wrong here."

"You can say that again!" Elizabeth breathed between set teeth.

Rather than backing away from Justin, Suzy cocked
her head and put one hand on her hip. Perhaps, Elizabeth speculated, she needed to be that close to see
him clearly through her glasses.

"Justin, I have no idea what you were asked to. All
I know is that a woman named Diana Daniels paid
your way, sent the packs and said you'd be joining us.
Naturally, I assumed you'd come for a holiday."

Two more attempts at grilling elicited no further
information from her. Suzy seemed genuinely in the
dark about the entire thing. Yet back there on the
dock, Elizabeth could have sworn . . .

She frowned, not sure what she could have sworn to.
Maybe she just wasn't used to Suzy's curious vague-
ness that, at times, seemed like an act. . . . She remained speechless as Suzy trotted off and left them to
themselves.

The sky was now a deep orange color, and shadows
were starting to thicken under the trees. The rest of the
people were dashing around, hefting packs and setting up for the night. Several orange, blue and green

tents had already popped up among the greenery. Suzy's massive partner was placing stones in a circle atop a bare rise of rock. Others were bringing dead wood and piling it nearby. Apparently the rest of the people were perfectly serious about camping out here for the night.

An unprintable expletive escaped Justin's lips. He turned and paced the space along the shore like a vigorous, headstrong animal brought up short against a fence. Elizabeth scanned the surrounding shores frantically, but, true to Suzy's word, there was no hint of any human presence. They might as well have been a million miles from the dock they had set out from that afternoon.

"I've been had!" Justin exploded, leaving large wet footprints behind him as he walked.

"*You've* been had! What about me?"

The gray eyes fixed on her scornfully.

"I sincerely hope you've been had, too, Elizabeth. Once in a while the shoe should be on the other foot!"

Elizabeth let fly a scandalized gasp. How dare Justin even hint that *she'd* taken advantage of *him*! How dare he! Her suit jacket fell open at the waist. "Why, you—"

"Hey, tents, folks. It's getting late."

Suzy spoke firmly from behind the growing stack of firewood—as if she had been keeping an eye on the quarrel. A primitive desire to physically attack Justin swept Elizabeth. With effort, she contained it. There was no escape. She and Justin would have to stay, at least for tonight.

"Wait until the morning. We'll see who's been had around here. Just wait!" Elizabeth hissed, turning on her heel.

She stalked up to where the bulk of gear lay, her wet pant legs grabbing at her calves like mocking hands. The first thing she needed was a change of clothes.

"Where's my suitcase?" she asked crisply when Suzy came within range.

"With the other baggage we didn't need."

Suzy knelt down and began to set sticks into a tiny pyramid and scatter dried pieces of bark at the base.

"What do you mean, didn't need?" Elizabeth felt her skin tightening on the back of her neck. "Where is it?"

"Back on the bus, quite safe. Suitcases and purses are no good in the bush."

Slow comprehension dawned, followed by outrage, then panic.

"You mean . . . my personal luggage with my personal things is not here?"

"Exactly. That case was far too awkward for a canoe. Your packs have everything you'll need for a camping trip."

Instantly, Elizabeth realized she was separated from her oatmeal soap, her cleanser and moisturizer, her handmade hairbrush, her French-lace nightgown and her magic mousse. Especially her magic mousse! Immediately she felt gritty, from her squishing toes to the roots of her hair. If she couldn't have a hot bath and repair herself, by morning she'd be an unkempt mess not fit for public eyes.

With dread, she eyed the pack assigned to her. Almost mockingly, it bore her company logo, a sprig of blossoms in a soft green oval. There was no mistaking that the sack had been designed specifically for her. Perhaps Diana was a sadist, pure and simple.

Her peripheral vision caught Justin stilled midstep as he overheard the exchange with Suzy. The corners of his mouth drew in. Then he grew very, very calm. Elizabeth knew calm was his most dangerous condition. *In the morning,* she thought, *we shall see some fur flying.*

She breathed deeply for control, taking care, as always, not to lose her temper in an unseemly manner while strangers were watching. She and Justin were two rigid figures standing out from all the activity around them. Their clothing, bedraggled though it was, still presented a brave air of fashion that suddenly seemed absurd next to an overturned stump and a clump of bullrushes growing in a pocket along the shore. Elizabeth knew that things were almost out of hand. She did not intend to become any more absurd than she was now. In the morning, she promised herself, she would get back to the city, even if she had to walk all the way. Then Diana Daniels had better have an explanation!

Right now, however, she had to make the best of being stuck here for the night. "We'll discuss this tomorrow," she said tightly in Suzy's direction. "In the meantime, would you, uh, direct me to my tent and I'll have a look at the pack?"

The heads of three people around the crackling fire snapped up in unison.

"I beg your pardon?" Suzy breathed, her eyes widening slightly.

Elizabeth repeated her request. Suzy stood up, dusting bits of bark from her palms.

"I'm afraid we each set up our own tent around here, and we carry our own packs. I'll be glad to show you how the tent goes up if you need help."

Elizabeth had taken service for granted for a long time. She realized instantly that to expect it here would be to expose weakness. Her pride prickled. She shook back her sleek, wind-tousled mane.

"I can carry a pack and put up a tent if I have to."

Without waiting for a reply, she set off, dragging the awkward load. Anything to get what she really needed—a blessed change of clothes.

Walking was not quite the word for what she did. Knee-high bushes grasped at her legs, plucking tufts of silk from her trousers. Trunks and twisted branches loomed at her face. Her slippery leather soles sent her reeling again and again. Twice she fell, tearing the cloth along her thigh and getting huge dirt stains on her seat. By the time she had made it two dozen yards from the camp fire, she had grazed her ankle and felt half-ready to cry.

In exasperation, she flung down the pack and pulled the tent from its bag. A mass of fabric fell out along with assorted pegs, ropes and poles, none of which she had the least idea how to use. She moved them all around with her toe until finally a light-haired young man in a baseball sweater came over.

"Ernie's the name, assistance is my game. Maybe you'd better set up somewhere else. This isn't so level."

"I don't care how level it is," Elizabeth said angrily. "I just want to get the thing up. How does it work?"

Ernie assessed her ineptitude and got speedily busy. For someone who seemed nothing but arm joints and shin bones and an Adam's apple, he untangled the mystery of strings and pegs with remarkable efficiency.

"Your castle, madame," he announced, waiting for Elizabeth to return his grin.

Not in a grinning mood, Elizabeth thanked him curtly. His face fell. Another expression, part resentment, part mischief, crept into his eyes.

"Well, look out for rattlesnakes," he tossed over his shoulder, and vanished through the trees.

"What!"

Elizabeth stared after him for a petrified moment, then caught herself. She wasn't going to fall for that one! She grabbed the pack, which seemed to weigh two hundred pounds, and nearly took the whole tent down again squeezing it through the flap. She crawled in and zipped the opening behind her. The floor tilted dizzily to the left, and there seemed scarcely enough room to lift her head. Oh, when she got a hold of Diana Daniels, she would be dazzlingly graphic about how she had spent the night!

To her dismay, the pack contained only rough, baggy cotton clothes, just like the ones the rest of the campers wore, and no makeup whatsoever; only the most basic survival kit of cleanser, moisturizer with sunscreen, toothpaste, soap and shampoo. No hair dryer. *And no mousse!*

A horrid premonition shot through Elizabeth's mind. In the morning, she wouldn't be able to shower, blow dry or mousse her hair. It would be as stringy as twine and quite as flat. Justin's eyes would fall out on the ground.

Rooting ferociously, she came up with a green cotton fisherman's hat. If she could keep it on until she got home, she might just escape the disaster of being seen publicly with limp hair.

She squirmed out of the wet pantsuit and into trousers and a shirt of a very uneven, washed-out blue. Very ugly but at least dry. The pair of brownish canvas running shoes didn't match at all, but they fit, and she had already acquired a fine appreciation of rubber soles.

By now the scent of food was wafting through the air, and Elizabeth realized she was starving. *Starving and exhausted,* she amended a touch melodramatically. As she ventured back toward the fire, she felt as if the whole world were gaping at the first unflattering outfit she had worn since turning a profit with her company. On top of this, her face felt stiff and she knew her sculpted cheekbones had almost worn clean off.

No one gave her a second glance or looked at Justin when he showed up, similarly attired in nondescript green trousers and a long-sleeved sweat shirt one size too large for him. His face was a cold mask that informed Elizabeth at once how angry he was inside. *Good old Justin, as wooden in the neck as ever.*

Suzy, aided by her huge canoe mate and others in the group, raked the fire into an even bed and placed a blackened grill upon it. Cans of stew were opened and dumped into a large pot that had materialized from a large brown pack that seemed to contain food and kitchen supplies.

The fire was set between a ledge of rock and a fallen log so that the campers could sit in two rows facing each other. Elizabeth flinched each time a spark popped in the coals; she had never been close to an open fire that wasn't in a fireplace. The evening light had faded to a luminous gray tinge. A high-pitched whining cloud attacked Elizabeth, and after her first moment of astonishment, she began to slap furiously at the myriad insects assaulting her.

"Ooh! Get these things away from me! Isn't there any insect repellent?"

"Sure!"

Suzy reached into a pack and handed Elizabeth a bottle that smelled like a cross between lighter fluid and barn disinfectant. Elizabeth interrupted her little dance of torment long enough to spatter some of the unknown liquid over herself, trying to spare her skin as much as she could. The mosquitoes thickened, seeming to love the stuff.

"It doesn't work," declared a voice from the other side of the fire. "The only way is to toughen yourself up. Let 'em bite till your skin gets tough like horse-hide and they can't pierce through. Meantime, they won't bother you if you stand in the smoke from the fire."

Elizabeth was so scandalized she stopped slapping long enough to peer through the flames. A thin fellow with the face of an ascetic under a crown of spiky red hair stared back at her unblinkingly. Clad only in shorts, his bare chest and bony knees presented an invitation to every biting insect in the north woods. He stood in the fire smoke, arms folded, chin lifted as if he had stepped out of a James Fenimore Cooper novel.

"Cities have made us soft," he declared with a fine disdain for everything that had been invented after the wheel. "We have to take opportunities like this to get back where we started from. That's what I intend to do."

He spoke as if he expected Elizabeth to strip off her sweat shirt and join him. Yet she noticed most of the people were bunched, coughing and watery eyed, on the smoky side of the fire. Her immediate future loomed before her. Two weeks, at least, of dodging the public until the red blotches on her face repaired themselves. A whole day as soon as possible at Natalie's Spa, taking the complete volcanic-mud-and-herbal-pack treatment. She'd book for tomorrow afternoon if possible. Natalie would click her tongue in that tart French manner and ask Elizabeth why she was determined to ruin everything that she, Natalie of Paris, had worked to accomplish. If it happened again, Natalie might strike her from her list of exclusive customers. Natalie did not deal with people who refused to care for themselves with the same zeal she herself put into her treatments.

A puff of wind scattered the insect attackers and blew smoke into Elizabeth's nostrils. She coughed and swatted at her stinging eyelids. The anger inside her climbed another notch at all the sharp and unwelcome sensations her body was being subjected to: heat, muscle ache, blisters, wet feet, biting bugs, smoke, hunger. She had not struggled so hard and made so much money to have to put up with this. She refused....

Her galloping temper was halted by the sight of Justin's set face. He wasn't slapping openly as she had done but brushed at his neck and his arms with short jerky movements. When the smoke reached him, he turned his face away as if struck, then turned it back. He himself seemed ablaze from the inside with pure indignation.

Good for you, Justin. See what it's like to have a little discomfort in your life!

Kate, a plain, stoutish young woman with black hair in a heavy braid, began ladling stew from the pot into tin bowls and handing them around. Elizabeth took hers with distaste. However, she was famished. She began to down it, quelling in her mind all her misgivings about the preservatives, red meat and refined carbohydrates she was putting into herself. From long experience she knew that whatever she ate invariably showed up on her skin, so if she only put the healthiest, freshest, most natural food into her body, her skin would reflect their goodness. At home she lived mostly on fresh fruit, salads and raw vegetables, a luxurious counterpoint to the cheap, greasy provender of her childhood.

Absorbed in her supper, Elizabeth barely heard the chatter of the other campers and ignored them completely until darkness fell—a darkness awesome and total, unlike anything she had ever experienced before. When the realization finally penetrated that the streetlights wouldn't go on, Elizabeth, despite herself, edged onto the end of the log with the other people, wanting to be near the warmth and light of the fire.

Justin had eaten his dinner in angry gulps and washed his plate with a disdainful slosh of the soapy water set out for that purpose. Now he stood apart from the circle, his arms folded across his chest, the firelight reaching him only enough to make his eyes glitter and etch his cheekbones in a few ruddy strokes. His shoulders were grimly tight. He looked as if he could punch through a cement wall with a single blow.

Quiet descended upon the campers and they sat, murmuring among themselves and poking lazily at the fire, until Suzy stood up and stretched.

"Bedtime, I think. Everybody looks a little wiped from the first day out."

Bedtime. Elizabeth hadn't the faintest idea where her tent was or how she'd ever get to it. Suzy, seeming to know this, led Elizabeth and Justin back through the brush. Elizabeth slipped and swore in a most unladylike fashion. Justin stumbled also, but not a word came out of him. Elizabeth guessed his mouth was too tight with lordly frustration.

Other people seemed to have had the foresight to bring flashlights to dinner, and those same flashlights bobbed eerily through the trees around them. Suzy got Elizabeth to her tent and waited until Elizabeth had located the flashlight included in her pack. The inside of Elizabeth's tent was strewn with the contents of the pack, which she had previously pulled out while in a temper. She struggled to unroll the new sleeping bag, and when she had finally succeeded and had crawled in, she found herself on a tipsy slant, head down against the wall. She had to crawl out, shift the bag around and crawl into it again.

Her spine scraped against something she eventually realized was a root. She moved off to the side to try to avoid it. When she lay still, she heard nothing but a sound like the distant rushing of a train. After many minutes of puzzlement, she realized it was the air rushing through the trees.

There were plenty of other noises, too, but she was too groggy to pay attention. The stresses of the day finally overwhelmed her and put Elizabeth to sleep as if she had been slugged over the head. Her last thought was a dim image of Justin illuminated by the fire-light. She hoped a root was sticking into his back, too.

CHAPTER SIX

ELIZABETH OPENED HER EYES to weird orange light filtering through a ceiling that was only three feet or so above her. She ached all over. Someone had left a knife sticking through her spine.

Justin Archer, I'll get you for this!

She dragged herself further awake. No, no. It wasn't Justin this time, however much he'd like to stab her. She'd been stranded in the bush by that freak of an actress, Diana Daniels.

Groaning, she tried to turn over. The knife blade turned, too, slicing through her ribs. Elizabeth stuck her hand behind her and found the woody knuckle poking its rudeness into her anatomy.

Yesterday's events came back in full. Disbelief, then indignation boiled up. She'd had just about enough of Diana Daniels. She was going home at once!

Neck, shoulders, back screaming, she sat up. The tent bounced and quivered when she scraped the wall. The sleeping bag clutched her like smothering nylon hands until she wrestled the zipper to her thigh.

"Ooh . . . my face, my hair!"

Worse than all the aches was the feeling of being grainy all over. Each morning Elizabeth was accustomed to stepping from her bedroom into her rose-tiled shower, where hot water would pour forth in needles from the shining silver shower head, and

lemon-and-balsam shampoo would stream lacy bub-
bles down her shoulder blades. Upon coming out of
the shower, she would take a fluffy towel from the
heated towel rail, apply lavender body lotion and put
on a soft silk robe while she blow dried her hair. What
did people do in the bush? Did they ever wash?

Seeing no help around, Elizabeth wriggled into her
clothes of the previous evening. Her oyster pantsuit lay
ignominiously balled in the corner, making her gri-
mace. She was not so far from her origins that she
could overlook the waste of such an expensive outfit.
She used money, and she enjoyed it, but she never,
ever threw it away.

When she had buttoned the shirt, she scrabbled
about in the pack until she found the comb. Automatically, she applied it to her hair and had it only
half-untangled when she discovered there was no mirror. She was stuck here with no way of telling what she
looked like. If how she felt was any indication, she
must look awful!

The force of her panic took her by surprise, unbal-
ancing her. How could she, Elizabeth Wright, head of
a burgeoning cosmetics empire and its personal sym-
bol, look a mess? For almost a decade she had not
appeared in public with so much as a wayward hair,
knowing the damage one really bad photo could do.
Who'd want to use Wright products if their creator
resembled a haystack?

In agony and fury, Elizabeth did her best, spending
ages. Her hair had already given up the struggle and
lay so limp that all she could do was cram it up under
the hat she had unearthed in the pack. Bravely, she
flipped up the collar of the shirt and pulled the utili-
tarian leather belt tightly around her waist, hoping to

give the bagginess at least a dash of chic. Without mascara she knew her eyelashes had probably disappeared. She would have pinched her cheeks like a Victorian lady, but she knew she needed no aid to maintain high color there.

At last she squeezed out of the tent and strode down to where the breakfast camp fire was in the making and several people were splashing about in the river. Justin was converging at the same moment. His hair had sprung out from his head. A dark shadow, probably the first of his adult life, covered his jaw. He looked ready to spit nails.

"I demand to leave this place at once. Radio in a helicopter. Anything. The expense doesn't matter."

Elizabeth slid hurriedly up behind him, keeping out of his direct line of vision. They cornered Suzy between the fire and the food packs, where she was laying out strips of bacon.

"Two helicopters," put in Elizabeth in her most fearsome "don't-mess-with-me" voice. "I'm leaving, too." She maneuvered herself so that a squat pine was between herself and Justin.

Even Elsie would have jumped—fast. Suzy only arranged the bacon on the grill. She wore khaki shorts this morning, and her hair was pulled into a ponytail.

"I thought I explained to you last night. This is a two-week camping trip. Nobody can leave before the end."

"I don't give a damn what it is," Justin exploded. "I'm leaving today. So please see to it!"

Pulses were working on both sides of his temple. One hand kept pushing at his newly tight curls as if they hurt his head. As soon as he became conscious of

Elizabeth's stare he jerked around, putting his back to her as if the sight of her hurt him, too.

Why... it's his hair and his beard stubble, Elizabeth realized in a rush. *He feels as awful as I do. He doesn't want me to see him!*

Despite her own condition, her eyes rounded slightly. Imagine catching Justin off balance because of his appearance!

Suzy rose slowly to her feet, wiping her hands on the back of her shorts. She seemed taller than before.

"Look, there's no radio here or any other sort of communication. Neither of you are hurt. There's no emergency and therefore no reason to disturb the trip. Both of you had better accept that right now!"

Justin stopped brushing at his hair and his jaw thrust out. He was a man unused to having his wishes thwarted. *Justin at his most stubborn,* Elizabeth thought. *And his most obnoxious.*

"Look, Ms Suzy, I'm afraid you don't understand. I have a business to run and no time for this sort of idiocy. I'm going today even if I have to paddle back to that wretched marina myself. There's no way you can stop me. I'm sure I can charter something from there."

"And I'll paddle with him," Elizabeth announced, not caring whether Justin liked it or not. "You can't keep us here."

One of Justin's shoulders lifted, but in the midst of his nose-to-nose confrontation with Suzy, he was in no position to argue with Elizabeth. And there was no way Elizabeth was going to let him leave her behind.

"No one is keeping you here," Suzy said quietly, lifting a strand of hair off her lenses. "But I hope you noticed how strong the current was yesterday. It would

be against you. Tough paddlers might make the marina in, say, two days. Amateurs such as you would
never make it, much less find your way among all the
islands and channels. You'd be lost within ten minutes of leaving here. So if you fancy the prospect of
starving to death in the bush, please go ahead.''

Every camper was staring at her. A dead log floated
by—swiftly. A hawk swooped, crying harshly. Maybe
there were buzzards out there, Elizabeth thought,
shivering slightly. Her prickling hair roots told her that
Suzy's words were all too real.

Justin was apoplectic. Muscles bulged on the side of
his neck. Blood rushed under his skin. With effort, he
sucked in air and placed his hands on his hips in defiance. He gave her his hard-boiled, horse-trader stare.

"Okay, Suzy, you score. I want off this river. How
much is it going to cost for you to guide me out?"

*Oh, that's rich, Justin, thinking you can just buy
everyone off!* Elizabeth thought this even as she mentally calculated how high she was willing to go for her
own escape.

All the other people had left what they were doing
to drift over. Two swimmers, a man and a woman, wet
hair slicked back, were hanging on to a rock a few
yards from the camp fire. Ernie, who had helped
Elizabeth erect her tent, had come through the trees,
his pack all neatly strapped down, his tent tucked under the flap at the top. And Suzy's massive partner
had turned aside from tearing a large dead branch
bodily from a pine. Disbelief etched their faces and
distaste wrinkled their brows. The unflappable Suzy
at last appeared to be growing vexed.

"Look, Justin, how many times do I have to tell
you? This is a holiday. Everyone here has planned time

out of their lives for this, sometimes months ahead, and paid with hard-earned money. If Diana Daniels sent you here and paid for your trip, I can't help that. But I have no intention of making these people sit around for three or four days while I guide you out. So face it. You're both in this for the duration.''

"No!''

They protested in the same instant. Forgetting her looks, Elizabeth thrust the branches of the tree aside to leap forward. This was too much! "I have dozens of people depending upon me for direction,'' she began to splutter. "For all I know, they'll twiddle their thumbs and take a free ride till I get back. The last thing I'm interested in is a canoe trip!''

Though her employees would work perfectly well on their own, Elizabeth felt bound to point out that she had just as much at stake as her arch-rival. She knew from experience that dear Justin was always out for number one.

The fire leaped and crackled. Bacon began to sizzle. Suzy opened a shockproof egg carton and counted out a dozen eggs.

"You must have made some arrangements. After all, you did come along voluntarily.''

She cracked the first egg and dropped it among the bacon strips. It made an enticing hissing sound. More people deposited tidy packs, complete with tiny tent bag, near the overturned canoes. All of them were tossing sharp glances at Justin and Elizabeth. Now their puzzlement was gone. They knew for sure they didn't want two stuck-up spoilsports ruining their fun.

The swimmers shook water from their eyes, toweled themselves dry in anticipation of food and joined the group now ranged opposite Justin and Elizabeth.

The division could not have been more clear, but Justin and Elizabeth were too stirred up to care. Elizabeth glared at her red canoe as if pure mental force could make it carry her out of there.

After a moment she drew a deep breath, as was her habit when agitated. She hadn't gotten where she was by losing control of herself in difficult situations. She had read all the management-technique books and could think quickly on her feet. If Suzy was protecting the group interest, then the thing to do was to persuade the group to outvote Suzy. Besides, it would be sweet revenge on Justin to acquire by intelligence and persuasion what he had failed to get by self-important bluster.

"Listen, all of you." She turned to the campers, sounding calm and businesslike. "As you've already heard, money is no object. You've seen our predicament—" she included Justin just to gall him "—so I'll make a bargain. You agree to go back with us to some sort of civilization and I'll see you all have a new trip. Way better than this. How about—" she racked her brain; she knew scarcely anything of outdoor activities "—a houseboating trip? Or maybe a nice lake with a hotel so you wouldn't have to sit in the smoke at night to get away from mosquitoes? Yes, a hotel with a lovely sandy beach." It would cost a fortune but the coup would be worth it. "There's nothing but rocks around here, really."

Several pairs of hostile eyes bored into her.

"Lady, just lay off, will you?" snapped a tense young man with a camera around his neck. "We're here because we like Suzy and because we like this river, and the whole point of the thing is to paddle the canoes and camp out. Most of us had to put in in

January to get our holidays now, so we don't have time to take you two anywhere. If you don't like it, why are you here?''

In spite of her best intentions, hot coals ignited in Elizabeth's stomach. No one had talked to her this way in years. Her fingers knotted as she fought to keep her temper down.

''We're here because we were tricked,'' she said through her teeth. ''And we just want to go home!''

Roy, who had stood bare chested in the camp-fire smoke last night, rolled his eyes. ''Well, then, we wish you had stayed home. We don't need two complainers lousing everything up!''

Justin showed every sign of lunging. His face locked into a scowl. Elizabeth thought she now knew what it meant when it was said that a person's eyes were burning in his head.

''Good cripes,'' she breathed, suddenly afraid of what Justin was going to do. She hadn't seen this side of him since that night long ago in the lab. Was she the only person in the world who recognized the tiger underneath the supremely civilized mask?

Tension thickened like a palpable cloud. Then, with enormous effort, Justin controlled himself. Fists clenched in an age-old gesture of frustration, he pivoted on his heel and strode off to glower beside a twisted stump.

This left Elizabeth no option but a similar retreat. As she turned away she felt all eyes upon her and was overcome with an acute awareness that her clothes were too ill fitting, her lashes too pale and her hair all in clumps under the crown of the floppy green hat, where she had hastily stuffed it.

"You'd better pack up your tents and packsacks," Suzy called, cheerful and impersonal again. "Then have some breakfast. Bacon and eggs today only. Porridge from now on. We'll be on our way as soon as we can."

The two remained immobile, Justin against the stump, and Elizabeth, feet planted wide apart, staring down into the deep river. Defeat was insufferable, but defeated they were. Though the tantalizing scent of sizzling bacon and frying eggs teased their nostrils, they refused to approach the breakfast fire or eat a bite.

Only when the entire group was assembled at the canoes and threatening to abandon them did they move. They huffed back into the trees, flung their things into their packs and pulled up tent pegs and poles, all the while enduring the humiliation of having their ineptitude watched by every eye. Finally, they deposited their packs on the rocks near the rest of the gear.

"Might be crosscurrents ahead," Suzy announced. "Anybody like to pair up with the newcomers to help them along?"

Dead silence indicated that each and every camper would rather share his or her canoe with a bad-tempered skunk. Suzy shrugged.

"Okay, you two. I guess you're together from now on. Good luck."

Justin and Elizabeth managed to get into their canoe only by soaking their feet again. Elizabeth realized now why everyone was wearing old canvas shoes without socks. For a moment, Elizabeth thought Justin was going to defy everyone and start paddling upriver. He hovered a long moment, his face set, his eyes hooded. Then, in unspoken agreement, they set out behind the departing troop.

"Well, so much for bribery and coercion," Elizabeth snorted, jamming her paddle into the water. "For once, Justin, your money didn't get you out."

"Or you. That was no cheap holiday you were offering. How much would you have paid, Elizabeth?"

Water sloshed against the stern from the force of Justin's stroke.

"Certainly as much as you would have. You didn't think I'd let you get out of here and leave me behind, did you?"

"Oh," Justin retorted darkly, "you never did have any trouble getting along by yourself. You're a survivor if I've ever seen one."

"I certainly am. Just you wait and see!"

Already the veneer of politeness they had maintained for so long was eroding; emotions were seething...emotions, neither of them had ever before acknowledged. If these emotions erupted to the surface now...well! Throwing her shoulder into it, Elizabeth thrust the canoe forward after the fast disappearing band ahead.

The river, if possible, grew wilder, rippling past enormous rock faces broken into crazy patterns, past snaking ravines choked with green brush and past dense clumps of evergreens, their tips all bent in one direction as if brushed by a giant hand. Great trees that had been blown down lay half in, half out of the water. A flight of mallards swooped before them; a sharp piny smell rode the breeze that plucked at the bow of the canoe. Elizabeth felt as though they had been dropped in the middle of a Tom Thompson painting. Was there no exit from all this primeval remoteness?

Suzy avoided the narrower channels and kept them to the open reaches. The laughter from the other canoes only underlined the reluctant, sulking silence of Justin and Elizabeth, who lagged behind. During snack break, the two showed no interest in their share of dried fruit and nuts; they would have had to join the sprawling circle of campers to get the treats. At lunch, they were about to turn away from the opened cans of sardines when Suzy laughed.

"Oh, come on. How can you possibly enjoy this trip if you don't eat?"

She was actually teasing them, brown eyes merry behind her lenses. Justin flung her a scathing look and stood back with his arms folded stubbornly. Elizabeth was torn between wanting to stand aloof and longing for nourishment. As she hovered, a rumbling gurgle cut the still summer air.

Heads swiveled toward the source of the sound—Justin's stomach. His face reddened; his body turned rigid. The sound triggered, at last, Elizabeth's sense of the ridiculous.

"You can be an idiot if you want to," she murmured to him. "I've got to eat."

She accepted a can of sardines and a fork. If Justin's eyes could have blasted holes in her head, they would have left huge craters.

So, then, why did she feel disloyal? As if she owed him anything!

The sardines, oily little creatures that they were, improved Elizabeth's temper enough to let her sit down on a boulder and take a closer look at the people she was stuck with.

She recognized this morning's swimmers, a fair young man and a leggy, dreamy-eyed girl, neither looking more than about twenty years old. Now they sat glued together behind a small bush that screened them. Sometimes they ate their food, but they seemed more interested in nibbling on each other. Now that Elizabeth thought about it, they had not been apart for a moment, either on the bus or by the camp fire last night. Remembering the cramped confines of the tent, her ears warmed slightly at the thought of how they must have spent the night. The sight of their mutual absorption evoked a curl of indulgence inside her—along with a flick of alarm. The sight of puppy love always had this effect on her. She wanted the young people to be happy, yet she also fought the urge to rush over and take them in her arms and cry, "Be careful, be careful. You don't know the awful things that can happen."

Suzy's canoe mate, addressed by the others as Moose, hulked about, making all the other males look miniature in size. Not even a ripple of fat padded his broad midriff. He had a somber, immobile face partly hidden by a mustache that dropped to his chin and made the expression of his lips impossible to decipher. Moose had not spoken so many as three words to anyone but Suzy since the journey had begun, and he seemed to be always watching Suzy, from wherever he was stationed.

Roy, no doubt toughening himself up, sat shirtless, letting the sun blaze down upon his naked shoulders while he tossed food into his mouth without benefit of utensils and with only a leaf to wipe his fingers on.

The fellow who had spoken sharply to Elizabeth earlier was lying on his stomach taking photographs of the water and the life within it. His camera was of excellent quality, and his concentration was that of a professional. Elizabeth's mouth curled sardonically. If this fellow had half a brain, he'd have figured out that both she and Justin were capable of making or breaking the career of a commercial photographer. This morning's rudeness was a monumental blunder.

"Anything for the contest, Spence?" sang out a long-legged blond girl as she plopped down beside him. She had bobbed energetically around since their arrival at the site and had been in charge of lunch. Her constant activity contrasted with the self-effacing stillness of the stolid Kate, who had served up the food the night before.

"Only something for the human-interest category. You!"

Spence whipped his stocky form around with the speed of an eel and snapped three pictures about a foot from his companion's open mouth. They both started to laugh and Spence slapped her on the back.

"You look great when you're surprised. I'll enter you in the nature category, too. As a frog!"

In the midst of their giggles, Elizabeth felt her skin tightening in apprehension. A photography contest! If this fellow pointed his camera in her direction once, just once, she'd have to do something drastic.

To her left, a plump, rather short female, lost under a mass of coffee-colored, frizzy hair, pattered up to Suzy and displayed a pinkish, glassy-looking stone in her palm.

"Rose quartz, isn't it? I'll keep it for my rock collection."

"Yep, rose quartz, Libby," Suzy agreed, taking the find, then turning to the group. "In case anyone here doesn't know it, we're sitting on some of the oldest exposed rock in the world, the lower edge of the Canadian Shield. It was ground down by glaciation in the last ice age. The tremendous weight of the ice sheets pushed most of the topsoil clear down into New York State. The trees and bushes you see are clinging to thin layers of new soil that has built up since then. As you can see, the environment is very fragile, and when it's disturbed it takes years and years to recover.''

"Yeah, even the trees have to hang on for dear life," giggled Ernie, imitating a scrawny little evergreen beside him that was sticking out from a slanting crevice.

Oh, great, thought Elizabeth. *We're going to be subjected to nature lessons every couple of miles. I wonder if we're expected to pass a test at the end.*

Her survey of the group made Elizabeth more aware than ever that she and Justin had not been introduced around and were not likely to be, considering the state of relations that had been established. This was a most unaccustomed state of things. She would have to deal with all eleven people, including Justin, on this trip. Of them all, Justin would be the hardest.

When they were back on the water, the sun grew very hot. It beat on Elizabeth's back and on her head and caused the river to give off a silver glare. Her arms, already aching from the unaccustomed exercise, grew more and more leaden. As muscles pulled painfully across her shoulder blades and chest, she felt like draping herself over the bow in weariness, but she knew she could not. Behind her, she could feel Justin paddling as if his arms were pistons, each stroke an expression of his wrath at being trapped against his will.

Damn him! Why can't he be human enough to groan or something!

Her own anger did not approach the inflexible ire possessing Justin. He was a hard man, she decided all over again. And it occurred to her for the first time that his rigidity probably made it quite difficult for him to get on in life.

Her forearms felt very warm, and her attention was drawn to her skin. To her horror, a pinkish hue was beginning to make itself known, despite all the no-name moisturizer with sunscreen she had slathered onto herself to protect herself from the frying rays. She was already speckled with itching bites; sunburn made the disaster complete. Oh, if only there were some way to escape!

The afternoon paddle was brief, though to Elizabeth, it felt like a hundred miles. The whole time, she felt Justin was glaring into her backbone, and it made her paddling even more jerky and uncoordinated. Her distraction caused them to scrape the canoe sharply on a slightly submerged rock.

"Hey, you're supposed to be watching out up there."

Justin gave a mighty stroke that slewed them sideways.

"Well, you don't have to take out your feelings on the boat, just because you're fed up. You could dunk us both."

"Since when have you been concerned for my feelings, Elizabeth?"

He spoke sternly, as if, for once, he meant exactly what he was saying.

Gasping, Elizabeth snapped around, making the canoe tip so far that water splashed in over the gunwale. She grabbed both sides to save herself and, in the scramble, dropped her paddle.

"Oh, damn!" she spat out, all the exasperating experiences of the day taking their toll. "Come on, Justin, it's floating away."

She twisted in her seat again and found him glowering at her with his jaw set, as if the paddle could have floated to China, for all he cared.

He is angry with me, she thought in an incredulous flash of insight. *He's been angry with me for years. How dare he!*

She glared back, her knuckles white on the gunwales, the canoe rocking mulishly. "Don't start talking about feelings, Justin," she flung back in a half-controlled voice. "Unless you're talking about greed, I'm sure you haven't a clue about the subject!"

Oh, God, the very last of their thin propriety was crumbling around them. Elizabeth had not realized until now how much she had been longing for an all-out, open fight. Years of resentment had lodged in her chest, constantly irritating her. Now, in the hot sun, trapped on this damnable river, she felt that her anger was finally forcing its way out. Justin's head flung up, like a horse suddenly jabbed with spurs.

"Don't you talk about—"

The lovebirds, Tim and Eileen, glided out from behind the island on Justin's left, where they had been, no doubt, dallying for a smooch. They spotted Elizabeth's paddle slowly spinning end to end as it headed, all on its own, after the distant canoes of the rest of the party. They looked as if they were going to offer to retrieve it, but the taut positions of Justin and Elizabeth warned them off. The paddle caught on a half-submerged log. The lovers sped swiftly and prudently off.

Guiding the canoe jerkily, Justin got them over to the paddle and balanced in the opposite direction while Elizabeth leaned over to grasp it. Then, needing to take out their irritation in action, they set out again, tearing their blades into the water, sometimes hitting, sometimes missing, making great splashes and wasting energy while the canoe veered recklessly this way and that. It would do a lot of veering in the future, Elizabeth reflected, for it seemed constitutionally impossible for Justin and her to work together in a coordinated manner.

Elizabeth strained ahead, her mouth set. She thought she had dealt with her anger toward Justin long ago. Now she found herself burning with antagonism all over again. Much of her determination to get Diana Daniels's services was really tied up with getting back at Justin and finally settling her emotional score.

Now they were thrown forcibly into each other's company and were being driven half-mad with the frustration of being trapped on this stupid expedition by whatever sadistic twist of mind Diana hid under all that superstar charisma. Worst of all, they were forced to watch the cool ironical exterior they had adopted toward each other fall to fragile pieces at the first hint of pressure.

I wish every blackfly in the bush would go after Diana Daniels! If I could get my hands on her, I'd stick her in a canoe and made her paddle for a month. Against the current, too!

They spoke no more until they reached the place where the others were beaching their canoes for the night. The sun-heated rock seemed to sizzle under

Elizabeth's feet. As soon as the others were un-loaded, they leaped into the water and cavorted around. Justin and Elizabeth, sticky and sweaty from their labors at the paddle, only hunched their shoulders like unhappy storks.

"I guess that's the only way to get clean around here," Justin mumbled as he looked at the splashing campers in disdain.

Elizabeth had the same problem. The only water around was in the river. She'd just have to figure out how to use it effectively.

Her temper was not improved by a marathon struggle with her tent. However, she at last succeeded in getting it upright, and she dragged her pack inside. Her own logo mocked her from the pack flap. Oh, how she longed to soak in her whirlpool tub!

Taking the small toiletries bag with her, Elizabeth headed gingerly to the far side of the island, where she was sure to be sheltered from prying eyes.

She picked her way very carefully. The ground seemed to be one big booby trap waiting for her to twist her ankle. The granite heaved and rolled and yawned open without the least logic. Twigs broke under her feet. Dense bushes tore at her clothes. Tree branches lurked in the shadows, ready to knock her cold.

At last she emerged on the far side and looked dubiously down at the water. It gleamed clear amber, dappled with the reflection of the young birches behind her and showing a gradually descending ledge of rock that dropped off out of sight about four yards out. Elizabeth had never used water in its natural state in her life. Her head rang with warnings about acid rain, pollution and dread disease. Could you get typhoid, for instance, by putting your face in it. Or cholera?

Well, typhoid or no typhoid, she had to wash.

She edged forward from the shore, wondering how she was going to manage it. The rock down there was sure to be slimy; what if she slipped off the ledge and went in to the eyeballs? Another legacy of her city childhood was that she had never learned to swim.

Desire for cleanliness won out. She took her chances.

Extracting her washcloth, she wet it and began to dip water toward herself, feeling it blessedly cool against her skin. Half-kneeling on a patch of moss, she washed her arms and her legs. When she got to her face and neck, she had less luck, dripping huge amounts down her T-shirt. She was going to have to take it off.

She peered about. Voices came from the other side of the island, but there was no sign of people here. She lifted the shirt over her head and began to sluice water over her shoulders and down her breasts to the top of her incongruous lacy bra. She had just flipped her hair back from her eyes when she was almost startled off her perch by a nearby splash.

Justin, clad in the shapeless bathing trunks from his pack, had just knifed cleanly into the water. He, too, had chosen the far side of the island, where he assumed he would be unseen.

Elizabeth was caught, washcloth in hand, frozen behind a branch of evergreen. Justin had dived deep, surfacing several yards from shore, shaking water from his dark hair. Unaware that he was being observed, he struck out, powerful strokes cutting the water, the wet muscles of his back gilded by the low-ering sun.

Elizabeth could not move. One single thought ex-ploded in her mind. *How could a man be so beauti-ful!*

It was an instant, unbidden, gut-deep reaction. Water sliding down her rib cage, Elizabeth simply stood there, watching this new Justin, who thought he was alone.

For the moment, he seemed to have forgotten his predicament. His face, stripped of its habitual arro-gance, showed only a kind of hard pleasure in the ex-ercise, as if he were driving himself to shake off the complications of the day. He chose the distance be-tween two points of rock and swam between them, back and forth with cool, relentless precision. Here, without facade, was the Justin who worked hard, who, despite his infuriating airs, ran his empire with a sure, shrewd hand. This part of him, at least, was real.

The ripples from his strokes lapped to her feet, but still Elizabeth could not move. Water trickled from her spine, soaking her waistband. A dragonfly hummed past her shoulder, its wings so close it sounded like a tiny airplane. In the center of her line of vision Justin exercised the lean, lithe body that had been honed by squash and tennis and all the other fashionable sports of the upper-echelon businessman. He moved through the water with the sleek, natural grace of a seal. The working muscles of his buttocks moved rhythmically under the wet fabric of his swimsuit. Strong brown ankles flashed, propelling him forward through the water's surface, which now reflected tree shadows and long fingers of light from between the western pines.

Suddenly, he turned over to float on his back, head up, so that his profile was outlined against the water. Strands of hair lay across his forehead. Dappled sunlight struck off his broad chest. Small motions of his hands edged him in Elizabeth's direction.

I've got to get out of here!

She could not tell why the thought struck with such panic; she only knew she had to get away. As she bent to grasp her T-shirt, her instep came down on a twig, snapping it with a loud, resounding crack.

Instantly, Justin flipped over on his side, his eyes sweeping the shore. His gaze caught Elizabeth, washcloth in one hand, T-shirt in the other. Her skin was a delicate pink except for the deeper shade along her arms and neck, where the sun had worked. Her floppy hat was tilted rakishly on one side of her head. Her firm breasts strained against the insubstantial little bra.

Justin stopped dead in the water. An instant of raw physical communication flashed between them before either could prevent it; a longing as naked and obvious and intense as if they had shouted the words across the water...a primitive animal response to each other's displayed bodies.

A hot rush invaded Elizabeth's abdomen, striking her immobile, even to her mouth, which had fallen half-open in shock. Justin's gaze touched her lips, her shoulders, and then slid down to her breasts. Elizabeth felt it as surely as if he had touched them. Her heart began to bump irregularly. Her throat closed. She might have been carried back six years to the first time he'd looked at her like that—when she had come for her interview.

I won't have this. I won't, I won't!

She forced her breath out in heavy rushes until she got control. Swiftly, she backed up through a screen of leaves, then made for her tent, fallen logs and broken granite no obstacles now in her urgency to be away.

By the time she'd zipped the flap tight, the strange sensation had vanished, and Elizabeth was almost certain her mind had been playing tricks. Yet her memories, after long suppression, had been revived. She was forced to acknowledge that that was how it had been back then. The heavy, beating physical attraction had addled her mind and sometimes possessed her so strongly she only had to glimpse at Justin in the hall and she could hardly move. Her hormones hadn't boiled up like this in years.

"A flash of my misspent youth," she told herself firmly, wryly, and went to work toweling herself into some semblance of order. Well covered against Justin, and the mosquitoes, she trudged at last toward the supper fire. Justin was sitting far off to one side, a shirt thrown over his shoulders, running his fingers over and over through his damp hair.

In a moment, she knew why. As his hair dried, it sprang inexorably into a tight halo of curls. Elizabeth gaped, realizing that, like herself, Justin was totally dependent on the blow dryer for his sleek, sophisticated look.

"Hey," crowed Ernie, already the camp clown, "look here. Hello, Curly!"

Elizabeth half choked on her own shocked amusement. Justin's hand leaped away and his brows flew into a scowl that was helpless against all the eyes looking at his head. Forgetting her own sad state of dishevelment, Elizabeth began to feel much better at once.

CHAPTER SEVEN

"PUFFBALLS ARE EDIBLE in their early stages, and they fry up beautifully. Myself, I like the inky caps best, though they turn a dreadful black in the pan. We don't know whether a lot of these other mushrooms are poisonous because no one will volunteer to try them. Don't any of you fool around with them, please. They're probably deadly."

Elizabeth shut her eyes and opened them against the relentless sunlight. Breakfast was past. Suzy was leading her flock down among the rock crevices and was magically uncovering varicolored mushroom species from under shrubs, rotted logs and patches of moss. Elizabeth was staying put on her ledge of rock, bleary eyed from the short sleep. She'd gone under instantly; the full day's exertion in the fresh air had knocked her out as surely as if she had been clubbed over the head. Yet each time Suzy found a mushroom, Elizabeth took notice. How could so many of the little capped creatures be around without her even suspecting them? Previously, the only mushrooms Elizabeth had seen had been either in her spinach salad, or dancing to the strains of Tchaikovsky in Walt Disney's *Fantasia*. In spite of herself, her curiosity was pricked.

Justin sat several yards away, his hands on his knees, his gaze broodingly directed across the chan-

nel. His pack was full and ready to go. He had given
in at supper last night and had eaten his ration of
macaroni and tuna. This morning he had also eaten
his oatmeal and was now nursing a cup of instant coffee in his hand. A bit of twig served as a stir stick.

How the mighty are fallen, thought Elizabeth. She
herself had found the oatmeal not bad. She didn't
drink coffee, but she had discovered some bags of
rose-hip tea among the supplies and was sipping the
healthful brew. Her shoulders ached, and she could
feel rings of bites on her neck and wrists, where she
must have been exposed as she'd slept. She was developing a bit of respect for those explorers who had
braved the biting hordes of insects in darkest Africa.

From under the brim of her hat, Elizabeth could
make out a few mare's tails scraping the sky. The river
stretched east and west—and probably north and
south, too, for all she knew. On a rock nearby, three
gulls quarreled in peevish voices. Across the channel,
a clump of evergreens resembled a tribe of robed,
slightly bent figures making their way in the direction
of the wind. Behind them were more trees, and more
rock, and then yet more rock, making Elizabeth somber. It had finally sunk in that she was truly trapped
on this camping trip. Part of her was still outraged.
Another part, ever resilient, was calmly listening to the
mushroom lecture.

Already, she had guessed that the rhythm of the trip
was geared to leisurely starts and rigorous after-
noons. The campers packed early, then puttered after
breakfast, enjoying themselves. She and Justin, still
the camp pariahs, were left to their own devices.

Justin drained the last of his coffee at a gulp and got
to his feet. His beard shadow was twice as dark, giv-

ing his face a desperate look. He had not acknowledged Elizabeth yet this morning. He looked as if he
might dive from the shore any minute and swim to his
freedom.

Elizabeth knew what he was feeling. She suffered
from it herself. Frustration. Her habit of being in
charge had been rudely thwarted; there were no longer
any soldiers to order about, and the customary sup-
ports had been kicked away. There was nowhere to
turn and absolutely nothing one could do.

Justin had his hat on today, jammed down over the
curls Elizabeth knew were underneath. He wore
shorts, exposing moulded knees and solid calves to
Elizabeth's sidelong scrutiny. The dusting of dark
hairs was thicker than she had anticipated, causing the
incident from last night to nibble along the edge of her
consciousness. Her right dimple flickered cynically.
There was no way she was going to deny that Justin
was a glorious chunk of muscle.

When it came time to depart, she and Justin were
the last ones off. While they stood apart, waiting for
the others to get going, Justin rubbed savagely at the
heavy growth of stubble obscuring his jaw and kept at
it until Elizabeth grimaced.

"Please stop, Justin. You can't scrape it off with
your fingernails, you know!"

"I would if I could," he retorted, all his distaste for
physical discomfort grating through his voice. "Do
you know there's not one single razor in this camp?"

The gravity of this announcement provoked wayward amusement in Elizabeth.

"I don't doubt it. You'll just have to look like an
unemployed pirate for a while."

He did look disreputable with his hat on crooked, his jaw blackened and his T-shirt raveled at the neck. Without the wardrobe and the polished grooming, this might almost be a different Justin she was looking at, someone she didn't know. Perhaps that was why she found it so hard to take her eyes off him.

And don't you dare be fooled by lack of a few props! she admonished herself.

As if to back her silent warning, one brow rose up in that familiar way and his lips came together.

"Then I had better stay away from cameras for a while, Elizabeth. The same as you."

Touché! A flare of heat blossomed inside her. She was suddenly aware of every limp hair on her head. Her face felt as round as a pumpkin's and her eyes entirely lashless. Such was the effect of years of being supersensitive to her own appearance. Since Justin was waiting for her to turn away in embarrassment, she met him unflinchingly, full in the eye.

"Oh, I shall, Justin. But if we do meet a photographer, I'd advise you to smile. Then you won't resemble a bull with his tail in a vice."

His other brow flew up. Suddenly, there it was again, that completely involuntary sensual communication: sparks that came quickly and left equally quickly, leaving a gap in the air between them.

Elizabeth swiftly dropped her eyes, feeling her scrubbed face and nondescript clothes more than ever. Without her usual decorations, she was also without the shield she had taken for granted these last years in her dealings with Justin Archer. Was he, in his dishevelment, in the same predicament?

Yet the worst sting was seeing his face settle into a blank expression that denied his obviously strong emotions.

"We'd better get going," she said, sighing resignedly. "Unless you'd rather try paddling back to Toronto."

"Wouldn't I just!"

The roughness in his voice, she thought bitterly, was naturally a result of the traumatic separation from his office.

Justin was apparently in no mood for a rigorous jaunt, and Elizabeth wasn't exactly pleased at the prospect, either. Justin fell grimly silent, paddling as if he regretted each stroke that took him farther into this unknown wilderness. The small craft moved through the water in little angry jumps.

Today the islands were smaller, crammed together in the choppy channels. Many were altogether bald. Others sprouted thin fringes of vegetation from their crazy quilt of cracks. Dead trees loomed from the water, ready to clutch the bow. Rocks lurked just below the surface, waiting to scrape a hole in the bottom. Fifteen minutes out and Elizabeth's body ached all over from the previous day's exertions. Suzy was working them harder today, increasing the distance covered—as if one island looked any different from another, Elizabeth thought with a burst of petulance.

For some reason, she and Justin just couldn't seem to work together. The timing of their strokes wouldn't match. Elizabeth let the bow swing too close to obstacles, so that once or twice the canoe collided with a tree. Justin refused to call for a switch in sides until the stern sailed sideways and Elizabeth had to scramble. After lunch, they lagged even farther behind because of curt spats over which channel to take. Despite her best efforts to forget it, the lightning communication of that morning was emblazoned in Elizabeth's mind. Her sharpness, and probably Justin's, too, was an attempt to deny it had ever happened. Their arms protested in their sockets, and the other canoes got farther and farther ahead. Toward the end of the afternoon they lost sight of them altogether for some nervous minutes before seeing them emerge from behind an outcropping up ahead.

"Hurry up, Justin. We'll have to paddle like crazy to catch up. I, for one, don't want to be stuck by myself out here."

With you, was the unsaid part of the statement.

Justin jerked the canoe under her with the force of his stroke, listing it heavily to one side as he leaned to gain purchase. A steep-sided island loomed up ahead, its rock face convoluted where the ancient lava had coiled and cooled. The other canoes had looped around its far side, avoiding the nearer channel, which narrowed into a rushing, rapid-spewing foam. Without so much as a by-your-leave, Justin started purposefully toward it. Elizabeth dragged her paddle in alarm.

"You know Suzy told us not to try any rapids without her say-so."

"Stuff Suzy."

They bobbed closer. The rapid developed a deep-throated roar. Elizabeth didn't like the look of it one bit.

"Justin, stop it, for heaven's sake. We don't know anything about running water like that."

"Then we'll have to learn fast, won't we? Wouldn't want to fall behind and get stranded."

So that was what was bugging him—her chance remark conveying how much she detested his company. More than just simple frustration was being stirred up in him today.

Elizabeth actively jammed her paddle into the water in an attempt to slow them down. The effect was to make the canoe swing sideways.

"Justin, you can't steer us through that. I demand you go the safe way."

She twisted halfway around and was shocked at his grim, half-mocking grin. He was determined to take out his mood on the boiling water.

"Oh, you demand, do you? We'll see about that. Put your paddle in, or we're going to go whoopsy over that rock."

"Wha—"

She spun back, rocking them precariously. They were indeed gliding broadside toward a jagged stone tooth planted in their path. Justin was deliberately letting the canoe go in order to make her get on with her job. She grabbed her paddle and began splashing furiously until the canoe straightened out. By that time they were careening toward the rapid, helpless to turn aside. A terrified pounding started inside Elizabeth as the bow slipped into the first white water. Up close, she could see how the water was being forced between a broken jumble of rocks.

The canoe began to bounce and buck, carried along at breakneck speed. The bottom scraped and banged as it glanced off submerged shards of granite. A glistening boulder loomed up ahead, with the canoe tearing wildly toward it. To its left, a great smooth tongue of water arched downward into a cauldron of foam that looked as if it would pound to sawdust anything silly enough to get caught in it. The canoe, out of control, veered toward it, then, at the last second, away, certain to be dashed to pieces on the boulder.

As the bow plunged out of sight in the foam, Elizabeth began to shriek. Her paddle was useless. All she could think of to do was lean over and grasp the sharp tip of the rock with all her strength. She hung on until she thought her arms would break. The canoe checked itself, throwing its full weight on Elizabeth's arms, swung one hundred and eighty degrees, then shot safely past the obstacle on the other side.

But now the canoe was stern first, awash with water and listing heavily toward the side Elizabeth was hanging over. In a moment she would be snatched out and flung forcibly down the rest of the chute, her body smashing from stone to stone until she was spat out at the bottom.

"Straighten up, straighten up and paddle!" Justin shouted.

As her body snapped back, Elizabeth caught a glimpse of him. The nasty smirk had been wiped totally away by the rude strength of the rapid. His teeth were bared. Every muscle in his body was contorted with effort. But his gaze wasn't on the river; it was on her.

How he did it, she'd never know. Even with her wobbly aid, it must have taken the strength of ten to propel them out of that seething raw whiteness and into a calm backwater. The canoe, half-filled with water, had all the mobility of a dead mackerel. It floated sideways and grounded on a rock. Neither of them made the least move to free it.

When Elizabeth could breathe again, she hitched around. Justin was staring at her fixedly, his paddle half-across the gunwale, frozen in the middle of a stroke. His ribs were heaving from his superhuman effort. His eyes bore the widened glaze of someone who had just been hit on the side of the head with a plank.

"Justin?"

Her voice sounded cracked, as if it belonged to another person.

Justin's mouth snapped shut, and his paddle came all the way out of the water to rest in front of him. Yet he couldn't shake the stunned look from his eyes.

Why, he didn't want me to drown!

And he'd nearly popped his arteries trying to keep the canoe from going under.

Elizabeth's own heart, thudding from the struggle, seemed to stop as an unnamed, totally unexpected emotion roared through her like a train. This frightened her more than her recent narrow escape.

No, cried a voice inside her. *No, no, no!*

She would not have this thing. Not again.

To blot it out, she got angry. Swiftly, blindly, ragingly angry. They had got into the rapid in the first place because of Justin's desire to bull through everything as he bloody well pleased.

"Well, Mr. Macho does it again!" she exploded. "Take the short cut, eh? You could have killed us both. I hope you're satisfied!"

The heaving of his chest instantly subsided. His face bunched up. He openly welcomed her anger, grasped it, for it wiped everything else away.

"Yes, I'm satisfied. We got out with our necks, didn't we? You might at least acknowledge that!"

"Oh, thanks a lot for saving my hide," she spat, choking back the real emotion underneath. "Now you want gratitude when I warned you like crazy not to go in there. That's rich! It's about time you found out that things here are a bit different from the squash court!''

Behind them, the rapid tossed up its relentless spume, reminding Elizabeth all over again of her tearing fright, now mixed in with her resentment at being trapped on this trip against her will. Justin was soaked from head to toe, and sweat shone in droplets under the crooked brim of his hat. In the veins of his forearms, blood still pulsed hotly as if it hadn't yet realized the battle was done.

Elizabeth, in similar condition, failed to feel at all sorry for his dripping state. It was about time that Justin Archer came a cropper!

For once, Justin had no answer for her. When he said nothing, she let out a soft, disgusted breath.

''Let's go. I think the others are making camp.''

Straining to move their sluggish craft, they set out across a stretch of open water toward the distant row of beached canoes. Long after the other campers were searching out tent sites, a bedraggled Elizabeth and Justin labored into the shallow water and stepped out, not caring that they were in up to their knees, since they were sopping anyway. They upset the canoe sideways trying to get their waterlogged packs ashore. Justin let out a muffled curse as he grabbed for the escaping paddles. Elizabeth's hair fell out from under her hat in twisted strands across her eyes.

''Aha!''

Behind them a camera clicked and clicked again. Excruciatingly sensitive to the sound, Justin and Elizabeth whirled simultaneously, appalled by the merciless, winking eye of the lens.

Inside of a second, Justin was up the bank and gripping Spence by the wrist. Spence gasped, his precious camera dangling loosely around his neck.

"I don't want you taking pictures of us. Now let me have the film."

Spence's eyes goggled wider and his squat body went taut. The camera banged against his ribs.

"The film!" demanded Justin in a terrifying voice. "I'll buy you fifty bloody rolls when we get back!"

"It's my film. My—"

Justin was so intent on snatching Spence's camera that he failed to see a hulking shadow close in on him. In turn, the arm gripping Spence was taken into the vicelike paw of Moose.

"Enough of that!" Moose growled. "Spence can take pictures of whatever he likes. You let him go!"

Up to her knees in water, still hanging onto the sloshing canoe, Elizabeth was petrified. Never, in her wildest fancies, had she imagined another male challenging Justin. But this male was half again as wide and six inches taller. What was Justin going to do?

She saw that Justin was as astonished as Spence had been twenty seconds before. He stood as frozen as if he had been chipped out of the local granite and planted on the shore. One foot was still in the water, the other braced sideways over a crevice. His hair sprung loose across his forehead, and his mouth remained half-open in the middle of the next word he was about to bark at Spence.

Moose's face was folded into a bulldog frown. His mustache bristled, his shoulders were set and his hamfisted free hand was ready and waiting. Spence became a forgotten adjunct as the two men stood locked in their positions of threat and counterthreat. Hostility thickened in the air between them. All the muscles in Elizabeth's midriff turned stiff as wood.

The entire island went still, all the campers similarly caught in the middle of whatever task they were doing. Every eye was on the scene. The formerly jolly troop stood about with faces shocked and eyes riveted to the scene.

Justin's neck bulged with cords of anger. It would take only the rustle of a leaf, the snap of a twig, to send him crazy. Elizabeth saw the large muscles under his wet shirt gather for a spring.

"Don't!" she cried out. "Oh, Justin, don't!"

His back went rigid. Then, he began to release the muscles, one by painful one. Not taking his eyes off Moose, he loosened his fingers. Spence stumbled backward, his face drained, his camera clutched to his breast.

Instantly, Moose let go of Justin and walked away, not even checking to see if Justin meant to come at him from behind. When Justin turned back to the canoe, his face was black and knotted, wiping away entirely any vestige of Justin the debonair. Elizabeth's heart was pounding within her. With great difficulty she forced herself to breathe.

"That was—"

"Never mind!"

She had been about to say that he had been wise, but she saw at a glance how fresh the wound was to Justin's pride. Pride! Always pride with Justin. Well, today he'd almost gotten his stiff neck broken!

Her sympathy of a moment ago was transformed into raw and intense irritation. Threatening Spence had been stupid, tangling with Moose more monumentally stupid still. Justin had done the rational thing

and stepped down. Yet he seemed to detest himself for
having done so. He was still the spoiled man who had
to be biggest, the best, and have his way in everything. She'd keep her civil words. Let him stew!

She put up her tent as far back in the woods as she
dared, not realizing that Justin's was just over the next
rock. He, too, was retreating, as if association with the
rest of the troop would contaminate him.

Suzy, meantime, was delivering an impromptu lesson on lichens and moss. Elizabeth, who thought lichens would probably come last on her list of all
possible interests, actually paused in the middle of
hanging out her sopping clothes. Imagine those
grungy dark flakes underfoot being called rock tripe
and made into stew!

Justin hung back from the group, leaning against a
rock ledge, his wet T-shirt drying on his back.

"Don't sulk," Elizabeth said to him in passing, and
he jerked upright.

"All right, everybody," called Suzy. "Camp chores.
Come and get yours."

Most people volunteered, and those who didn't
found themselves quickly assigned to tasks. Elizabeth
was to mix the powdered fruit drink. Justin was given
a crosscut saw and told to cut up a large dead pine
branch for the evening camp fire.

Though he looked close to rebelling, he stepped
away wordlessly and went to work. The saw had double handles, and Roy, without asking, took the other
end. Toughening his arm muscles, Roy threw his
weight into the task, causing the flexible saw blade to
buckle each time it slid toward Justin. To counter him,
Justin pushed back with all his might. It was clear
neither was highly experienced at wood cutting. After

a few moments without much damage to the branch, Justin stopped.

"Slow down or we'll never get through."

He had assumed his customary air of command as if determined to be in control, no matter what. His tone did not endear him to Roy, who kept right on as he had been doing before. Justin pulled on the handle, dragging the saw to a stop.

"Look, the blade is whipping all over the place. Do it like this."

Justin meant to be civil, but he was used to running the show. Roy, however, was not one of Justin's employees and was impervious to the commanding steely gray eyes. He promptly let go of the saw.

"Since you're such an expert, I think you'd better finish it alone," he said coolly, and strode off, bare soles flapping on the rock.

Justin cast a black look at Roy's back and went at the branch single-handedly. Elizabeth grunted to herself from where she was dealing dubiously with river water and plastic containers. Justin's forceful thrusts at the pine indicated more clearly than any words that here was a man who never admitted he couldn't do anything by himself.

Justin sawed furiously until, without warning, there was a sharp crack. The branch, eight inches thick, separated from the tree, and the cut end landed directly on Justin's foot.

Elizabeth winced the entire length of her body—and so did Justin, though he didn't let even a squeak of pain pass his lips. Molly and Kate came running over.

"Hey, that was quite a bang. Are you hurt?"

Justin stood immobile. Instinctively, Elizabeth knew he was humming with pain through every fiber of his body.

"No! I'm all right. Leave me alone!"

He picked up the branch and dragged it over to where the camp fire was being started. He walked slowly but evenly, setting each foot down on the ground with a casual ease that fooled everyone but Elizabeth, who knew how much his foot had to be hurting. She straightened up from mixing the drink.

"No kidding, Justin, you better have your foot looked at."

He cast her a murky stare. "My foot's okay. Lay off!"

"All right, Mr. Tough Guy. Suffer! See if I care!"

"Oh, I can see that right away, Elizabeth. Please don't bother your head about my supposed injuries."

Stung in spite of having initiated the exchange, Elizabeth drew back, accidentally sloshing fruity orange liquid onto her shoes. If something wasn't done, Justin's foul mood might just contaminate the entire camp. No wonder the others hadn't wanted him along.

Unaware of this slight unconscious shift toward aligning herself with the campers, Elizabeth was searching for a reply when Justin picked up the saw again. Doggedly, he started on the branch and began to saw it into sections short enough to be piled on the camp fire. Out of the corner of her eye, Elizabeth watched him with a sort of grim satisfaction.

Good for you, Justin. How do you like dealing with real life for a change?

How do you like it yourself? asked a little voice at the back of her brain. *Nearly getting drowned can wake a person up on a boring afternoon.*

Justin finished the entire log by himself, expending many times the effort he would have had to, had he been able to get along with a saw mate. Elizabeth washed sticky stuff from her hands, while casting covert glances behind her. Justin was busy trying to prove he was the toughest banana among them. Masculinity, Elizabeth thought, had its comic side.

Justin piled the cut wood beside the fire, put the saw down and retired to his brooding-eagle stance against an uneven stub of granite. His eyes shot daggers at the group, as if each one was personally responsible for imprisoning him here. Elizabeth wondered whether Justin was capable of taking revenge on the lot of them the moment he got back to civilization, all for having the temerity to wander inconveniently into the great man's path.

Because Elizabeth was instinctively ducking her head to hide her disheveled state when anyone looked at her, she failed to notice Suzy pausing behind Justin and peering at his hands hanging at his sides. Immediately, Suzy pulled from a pack a kit box with a red cross on top and handed it to Elizabeth.

"Your friend has managed to put blisters all over his palms. Your hands are the cleanest. Go fix them up."

Suzy walked off to another task before Elizabeth could get her mouth open to protest. She was darned if she was going to minister to the self-inflicted results of Justin's pigheadedness. She baulked long enough to attract a shocked look from Kate through the slowly curling wisps of smoke off the new camp fire. Disgustedly, she picked up the kit and stalked over to Justin.

"All right, let's see your hands. I've been ordered to save you from gangrene!"

Justin's lips compressed. He began to slide his hands behind his back, a curiously boyish gesture.

"Oh, no, you don't. Not with me!"

Elizabeth made a snatch for his wrist and turned his palm upward. She gasped at the dark, blood-stained blisters showing through the grime of tree bark.

"You don't need to bother," Justin grumbled. "I'll live."

"Sure. All we need is for you to get a serious infection. Has it occurred to you that it would probably take a week for these people to get you anywhere near a doctor?"

He had no reply to that one. His face stilled for a second at the urgent worried note Elizabeth wasn't even aware of. Resisting no more, he turned his head away as if suddenly distracted by the horizon.

"Maybe this is just what you need," Elizabeth continued, now with some satisfaction. "Reality therapy. Disaster here is a bit more substantial than slipping sales figures or a bad angle on your award photo. Spread your palms."

He did as ordered and stood unflinchingly while she applied alcohol and then iodine, which must have stung like a horde of wasps.

"Then don't forget we're in this together, Elizabeth. Sauce for the gander and all that. Chew on that one while you sit in your tent a hundred isolated miles from anywhere!"

"I don't forget anything!"

Her eyes flew to meet his, then wavered betrayingly. There were more things to remember than either of them cared to. . . .

CHAPTER EIGHT

"FIRST—ONE TWIG CRACKED," breathed Ernie, his hands waving melodramatically in the firelight. "Then...another twig cracked. Then another. A horrible sighing sound moaned through the woods. Was it the wind in the trees...or the man-eating Fang Spirit growing angrier and angrier?

"The two trappers knew what it was. Their hair stood straight on end. Their eyes popped out of their heads. They started to run, crashing through the trees, stumbling and falling and getting up again! Their hearts were pounding in their chests. The brambles tore the clothes from their backs, and their hands were all bleeding from the bushes.

"The terrible sighing sound turned into a wail...the most bloodcurdling wail the trappers had ever heard. It got closer and closer. In the distance, they began to hear footsteps. Giant footsteps were coming up behind them. Thud, thud, thud! Closer and closer. Faster than any flesh-and-blood animal could run. Eighteen feet at a stride. The wail turned into a shriek. 'Ooooooooooh...oooooooooooooooh!' In a minute, it would get them!"

Ernie's eerie cry punctuated his harrowing tale. A shudder ran around the circle of campers, who sat riveted by the camp fire.

"The trappers were so scared they started foaming at the mouth and grabbing at each other. They tried to jump a creek, but the ice-cold water pulled them down. Their wet clothes dragged at them. Their legs pumped and pumped, but they could hardly move. The big footsteps were right on the bank behind them. The screaming ripped at their eardrums. 'Ooooooooooh! Ooouuuuuuaaaah!'

"And then—what do you think happened?"

Ernie paused, taking full advantage of the nerve-tearing tension he had built up around the camp fire. Supper was long over, and darkness had fallen in all its black entirety. The only light came from the leaping orange flames, which cast lurid shadows across faces, making everyone look like a member of some strange tribe assembled in readiness for a barbaric ritual.

It had started harmlessly enough, with people trading ghost stories. Then Ernie insisted he had a genuine gold-plated scalp peeler. He did. He was telling of the Fang Spirit, a sort of primeval cannibal that crouched in the deep woods of Canada and picked its teeth with human bones. Elizabeth had never heard of it before. She fervently wished she wasn't hearing of it tonight. It was the last thing she needed to know about while camping umpteen miles from nowhere.

Nevertheless, she, too, was captivated. Here, with only the fire for illumination and the crying of the wind for accompaniment, a simple story was more compelling than the most gruesome horror movie in Sensurround with a city budget's worth of special effects. Ernie's eyes glittered wickedly amid the swirls of flying sparks, and his arms waved about, thin and specterlike. He had a good thing going and was making the most of it.

We're spellbound! Elizabeth suddenly realized. She was now excruciatingly aware of the creaks of the trees and the moans of, she hoped, the wind.

Hungrily, she had devoured her meal, then had sunk down by the shore as the day's shocks began to catch up with her. Out of the corner of her eye, she had seen Justin putting away his share of the chili. His whole rigid body had hummed with offended pride.

As dusk descended, people gathered close around the fire, having grown mellow from plenty of food, and tossed jack-pine cones into the fire to watch the heat open them. Suzy had pointed out that only a forest fire would free the seeds, and this was nature's way of regenerating quickly. Justin approached not at all, though the logs he had cut were now crackling away under wavering banners of flame. The other stiff figure of the group was Spence, not quite recovered from the contretemps of that afternoon. He sat with his arms tightly folded and his camera nowhere in sight. He was younger than he appeared, Elizabeth noticed, and would be deliciously hard-bitten in middle life. The finest of cold disdain toward Justin and herself exuded from him.

Now, with Ernie nearing the climax of his tale, Justin still hadn't joined the circle around the fire. However, he hovered just on the outside, gazing at Ernie quite transfixed, his previous sullenness swept aside.

"What happened?" Libby asked, quite faint from the suspense. These people, weaned on television, were putty to the storyteller's art.

Elizabeth felt the roots of her hair crawl in anticipation but could not unfix her eyes from Justin. She saw his eyes gleam and his body thrust forward slightly, all else forgotten save Ernie's coming words.

"Why, the trappers tried so hard to get away that their heels gouged trenches out of the bedrock. You can see the marks to this day. They heard brush cracking and splintering. They heard saplings snapping and trees as thick around as your arm breaking clean off. All the time the wailing got louder and louder. Hungry wailing. Ravenous, starved wailing. They saw a big black thing coming. Big as a cabin, with two round burning eyes fixed right on them. They heard its snarl and they smelled its odor. When it opened its mouth, they saw its teeth by the moonlight, sharp as skinning knives, every one!"

"Oh, no!" Libby put both hands to her mouth, looking as if she was going to keel over.

"The trappers quit running and started screeching. It didn't do them any good. The Fang Spirit pounced into the water and came toward them. Inside of one second it had them by their throats. Argghhhhhaaaah! Inside of two seconds, it was crunching up their bones. Inside of five minutes, it was sitting on the riverbank, licking off its chops—and smiling!

"But—" Ernie jumped up off his seat, his mouth fixed into a huge, toothy, fearsome grin "—it wasn't full. The Fang Spirit is never full. In the dark of night, in woods just like this, it's on the prowl. So—" he leered as horribly as he could "—you folks be *verrrry* careful on your way to your tents tonight—and keep that flap zipped up tight!"

He ended with a knowing hideous giggle. There was about thirty seconds of silence followed by a collective whoosh of released breath. The campers came out from under the spell, shaking their heads and peering at each other sheepishly, then jauntily, to show the story was fun but of course they didn't believe it. Only their many fluttering hands indicated that, deep down, they weren't quite sure about that.

Elizabeth was still eyeing Justin. He was several feet closer still to the fire, his shoulders half-turned away from her and quite motionless.

Why, that story rattled him, too!

The novelty of this idea held her while the party broke up, murmuring fearfully. Campers hovered around the edge of the fire for several moments before summoning their bravado and plunging off into their various directions for the night. Elizabeth rose to make her own reluctant journey. Suzy stopped her.

"Justin's forgotten his flashlight. If you're going to your tent, you'd better take him with you."

Only Justin was left. The dying embers licked his cheeks with light but left the rest of his face in shadows, so that she could not make out his expression. His eyes flickered and gleamed as they fixed on her. She remembered that his tent was just beyond hers. They were the only two inhabiting that neck of the woods.

"Come on, then," she sighed, glad of a companion, any companion. Even Justin.

When Elizabeth switched on her flashlight, she realized it wasn't powerful enough to relieve her sudden fear of the darkness. Outside the narrow stream of light were branches and crouching clumps of brush. Anything, absolutely anything, could be hiding out there.

The journey, though not a hundred yards, seemed interminable. Fallen trees blocked their way, and decayed stumps lay about like the shoulder blades and pelvises of prehistoric beasts. Twigs crunched under their feet like tiny fragile skeletons. Crevices yawned unexpectedly. Flanks of granite rose before them and had to be scrambled up and skidded down. Elizabeth's toe caught in a root and she careened sideways against Justin. He caught her quickly and tipped her upright again so she could grasp a sapling for support.

"Sheesh! Wouldn't do to come drunk around here, would it?" Elizabeth laughed shakily after having almost turned her ankle.

One of his hands was still holding her shoulder; his breath feathered her face. Her heart hammered in her throat for no reason at all.

"No." The irritation had vanished from his voice. Though his tone was gruff, he sounded half-surprised—the way she felt.

Disengaging herself, Elizabeth began to pick her way more carefully, stumbling often on terrain three times as treacherous by night as it was by day. Shortly, they faced a wall of bushes that she was sure hadn't been there when daylight had shone.

Justin took the flashlight from her and plowed ahead, thrusting to the right and to the left. Without asking, he took Elizabeth's hand and guided her through the passage. When her bent shoulder touched his ribs, she thought she heard his breath whistle out. He drew her after him until they emerged on bare rock on the other side. The rock slanted sharply into a hollow dark with moss. Their two orange tents glimmered on the other side.

Elizabeth was aware only of Justin's hand. How warm it was. How strong and firm. And how long it had been since she had held it. The first time he had driven her home in his sports car, his fingers had closed so easily over hers in the little gap between the bucket seats. A little shock of wanting had shot through her then, too.

Oh, Justin.

"We have to get down the rock," she said aloud, withdrawing her hand abruptly.

"I'll go first."

With an agility she hadn't known was in him, he slid down the lichened surface and landed with a soft thud at the bottom.

"Now you come."

He had turned and was holding up his hand to her. Cautiously, Elizabeth edged downward, both hands on the rock beneath her to avoid Justin's grip. In the end, she slipped, flailed her way to the bottom and catapulted into his arms.

The force of her descent flung her full against him. For a long moment she clung, the breath knocked out of her by more than the thump. While she hovered, her body had the opportunity to take in the smoky scent of Justin's hair, the masculine solidity of his shoulder, the brightness of the moss at their feet in the light of the fallen flashlight.

And the fact that Justin was hard with physical desire!

The last time she'd seen evidence of that had been years ago. She'd had an office of sorts, a desk behind a curved, movable screen. The others had gone for coffee, and she had been reaching for the celery sticks she kept around for snacks. Justin had surprised her from behind, sliding his arm around her waist, drawing her back against him while his face nuzzled her hair.

"Hello," he had murmured huskily, his low voice thrilling the hairs on the back of her neck. His hand had been flat against her stomach, his suit jacket smooth against her shoulder blades. Unnoticed, the celery sticks had rolled, one by one, over the edge of her desk....

They broke apart, then clutched again, momentarily startled at the ghostly shapes hovering around Elizabeth's tent.

"It's only my...my clothes. I hung them on the bushes to dry."

Justin, having picked up the flashlight, kept it pointed toward the ground and, they stumbled the few remaining yards to her door. As soon as they stopped, the wind moaned desolately above them. Outside their pitiful circle of light, the darkness, unrelieved by star or moon, developed a smothering density. Elizabeth shivered slightly, deeply aware of Justin beside her, the outline of his knees and feet vivid from the flashlight, the rest of him invisible. She felt everything about him—his breathing, his bulk, his body heat radiating into the night. It was as if she had developed extra senses, all of them attuned to his presence. She still felt the mark of his hand on her shoulder. Her ribs throbbed from where he had caught her at the end of her stumbling descent. Her mouth was dry with knowing he could still feel desire.

Justin did not move away from her despite the whine of the mosquitoes starting to home in. The vast dark woods overwhelmed them, telling them they were but two fragile human beings allied together in the endless wilderness. Quarrels over shelf space seemed a million miles away.

The first insects struck, and still neither moved. Their emotions had been prodded alive; the chills of the ghost story had quickened their nerve ends. Now, in an age-old transmutation, it took only a moment for fear to become desire. Invisible currents danced in the air around them. Elizabeth felt her knees grow heavy. She swallowed thickly. His heady male scent was reaching out to her, dizzying her with its honeyed force.

She could not even see him, but she saw the flashlight waver, felt his hand dimly groping for, then finding the back of her neck. For a moment it just sat there, and waves of sensation shot through her shoulders and arms and down into her solar plexus. Then, with a low groan, Justin dropped his head and took her mouth with his.

Oh, God, it might have been last night that they had parted, not six years ago. How well she still knew the shape of his lips, the taste and texture of his skin and that certain tilt of the head that would just let her fit against him.

He did not embrace her. One hand remained hanging with the flashlight. The other cupped her neck, telling him where to find her. When their lips met, he seemed to be holding his breath. As soon as the shock of her soft mouth reached him, he exhaled sharply and began to ravage her mouth, parting her lips with his tongue, tasting her, seeking, moving his head with the urgent fervor of a man who had just found food after six long years of starvation.

Elizabeth was unable to breathe. Her eyes remained wide with the shock of Justin's action, yet all they could glean from the blackness was the darker shape of Justin leaning over her. Her heartbeat stopped, then suddenly rattled to life again as familiar melting waves rippled through her. Her brain struggled to start functioning again, and finally it caught. Memory spurted back. Elizabeth tore herself away, defending herself with anger.

"Oh, no! Not that again. Not just because... because I happened to be conveniently at hand!"

She felt Justin snap upright and step back stumblingly. She swore she heard his heart beating, and she could guarantee the dark heat staining his cheeks. She did hear his breath, sharp and fast; either strangled or panting, she could not tell. He remained silent an alarming amount of time, until he got his lungs under control.

"An unfortunate slip, Elizabeth. Temporary madness. Next time I'll try very hard to resist."

The old half-ironical tone was there, though uneven, as if hastily summoned.

And why does he sound so bitter?

Involuntarily, Elizabeth's hand flew to her lips, though she wasn't quite sure whether she wanted to wipe off the kiss or keep it there. Justin shoved the flashlight into her hand. She stood woodenly until he had followed its beam over deadfalls and moss patches to his own door. His broad back and long legs were lit from behind. His head was bent forward, keeping his face in an obscurity the small beam couldn't penetrate. In a moment, his own flashlight clicked on, making his tent seem a glowing orange bubble of warmth. Bending sharply, Elizabeth scurried into her own shelter. The sleeping bag was what she wanted, folded twice and zipped on all four sides.

Oblivious to the mosquitoes that had followed her into the tent, she undressed, still dazed by the severe and unexpected erotic shock. She unrolled her sleeping bag and crawled into it naked, then zipped it tight and switched off the flashlight. Through the nylon wall beside her, she could see the orange blur that was Justin's tent, then saw it go as black as hers. He was tucked in his sleeping bag, too. She thought of the soft fabric inside it sliding over his thighs, and she was jolted, as if Justin's lips had touched down again on hers.

Damn, damn, damn!

Yet she was unable to stop herself. Each time her mind dwelt on his kiss, the same sensual thrill skidded through her. It was as though she was trapped on a roller coaster. Just when she thought she had reached a standstill, the heady feeling would rise again and then carry her down another screamingly erotic incline. Elizabeth was helpless to prevent it. Now she knew why neither Kevin Longfield nor any of the other attractive men she had toyed with in the past few years had interested her in the least.

Her lips tingled. She scrunched her eyes shut and pressed her hipbone into a ridge of rock in hopes of being distracted.

Eventually it worked. Her breathing evened out, and her heartbeat slowed. The last of the eroticism was blotted out in a surge of fury, fury against herself for feeling this way again and fury against Justin for daring to kiss her.

Oh, why did he have to start this all up again? she railed in her mind. Why? Was he like a small boy

compelled to wind up the toy he had broken, just to
see if it had one more spring left in it?

*You forfeited all that, Justin, when you forfeited my
trust!*

Indignation kept her occupied for a good hour after that. Then it, too, faded abruptly when a branch
shook to her left. Her attention was distracted from
Justin enough to make her aware of the awful stillness of the north woods. A breeze started up fitfully,
soughing in the treetops, more like the breath of a
huge beast than an innocent puff of air. Crickets
shrilled, then went still, as if thinking it better to keep
a low profile. A strange cry, like that of a bird but
more harsh and desolate, echoed.

The Fang Spirit! Swallowing hard, Elizabeth balled
her fists. *Oh, cut it out. There's no such thing,* she told
herself sternly.

Rattlesnakes, grizzly bears, wolves? a small voice
asked.

They don't live on islands, she answered the voice
quickly.

How do you know? the voice hounded her.

The cry was repeated. Was it farther away...or
closer? How easily ravenous claws would slice the thin
fabric protecting her. Elizabeth felt her neck go
clammy.

For two nights she had slept like a dead thing,
oblivious to her surroundings. Ernie had ended all
that. Now she realized that the woods were chock-full
of mysterious rustlings and sighings and croaks. Her
ears seemed to grow huge, amplifying her hearing so
that she could have picked up the sound of a pine
needle dropping at fifty yards. Rigid with apprehension, she began to imagine bears and monsters and

cannibal spirits hungrily zeroing in on her. Oh, what wouldn't she give for the clang of a streetcar or the homey wail of a siren in the night!

Something scuffled, followed by a low animal cry. Elizabeth cringed, imagining in Technicolor a fanged beast pulling her out like filling from a pastry. Vague grunts down near the water petrified her. Her thoughts turned violently once again to Justin—this time in his capacity as a fellow member of the human species. Her pride was so far disintegrated as to make her want to call out—except she was too terrified to open the tent flap. Anyway, from his last words, she was sure he would gladly toss her to the Fang Spirit.

As the long night progressed, Elizabeth alternately quaked with fear and found that by deliberately conjuring Justin's kiss, she could get momentary relief from her lurid imaginings. Her anger at him went underground. This was no time to be mad at the only living human being within hailing distance on a dark night in the woods.

By dawn, she was a quivering dollop of jelly and was stuffed, fetus position, so far into her sleeping bag that the top half was empty. When the first gray light penetrated her tent walls, her nose emerged cautiously, then her chin, then one blinking blue eye surrounded by fair lashes. When she was sure no large, hungry predator had been attracted, she was further emboldened to sit up. All that had kept her going through the night, and all she could think of now, was that Justin was near. For all his faults, he spoke English and didn't eat people for breakfast.

She sat and listened. There was not even a breeze now. Perhaps Justin had been carried off in the night.

In an act of supreme courage, she eased the zipper down enough to peep out. The woods were still full of darkness but the lightening sky reassured her slightly. As she sat looking and breathing in the clean cool air, she saw a tiny movement. Justin was unzipping his tent, too. In a moment, he stuck his head out, all his attention directed toward Elizabeth.

Their gazes locked like those of two castaways sighting each other in the Arctic Sea.

Why, he's been lying in there all night nervous as a cat and thinking of me!

The look of great sheepishness that spread over both their faces did nothing at all to stem the glad flow of spirits in Elizabeth's breast.

CHAPTER NINE

ELIZABETH MANAGED A SPOTTY WASH that morning by clinging to a juniper with one hand and sloshing water on herself with the other. The first few handfuls raised goose bumps. Her whole outraged body remembered her Mexican-tiled Jacuzzi that lay under a skylight safely between herself and the racing clouds. Tonight, despite whatever scaly horror lurked on the bottom of the river, she'd have to screw up her courage and wade in. If she got dragged off by the ankle, she hoped her estate would sue Diana Daniels for every glitzy dollar she was worth!

After cleaning her teeth in a cupful of water and scrambling a full twenty feet away from the shoreline, as Suzy had commanded, to spit out the foam, she scraped one knee and got toothpaste down her T-shirt. Though the shirt was new, its cut and color smacked of army surplus. One scrub and it would look like a historical artifact.

Much of her hair had gotten wet from her splashing, and the damp knot crammed under her hat was uncomfortable, yet there was no way she was going to go to breakfast with strands hanging out. She would have killed for five minutes alone with a good blow dryer.

Justin was already on the edge of the breakfast crowd when Elizabeth arrived. His hair was curlier than ever, and he wasn't wearing his hat—as if he hadn't thought of it today. There were dark circles under his eyes, and the frown line on his forehead had deepened into an exclamation mark.

Elizabeth took care not to meet his eyes. When he looked her way, she became greatly preoccupied with tying her shoe. Only when he stepped up to get his portion did she steal glances at him, and the sight sent the memory of last night whirring alive inside her again. The rough shorts and nondescript T-shirt seemed almost stylish on his lean, stalking body. His visible tension made him stand out among the others, who were all lounging comfortably. There was a warm tan on his cheeks now, which added to his air of strength. When he finished his breakfast, he stood with his hands in his pockets, keeping himself determinedly apart from the crowd.

Forcing herself, Elizabeth climbed the rest of the way up the granite slope to where the oatmeal waited. She quickly took a bowl and spoon, eager to get away from his distracting image. Justin glanced at her, then glanced away so quickly Elizabeth knew that their encounter was also burning in his mind. She drew a great breath and closed her eyes. She hoped that when she opened them, her old attitude toward Justin would be restored and she would be back to her normal self.

But without warning, his kiss flared on her lips, stopping her spoon midair. She swallowed as her disbelieving eyes told her Justin's tan had deepened in the five minutes since she had arrived. She knew for sure a red line was moving up her own neck, as if she were a bottle being filled with pink ink. Quickly, before Justin spotted her blushing, she applied force of will to make the telltale red blotching fade. If this was going to keep happening, maybe she had better get sunburned fast.

Drat Justin! Who did he think he was that he could just reach out for whatever female happened to be within his grasp? Oh, she wished she could just take him by the neck and shake him and shake him and . . .

Justin squatted down to rinse out his tin bowl in the bucket provided and caught Elizabeth glaring at him ferociously. It took two or three seconds before Elizabeth realized what she was doing, but she was so stirred up she didn't waver. Justin's lashes flickered for an instant in automatic challenge, and his thighs tightened, as if he was readying himself for action. Yet when Ernie came up behind him, waiting his turn, Justin's gaze veered away. He put his head down again and finished quickly, spilling water over one of his knees.

Unexpectedly placated, Elizabeth's ire drained. She remembered her quaking gratitude for Justin's presence in the night and her limp relief at dawn, when she found he hadn't been eaten by the Fang Spirit and neither had she. With so many more dark nights ahead, it couldn't hurt to be temporarily fair-minded.

Besides, her lips were tingling again, treacherously. His kiss had been sweet, like a small, potentially poisonous fruit she did not have the strength to toss away. Not quite yet.

Suzy laid her hand against a tall evergreen overshadowing the bank.

"This is a white pine, folks," she began. "You can tell it from a red pine by the softness of its needles. Try it." She demonstrated by sliding between two close specimens. "They brush right across your skin like silk. You can walk through them even in your bathing suit."

Everyone began milling around the trees on the far side of the dying fire, brushing needles across their forearms, teasing each other with the green tips of branches.

"White pines are the true giants of our forest," Suzy went on instructively, straightening with that curious excitement she always showed when immersed in one of her lectures. "You think you've seen big trees along the riverbanks, but you've seen nothing until you've seen a stand of virgin white pine. They tower way above the rest of the forest canopy. A truly magnificent sight."

"Are we going to see any?" inquired Molly.

"Maybe. There's a stand on the islands we're going to out in Georgian Bay. In fact, a lot of people are getting up a petition to have the area made into a provincial park. Virgin white pine is very rare. You have to remember that most of Ontario has been either logged over or burned over, or just doesn't have enough soil to support a group of giant trees. And the few left along Lake Ontario are dying from acid rain."

An indignant murmur passed through the group, causing Elizabeth to examine the people more closely. They appeared to really care about trees. Elizabeth had cared about many things in her life, but never about trees. She had always taken for granted the shady city parks and the sturdy maples that relieved the heat on the streets she had grown up on. But what if all those trees got sick and died?

The prospect was too awful to contemplate, for as a street child, she had deeply loved those trees. She promised herself she would look into the business of acid rain as soon as she got back.

Suzy broke off a twig and handed it to Elizabeth to try. She ran it across the palm of her hand. To her surprise, a delicious shiver from the cool, smooth needles ran up her inner arm. Catching Justin looking at her, she dropped the twig to the ground just as a high-pitched, chattering buzz broke the stillness in the air.

"Rattlesnake!" shrieked Ernie, springing up. "Run for it or you're dead!"

He made for the canoes in great kangaroo strides, and the other campers stumbled after him. Elizabeth felt a white shock of terror strike her limbs. Almost instantly, Justin had her by the wrist and was dragging her behind him down the tilting rock. She stumbled and scrambled and bounced against him in their headlong flight to their canoe. They had it half-righted when Suzy's voice, ordering them all to stop, penetrated the furor.

"Ernie, you ought to be ashamed of yourself. It's nothing but a red squirrel!"

"Squirrel!"

Elizabeth and Justin dropped the canoe onto their toes. Kate and Libby, who had actually made it onto the water, hesitated, then began to splash frantically over the sides with their hands. They had neglected to grab a paddle and the current was gently winging them away. Suzy had not budged from her spot under the pines. Ernie hopped around like a youthful scarecrow, grinning from ear to ear.

"Ha! Gotcha!" he crowed, oblivious to the threat of mob violence. He was still riding high on the success of his ghost story, probably well aware of the effect it had had on many of the people during the night.

In a few minutes, everyone had climbed back onto the island and was giggling foolishly. Elizabeth extracted her foot from under the bow of the canoe. By daylight, her fears seemed laughable, though she could not deny how grateful she had been for Justin's nearness as he had raced with her away from the supposed rattlesnake. This, she decided, must be why she was finding it so strangely difficult to be angry with him.

"And I don't want to hear you maligning rattlesnakes again," Suzy scolded Ernie sternly. "They're an endangered species. If anybody should happen to meet one, the snake will be the one who's most scared."

When the tents had been taken down and the packs were heaped on the shore, Suzy ran her hand over Justin's knapsack, grimacing with distaste. Large damp stains showed on its sides.

"You got soaked yesterday. Didn't you put your things out to dry?"

Justin's mouth stiffened.

"Oh, for heaven's sakes, you can't drag around a load of wet clothes. They'll weigh a ton and get mildew. And by the way—" Suzy already had the flap open "—the water is fairly calm today. Elizabeth, I think you should take the stern and learn to do a bit of steering."

Justin stood speechless while Suzy tore into the pack, pulling out all the incriminating wet duds. By the time they got settled, the canoe looked like a moving laundry, and Elizabeth choked on laughter she dared not show. Justin was wearing only shorts now, having had his T-shirt ordered off and added to the drying load, though he was allowed to rescue his hat. Silently, he got into the bow, eyes frontward to avoid the festooned fabrics.

My, my, already such a different Justin from the blustering captain of commerce demanding that a helicopter be radioed in.

Mischief danced in Elizabeth's eyes as she saw from the set of his shoulders and the tightness at the back of his neck that Justin was not taking this as calmly as he appeared.

After they shoved off, under the amused eyes of the entire group, Elizabeth struggled with the J stroke, the draw and the pry, going at it with the same determination she went at everything, her inborn elegance of motion subordinated to firm-lipped discipline. Suzy, about to board her own canoe, watched briefly, then called out from the shore.

"Hey, it's supposed to be fun. Relax."

"Relax, my eye!" Elizabeth muttered. "They're all just waiting to see our arms drop off."

Was that an agreeing sputter she heard from up front? From Justin Archer, the human clothesline?

The other canoeists soon passed them. Elizabeth's canoe wobbled slightly to the left as she sent it out onto the grape-green water. The drying clothes seemed to take all the danger out of him.

Slowly, she worked into the rhythm of the paddling. The river lay quiet, a sparkling aquamarine color under the open sky. Today, it seemed almost . . . natural to be there. Her senses hummingly alive, Elizabeth began to notice the infinitely subtle variations in the color of the water as the sun scattered flecks of light in the hearts of the ripples. In the surrounding wilderness, she found much more to look at than she had previously supposed—from the slim Japanese perfection of rising reeds, to the ducks taking flight on their stubby wings, to the first clouds of goldenrod heralding the fall.

As they worked up to a broad sunny curve, Elizabeth emitted a faint grunt of surprise. Justin did not deign to speak, but his head came halfway around as if to ask, "What?"

"My arms," she explained. "They don't hurt anymore and they're stronger. I should have worked up a lolloping ache by now, but I'm paddling on as if it's nothing."

"I'm glad you're pleased. Another three hundred miles and you'll be a regular female Paul Bunyan!"

His voice conveyed a host of things—continued chafing at his situation, his usual sardonic tone when addressing Elizabeth and a certain swiftness of words that hinted at obscure discomfort, probably related to the previous evening. But underneath all that was a hint of wryness that might, by a wild stretch of the imagination, be called humor. This last note so softened the rest that Elizabeth could not respond sharply even though she supposed he was implying that she'd emerge from this adventure muscle-bound.

"All the better for getting me out of here," she commented mildly. Pleased at the way her reliable body had risen to the occasion, her confidence expanded.

The river stretched out and slowed as the channels became wider. The broad reaches required little attention as far as navigation went, and Elizabeth could keep the canoe fairly straight without great effort. Her well-trained nose had been sniffing the air since she arrived, trying to place the peculiar, exhilarating scent.

Now it came to her. Cleanness. The all-pervasive hint of asphalt and exhaust she had lived with since birth was gone.

Why, I'm breathing fresh air! she thought in wonder.

All her life she'd heard about air pollution but had scarcely given it a second thought, save to build more protection into her moisturizers. Now, here, she understood at gut level what clean air really meant. No wonder that, when she first arrived, she had slept as though she had fallen down a well. Her poor system had been stunned by all that extra oxygen!

She began to look about her with sharpened interest, delighted that she could identify, thanks to Suzy, red pines, white pines, jack pines, oaks, maples, birches and aspens, as well as alder and blueberry bushes. Up ahead, rhythmic flashes of light danced from the blades of the other paddlers. Sunlight shimmered in a living silver skin across the water near the bow, while the water itself was an ever-changing fabric of ripple and calm.

Yet again and again, her eyes kept returning from the landscape to Justin's back just a few tantalizing feet away. His shoulder was taking on the color of polished mahogany, and she noticed that his build was naturally athletic and compact. Hypnotized, Elizabeth watched the rhythmic bunching and releasing of his back muscles as he dipped his paddle into the water and lifted it out again, leaving behind a green swirl. She could not help but note that his muscles were clearly defined, without a hint of fat, which many of the other canoeists had. Yet, squash and tennis were responsible for Justin's sleek body, not any rough-and-tumble outdoor sports.

Before long, she forgot the interesting birches altogether, for her attention was absorbed by the long indentation of his spine, the triangle at the small of his back where the lightest fuzz of hair made her want to tangle her fingers. Such a supple spine . . .

"Switch!"

Elizabeth jerked awake, arcing her paddle to the other side. This call was a holdover from their first unfortunate day, when they had had to steer this way. Now they did it regularly to rest their arms and even out the exertion, Justin calling the intervals.

When they had settled into their rhythm again, Elizabeth tried briefly to divert her attention back to the forest cover. Lovely as it was, however, the forest cover could not compete with the magnetic fascination of Justin's naked back. With a tiny bright shrug, Elizabeth gave in. She might as well enjoy the scenery. After all, the sight of Justin Archer, half-naked and paddling a canoe full of drying laundry, was not a treat she was going to see every day when they got back to the city.

By the time they stopped for snack break, the sun had dried the clothes. The second the canoe beached, Justin began stuffing them back into his pack, ignoring the strong scent of sunshine that rose from them. When he dropped a shirt, Elizabeth picked it up without thinking and handed it to him. Her fingers tingled as she realized that the fabric had lain close to Justin's body.

"Thanks," Justin murmured, looking abstracted, ostensibly by his packing.

On the river again, they spotted a small rapid up ahead, bouncing and foaming in a dog-leg chute.

"Look at that. Better steer clear!"

"You bet!" This time Justin agreed heartily.

They swung the canoe far out into an alternate passage, where it floated past the danger zone as calmly as a wood chip bobbing in a pond.

Elizabeth laughed lightly, pausing to pull her hat down over her eyes. "That's a change. I thought you were going to drive us headfirst into this one, too," she exclaimed.

"We'll pick one our own size next time."

Astonishingly, he smiled. All the planes and angles of his face changed, and the old, charming Justin from the distant past shone out. Two days after he'd hired her, Elizabeth had so far forgotten herself as to tell him a joke about a drunk and a sunflower. Quickly, she had stopped, afraid her talk might still smack of the streets. That same smile had dispelled her anxiety and given her her first boost of confidence in the new world she had been so determined to conquer.

Elizabeth swallowed, not wanting this tenuous connection to break.

"Seriously, Justin, have you ever had any experience with this wilderness stuff before?"

Two days ago, her jaw would have stuck rather than ask a direct question. Knowing how Justin hated to reveal any sort of lack in himself, she thought he'd claim at least two Arctic expeditions. His paddle hesitated, then he shook his dark head.

"Not a jot. Only old Sergeant Renfrew movies."

Elizabeth giggled, something she would never, never do in public. Certainly not in front of Justin.

"Me, neither. Except for Queen's Park, I don't think I've ever seen a pine tree up close."

Justin went back to cutting a trail through the water. The long sinewy muscles of his arms stood out, attracting Elizabeth's gaze.

"You should do that more often," he said presently.

"What?"

"Laugh that way. It sounds good . . . out here."

Elizabeth closed her mouth and peered hard, but all she could see was the back of Justin's recently retrieved floppy hat, crammed down as hers was, for exactly the same reason. His tone had been conversational . . . carefully so, as if he were protecting himself. An absurd idea, of course, but Elizabeth hadn't heard his voice without that insufferable edge for years.

Curious.

They worked through the rest of the morning almost companionably, the sharpness between them having mysteriously subsided. Justin kept a lookout for hidden rocks while Elizabeth steered them shakily after the group. With their combined efforts, they even managed to keep up most of the time. Once, when Elizabeth almost nosed them into a clump of bullrushes, they both laughed, then stopped themselves. Elizabeth sniffed the air with rising vigor and forgot to flinch when the sunlight started to burn her nose.

Now that she was in the stern, the rhythmic unity she fell into with Justin caused a physical sensation she found quite odd. It was as if they were singing together with only the long, strong dips of their paddle blades for words. Yet, to be on a team with Justin Archer was such an unheard-of development that she almost didn't want to recognize the skills they were honing together. Surprised when Suzy called out the

stop for lunch, Elizabeth swung the canoe in with a bit
of a grandstanding flourish.

"By golly, I think we've got the hang of it. And I'm
hardly pooped at all." Elizabeth puffed up with conscious pride.

"We're getting toughened up, I guess. If they manage to keep us prisoners the whole length of the trip,
we'll make perfect boot leather."

The faint smile playing across Justin's cheeks took
the sting out of the appalling thought. To go home
looking like boot leather would be the end of Elizabeth Wright for the rest of the gala autumn season.
She'd have to move bag and baggage into Natalie's
Spa.

People draped themselves about the rocks while
lunch was laid out. They began helping themselves.

Funny, I already know their habits, Elizabeth
thought. Moose settled down silently. Ernie would
soon start clowning, she knew. His type had been the
life of dozens of high-school classes. Spence, the
photographic fiend, a far worse threat to her than
blackflies, peered through his lens with one eye as he
ate, his body slightly curved as if ready to throw himself bodily in front of any danger to his camera. Molly
and Libby were dabbling their feet in the water and
poking at the moss. Roy, spread-eagled under the full
sun, roasted his naked hide while eating with his fingers. The two lovers, Tim and Eileen, went off by
themselves. They could be plunked down in the middle of the Garden of Eden, Elizabeth mused, and still
care only to whisper sweet nothings into each other's
ears.

She turned her eyes away. They were so young. She
wished she could warn them. If only someone had

snatched her from her infatuation with Donny Clenman!

Elizabeth sat on a slab split from the rock face above. Justin, after picking up his share of the bread and cheese, looked around, hesitated, then came and sat down nearby, though not quite close enough to be actually with her. This was natural, since their stock did not appear to have gone up much with the general company.

Just as Justin had a slice of cheddar halfway into his mouth, Spence aimed his camera and fired. Justin half sprang to his feet, swallowed the cheese, then sat back down, saying nothing. Without incident, Spence turned his attention away and started shooting at Ernie, who posed as a squirrel on a stump so satisfactorily that Elizabeth, after she caught her breath, grinned, always a sucker for high-school clowns. She already knew from overheard conversation that Spence wanted to be a news photographer. What fine contempt he would exude should she or Justin offer him an assignment shooting close-ups of bubble bath.

Beside her, Justin ate with a sudden keen hunger and stared out at a swallow dipping to take a drink. When his food was gone, he picked up a stone and skipped it angrily along the water. Elizabeth saw he had not given up the idea of escape. When Justin wanted something, he could hang on like a bulldog. Yet he was managing to curb himself as Elizabeth had never seen him do before.

She smiled merrily, and her blue eyes truly sparkled for the first time since her arrival. "Cheer up. Maybe Diana will still show up with a royal barge and carry us off."

"Fat chance! Though that doesn't mean there still isn't some way to get out of here!" He fixed his eyes grimly upon Suzy.

Food and a satisfying doze in the sun improved everyone's temper, including Justin's. When they shoved off for the afternoon, the pace was leisurely. Suzy pointed out, to the wonderment of all, a great blue heron standing as if carved on a half-sunken log lying in a marsh.

"It's so...big," Elizabeth breathed. In the city, she'd never seen a bird larger than the street pigeons that plagued the ledges of her office building.

Justin, too, was gazing at it, allowing the canoe to float, his head cocked in a way Elizabeth had never seen before. She wished that she could see his face.

After a moment, he eased the bow in the direction of the others and they set off again. Against her better inclinations, Elizabeth was consumed with curiosity about whether he was really interested in the creature.

"Have you ever seen a heron before?"

"In a zoo, probably."

"Have you been to many zoos?"

Her private demon of inquisitiveness was awake and prodding her. In her kind of world one didn't get ahead unless one was inquisitive.

"I went to a fund raiser for the Metro Zoo a few years ago."

"Ever go to Riverdale as a kid?"

Riverdale was Toronto's former zoo, situated in a smelly, cramped downtown location. It had been dismantled. The new zoo, on the outskirts of the city, stood up to anything the world had to offer for comparison.

"Nope."

"Never?"

Elizabeth was incredulous. To her, it had been a magical other world were real lions had yawned and polar bears had cavorted in their pool. Yet Justin sounded as if looking at wild animals was the last thing his family would consider.

"We didn't go in for zoos."

His flat tone confirmed her suspicion. She paddled for a while in silence, digesting this. A few chance words had opened a vista on his childhood that she hadn't even suspected back when . . . when they were going together. Of course, earnest conversation hadn't been a big item on their agenda.

This was the first time their past had asserted itself into her consciousness that day, though doubtless it had been lurking in her subconscious, waiting for an opening.

The surface of the river shifted restlessly in a breeze as she tried to get a hold on their time together. It had been all a whirl, it seemed, of restaurants and parties and Justin's fast car hounding neon-lit streets. And then the explosive end. What had they ever really said to each other? she asked herself. What?

Odd how she could remember hardly a word. She could recall other things. If she tried, she could conjure up the feel of his lips and the smell of him and that raffish smile. She could conjure textures of him, a thousand little movements . . .

Of course, she wouldn't try. That part was forever under the rug, as far as she was concerned.

Nevertheless, she spent some more time looking thoughtfully at Justin's glossy curls poking out from under his hat brim, and she was startled when he asked a question back.

"Did you go to . . . Riverdale?"

"Oh, yes. Lots of times. There was this old baboon there that all the children went to see. He used to strut from one end of the cage to the other. We kids would nearly fall down on the cement laughing. He looked so pompous, wagging his bright-blue shiny bottom."

A chuckle broke out of her, thinking back to those crazy expeditions with her friends.

"Shiny blue bottom?" Justin echoed incredulously.

"Yeah. Blue as that Corvette you used to have. Remember . . ."

She stopped herself, but not in time. The reference could not be buried.

"I remember." His voice, trying to be neutral, was so laden with grating undertones that a palpitation of fear passed through Elizabeth.

He didn't continue, however. The image of the blue Corvette kept racing before Elizabeth's eyes. My, how the wind had blown in her hair then and how she had loved it. She closed her eyes for an instant and it all came back to her: the hum of hard tires, the growl of the motor, the thrilling thrust of the seat into the small of her back. They had swayed around corners, bucked up hills, yet she had felt perfectly safe.

She opened her lashes to slanting bars of sunlight in the water and the dim darting of a fish. She hadn't been safe with Justin then. Was she safe with him here, now?

In the clear day, the question seemed absurd. She was growing warm, and a pleasant tiredness crept up, sapping her of the energy to be alarmed. Besides, she was an experienced woman of the world now. Considering the way she and Justin felt about each other, the danger was long past.

"You never told me about the zoo," Justin said as she slowed her stroke.

"You never asked."

"How could I ask about a zoo when I never imagined you had ever been to one?" he returned in a faintly accusatory manner—as if he had really wanted to know about her life.

This was news to Elizabeth. She nibbled on the inside of her lip, slightly taken aback.

"We never really talked about anything back then." It was more a simple statement of fact than anything else. Yet it was also a revelation—and Elizabeth was surprised at the aftertaste of bitterness under her tongue.

How little a part words had played, she thought, except for laughter and Justin's easy, head-turning compliments. They had been too taken up with each other in a purely physical way.

Or, at least, *she* had been.

She sighed, then managed to divert them around a lazily floating log. The door on their tempestuous affair was supposed to have been shut long ago. How strange that she should now be paddling around the north woods with none other than Justin Archer—and against her will.

Yet today she didn't feel half like a prisoner. The day was so pleasant and the paddling so easy. Her bottom had settled into the seat of the canoe as if it belonged there, and she was keeping half an eye out for white pine. She hadn't given her business two thoughts all day.

Justin had not commented on her last statement, but his shoulders seemed to have risen slightly.

Oh, Justin, don't you ever dream, don't you ever hug and laugh just for the joy of it—without some ulterior motive?

The poignant cry erupted inside Elizabeth completely without warning. She wanted to drag the tension from his shoulders, make him answer.

Impossible, of course. Justin himself straightened and slipped the bow neatly past a submerged hardback already well streaked with canoe paint.

"I know one thing," he said decisively. "After this little escapade, Diana Daniels will have a helluva lot of explaining to do before she gets near my company!"

Elizabeth shed her attack of sentimentality in an instant.

"Hear, hear!" she chimed with heartfelt emphasis. "Same goes for me. If this is her idea of a business meeting, heaven knows what she'd do after she signed a contract!"

Justin swung around far enough to grin at her, their first bone-deep agreement in years. Together they beached the canoe with the others for the final snack break of the afternoon.

The goodies were spread out on a long glaciated tongue stretching between what seemed the main river and some sort of tributary. The choice between fruit coils and granola bars was as difficult a decision as any Elizabeth had made in her boardroom.

As she sat munching, with little crumbs of granola clinging charmingly to her lips, Suzy started talking about watersheds and how logging and the clearing of land affected the amount of water in a river and caused erosion and spring flooding, with rapid run-off that would normally be slowed and absorbed by the forest cover.

"Why, there was logging to the north of here not a dozen years ago. They worked off the Perry side road, about ten miles up this channel."

Justin stopped eating. Elizabeth had been unconsciously following the movement of his fruit coil to his lips as he gradually unpeeled it from its wrapper. His lids lowered against the slanting sun. After a moment, he began chewing again, as if the treat were twice as delicious as before.

When they were on the river again, their arms ached, but with a good ache well earned through a long day's effort. Elizabeth looked over at the other canoes, now gliding along in loose formation. No one exerted himself, and many hands trailed in the water. The people looked so relaxed and happy that Elizabeth felt a pang.

"You know," she said thoughtfully, "we have rather been making asses of ourselves with these people. It's not their fault we're stuck here. We could at least be polite."

Justin digested this while he rubbed an elbow.

"You're perfectly right. We ought to try to make amends," he conceded with unexpected reasonableness and grace.

Elizabeth was surprised. What was this she was hearing? Justin Archer showing signs of being a good sport? Justin Archer exhibiting social instincts not entirely directed at serving his own ends?

Some little wheel inside her did a half turn. She didn't really know Justin anymore. Perhaps he had changed—a little. Perhaps two or even three decent inclinations might be found in that great heap of self-ishness composing the bulk of him.

Why, she realized as they swung toward camp, they were almost companionable. Regret filled her. Wistfully, she thought how well they might have gotten along years ago, had he not been spoiled rotten beyond all hope.

CHAPTER TEN

IT HAD BEEN ALMOST . . . LOVELY with Justin this afternoon. Too bad . . .

Those were the words that formed in Elizabeth's mind as she lugged her pack up the shore and helped Justin stow the paddles under their canoe. She cast one last look at his broad back and absorbed the masculinity that radiated from him. Sighing, she turned to the now familiar routine of tramping off to find a tent site. In a very few minutes, her tent was up, causing her to regard it in surprise.

Why, I'm not a bad hand at this. Not at all.

Good feelings from the day percolated through her. For the first time she bent down and took a good look at the soft moss beneath her feet. It was dark but with masses of green spears, like miniature pine trees; a tiny forest she could crush between her toes. The lighter patches, like great fistfuls of tangled blue-green threads, were reindeer moss, which caribou actually lived upon. Suzy said moss came after lichen had broken the bare rock surface into tiny particles of soil. After the moss came the grasses, the shrubs and then the trees. Layer by layer, with painstaking, infinite slowness, the landscape was built up from nothingness. A fragile environment, easily damaged. Elizabeth decided to watch what she trampled and have a little more respect.

She straightened. There was a good hour before dinner, and the heat of the day lay heavy in the air. All of her, including her hair, had to have a thorough scrub. There was no more help for it. She would just have to wade into the river.

Keeping on her canvas shoes, she retrieved her plastic toiletries bag and searched out a secluded spot in the lee of a blunt outcropping, to screen her from the woods. She'd have privacy here, and she hoped that Suzy didn't catch her dripping soapsuds in the water.

Green plants grew thickly right to the water's edge. Below, the rock angled under the river's surface. Slowly, with the air of a soldier about to be shot, Elizabeth made herself step in. The water was colder on her thighs than she expected, but after the first shiver, it flowed over her skin with a gentle tug from the current. It was so clear that she could see her shoes in every detail braced on the slanting ledge below.

She scrubbed her arms and her legs, then bent over to pour water over her head with a soup pot borrowed for the purpose. She was just working in the shampoo when she heard the crunch of footsteps above her, behind the blueberry bushes. With one waterlogged eye she glimpsed Suzy and Justin. Suzy was gathering wood with Justin assisting behind her. To Elizabeth's astonishment, he was smiling attentively. Since they had no idea she was there, Elizabeth went still, her fingers sunk deep in lather.

"You have quite an unusual color of hair, did you know that?" he was saying to Suzy. "I could show you some places in the city to have it done. It would look smashing, believe me."

He was using his professional tone—warm, authoritative, slightly intimate—that always threw the ladies off their guard. What on earth had Suzy done, Elizabeth wondered, to merit a change in status from chief jailer?

He must have listened to our talk and decided to act like an adult.

Elizabeth's mouth flickered halfway into a smile, taking a large chunk of the credit for herself.

"Would it?" Suzy answered noncommittally as she snapped off thin, dry branches just right for kindling. Her peanut-colored hair was caught into its usual bushy ponytail—bristling a little more than usual, Elizabeth thought.

"Then you'd have to show it off. One of the better restaurants would be just right. I'd be proud to escort you to Selena's. She always lays on the best—especially for me. It would be to show my gratitude, of course."

Through the brush, Elizabeth saw him applying his most melting smile. It had turned countless women into cornmeal mush, including, a thousand years ago, herself. Her mouth dropped open. Suds trickled, unchecked, toward one eye.

"Gratitude for what?"

"For guiding me out of here. I do have a business to run, and I'm afraid Diana Daniels has played some kind of practical joke." Justin slid this in so easily that his tone barely changed its modulation.

"I thought we discussed this earlier," Suzy said dryly.

"Oh, we did. And after the way I lost my temper, I don't blame you for putting me off. I was a bit of a pain, and I apologize. Right now, I'm throwing my-self on your mercy.''

Honey dripped from his voice. His rich, slightly self-deprecating laugh said, ''How can someone as wonderful as you resist me?'' Elizabeth felt its heat sweep outward through the bushes and wash over her. With a tiny squeak, she realized what Justin was doing. He had merely switched tactics and was trying to overwhelm Suzy with the force of his prodigious charm.

Why, that skunk! And to think that today I almost believed... Her teeth snapped furiously together. *Oh, you were right about being a pain, Justin. Never a bigger one than right this moment!*

Taking a breath, she checked herself. She hadn't been taken in, really. She'd only relaxed her vigil. Only allowed herself to talk to Justin as if he were a human being.

She stood with water sliding down her thighs while Justin went deliberately to work, shrugging boyishly and leaning his large body slightly toward Suzy as if to intimate that only she could understand and solve his dilemma. Elizabeth must have seen him pull this act a hundred times with models and the press and adoring female members of the public, who then obligingly slathered themselves with Concerto Moon Dew in or-der to contribute to his profits. Already, from behind the distant food packs, Molly and Libby were gazing at him, unconsciously mesmerized. When he turned it on, his range had to be a good quarter mile.

''You *were* a pain,'' Suzy admitted bluntly, putting Justin at a momentarily loss. He wasn't used to hav-ing his bad points agreed with, especially by ladies who were supposed to be falling under his spell.

"Then I hope you'll let me make amends when we're back in the city," he smiled, skipping over her lapse and implying worlds in a few little words. "You said today that there's a side road down that tributary just back there. If you would please guide me out, it wouldn't take more than a day out of the camping trip and I'll be more than glad to compensate anyone."

By now, he was practically radiating stardust. How Suzy stood up to it, Elizabeth never knew, yet she just kept piling brittle wood into her arms.

"Naturally, you'd want Elizabeth to go, too," Suzy commented in an offhand manner.

In the pause, Elizabeth felt her heart scoot up somewhere under her collarbone and stick there. Justin scraped at the lichen with one toe and half cleared his throat. Several different expressions flickered under the hypnotic mask of his face, momentarily sobering it. Finally, as if he had made some tough internal decision, the corner of his mouth tucked in.

"You must understand that there is a friendly business rivalry between myself and Elizabeth Wright. Whenever possible we prefer to do things our independent ways. I'm sure—" he paused smoothly and significantly "—she'd wish to manage her own way out."

The strangled gasp from behind the blueberry bushes luckily coincided with the squawk of a jay. The trickle of suds had reached Elizabeth's eye but she was too apoplectic to notice. How could she have been so idiotic that afternoon to have thought Justin actually friendly.

"You and I could leave first thing in the morning," Justin suggested, with such lilting persuasion only a glacier could have remained unmoved.

"No."

Suzy might have been rejecting a bent fork for all the emotion she put into the word. Justin, nonplussed, covered at once.

"Oh, come on. Everybody will enjoy themselves while they're waiting for you. It'll be a nice rest. Or better still—" Justin leaned persuasively forward "—you could take me to Diana Daniels. Maybe you know where she is."

He could have made fudge with the sugar in his manner. Oblivious to the deerflies sampling her shoulder, Elizabeth went stiff from her lips to her toe joints.

The scuzzball! Trying to pull a fast one on me. If they try to sneak out of here, I'll fling my body across the canoe!

"I said no."

When any other woman might have been reeling from sheer exposure to Justin's masculine force, Suzy wasn't even looking at him. Even in the midst of her wrath, Elizabeth spared a breath of admiration for the intrepid leader.

Justin straightened, the tense muscles in his cheeks giving away his frustration. He was still smiling, but his face was growing dark. The beard stubble gave him a wild look totally foreign to anything Elizabeth remembered.

"I'm sure when you consider just a little—"

"The lady said no!"

From nowhere, Moose loomed up, breaking into speech for only the second or third time since the beginning of the trip.

"Exactly." Suzy piled a final branch atop her load and turned back toward the camp fire. "Now please accept that the trip is going to run its course, Justin, and stop pestering me!''

"Exactly," repeated Moose, shifting his massive shoulders. "You pester the lady and I'll mash your nose!"

Suzy stalked off with Moose in the rear, leaving Justin standing with his mouth ajar and his charm flat on its dynamic, irresistible face.

"So, Mr. Hotshot, how does it feel to find out just how much weight you carry out here?"

Justin whirled around so fast he nearly pitched himself into the river. His face froze in shock and surprise at discovering Elizabeth glaring furiously up from about six feet behind him. She was so angry she had forgotten completely about her barely clad state and the slowly dissolving soapsuds in her hair. Within ten seconds, Justin was the color of a sugar beet and his fists were clenched at his sides.

"Do you always eavesdrop?" he inquired nastily as he recovered his precarious balance.

"Only when people are making asses of themselves. It's more amusing that way."

Justin's violent color deepened. Spurred by a nameless emotion churning her insides, Elizabeth tore on. "You were trying to beat me to the punch with Diana. After all that solemn declaration that she'd never get near you."

"And of course you'd turn her down if she made an offer to you tomorrow."

Elizabeth ignored that, attacking again, her body sharply outlined against the moving water around her.

"What I would or would not do is beside the point. As you just found out, deals don't matter out here. Nor do corporate power, image or clout. So it's no use trying to throw your weight around, Justin, or your legendary charm. Nobody's going to fall for it." Then, driven, she added, "You're nothing here! You're so phony you echo when a pinecone drops on your head!"

Her outburst of anger was sizzling and unchecked. Shampoo ran down the sides of her face and neck, reinforcing the impression of foaming fury. The rush of emotion in her felt both frightening and astonishingly good, for it ripped up the lodged resentments of years and whirled them at Justin.

Justin was so angry, also, that he shoved himself halfway through a thicket of alder bushes in order to get face-to-face with her. Red blotches blossomed under his deepening tan, telling Elizabeth she had hit home.

"Well, the same goes for you!" he flung at her, his restraint blown as thoroughly as hers. "Where are all your self-serving labels now? Mess up your hair and take away the makeup and you're not so keen to pose for the camera, are you, Elizabeth?"

Elizabeth's eyes popped wide under her melting crown of shampoo. If she'd had the bottle in her hand she would have aimed it straight between his eyes. She wanted to shriek. She wanted to tear up waterweed and fling it in his face. She wanted to rage and stomp. When she jerked her head up, a mass of sudsy hair dropped onto her forehead and she slapped it back.

"That was low, Justin, really low!"

"No lower than you descended, my dear. Don't tell me you're losing your famous composure! What's the matter, isn't the audience good enough in the bush?"

"You should talk about composure. Justin Archer, the original plastic man, strutting and smiling and playing Mr. Big. Suzy had your number right off. Do you really think you have anyone fooled for a minute?''

Elizabeth could actually see the blood pulsing in the veins of his neck and forehead. He was making a Herculean effort to get control of himself, knowing instinctively the advantage it would give him in a fight. His teeth clenched tightly for a long moment, and then he spoke with a dangerous softness.

"I thought I had you fooled—for a little while, anyway. Then I realized it was the other way around, when you ran off with my formulas!''

"Your formulas!" Elizabeth felt all air knocked from her lungs. Her eyes bulged; her jaw flapped vainly in outrage as Justin's eyes bored into her.

"Yes, my formulas, Elizabeth. That you put together in my lab on my time. How does it feel to owe all your success to me?''

He thought that! He had actually thought that all these years! This was the grudge he was carrying while he was out to skin her for all she was worth.

"My success I owe to my own hard work," she fired back, at the same time stepping backward toward the shore. "I was smart enough to reap the benefits of my own hard work. All you did was try to steal them and make a fortune for yourself!''

With her final words, her heel struck the last slope of rock she was standing on, causing her to sit down abruptly among the greenery at the water's edge.

Justin, apparently struck mute, stood silhouetted against a tangerine wedge of sunset. His face became stripped down, hard edged, as if exposed to an invisible storm. His gaze burned its way from her soapy head to her pale shoulders, her breasts and down to her thighs buried in the crushed vegetation. His mouth opened, then closed again.

"I'd get out of that poison ivy if I were you," was what he flung softly over his shoulder as he turned on his heel and strode away.

"What!"

Elizabeth sprang upright, losing her balance entirely and plunging under the water. She surfaced, blowing and scrambling for footing, fingers of incriminating suds floating out in several directions. When she had skinned the water out of her eyes, she stood staring down at the imprint her body had made on the shore, flattening, in particular, a number of shiny three-leaved plants that looked suspiciously like the subject of one of Suzy's warning talks.

"I'll get you for this, Justin," she swore, as if Justin had personally tossed her into the patch. "I'll get you if it's the last thing I do!"

Struggling out, she found herself waist deep in ferns and stabbed by dead twigs on the underside of pine trees. Clutching her T-shirt, she fought her way out into the open. There, she toweled her head vigorously and sat down in the lowering sun to dry it. All the while, Justin's words rang inside her like an infuriating jangle of brass bells.

His formulas!

So after all these years, that was what was still eating him. After the way he had treated her, he still imagined he had claim on her work. Just because he had had the magnanimity to give her a job, a job she had done very well, he had expected to grab exclusive ownership of knowledge traditionally held in common and use it to make money. Oh, the arrogance of the male species! No wonder he couldn't stand her success.

Of course, the fact that she had made money from it couldn't be ignored. But she had at least packaged it simply, kept the price down and tried to make it easily available to any woman who wished to use it.

She spread out her hair impatiently, pulling it into separate strands, feeling it lose the fight for body under her very fingers. She missed her blow dryer as if a physical part of her were gone.

A dragonfly dipped near and, without warning, alighted on her knee. Elizabeth stared unseeing at its blue iridescence, barely aware of its six little feet delicately tickling her skin. For the first time she was considering the amount of energy the suave and smooth-masked Justin put into his rivalry with her. She had not truly suspected the amount of effort, the amount of . . . emotion he must have invested.

Something in her anger changed gears. She blew the dragonfly away.

Justin was out of sight when she stood up. The campers would be resting during this slow time before dinner. Elizabeth's rage had abated, some of Justin's stings stood out starkly in the landscape of her mind.

Curse his snooty arrogance, anyway!

Tugging the towel about her shoulders, she reconfirmed her convictions about him. She regretted every one of her silly softenings toward him this afternoon. He was as slippery and deceptive as ever.

Last night came back vividly and intimately. She had let him kiss her. Her face reddened again. This, more than anything, rekindled her fury. He had been trying to use her back then, and again now—trying to make her think he was as disgusted as she with Diana

Daniels, then attempting to slip away to get a contract with Diana on his own.

Elizabeth tossed her head. Contemptuously, she thought of Donny Clenman. It wasn't as if she hadn't had experience, hadn't had warning. It wasn't as if she didn't know better now.

Well, Suzy had certainly put him in his place!

Elizabeth's finely outlined mouth curved momentarily, remembering Suzy's superb coolness. There was a lot more under that ragged T-shirt than she'd ever suspected . . . a woman with the nerve to show Justin she didn't give a tinker's hoot just who he was.

But a moment later her amusement evaporated. If she had been forced to admit anything, it would have been that she knew just how Justin felt. She had been wealthy and powerful for so long she had forgotten what it was like to be an unimportant nobody. A familiar base had been kicked rudely out from underneath both of them, leaving them suspended in the air, flailing indignantly.

She swallowed hard and looked away from Justin's dark head bent over his pack. Her gaze lit on Eileen and Tom sitting entwined in each other's arms, feeding each other blueberries, utterly besotted.

A sharp pang writhed through Elizabeth without warning, a pang she was loath to think of as envy toward the loving couple. Instead, she called it wounded vanity. Last night, and today, she had supposed Justin might still harbor a civilized interest in her, a foolish illusion that had been blown to pieces in exactly the manner it deserved.

The rapid blotting out of the sun brought Elizabeth back to the real world. Low clouds were rolling up.

Suzy was trotting about the fire, getting the big pots going.

"Rain gear, everyone," she called out cheerfully. "We're in for a spot of drizzle."

And Elizabeth's hair wasn't even dry yet.

Fine rain began to spatter down, speckling the rocks, then turning them into glistening expanses in the evening light. The people, instead of bolting to their tents as Elizabeth had expected, just put on their plastic rain jackets and then went about their usual camp chores. Elizabeth retreated immediately to her tent but soon realized that if she stayed, she would starve. She fished out the rubberized poncho in her pack, slipped it on and ventured out to the fire. Despite the drizzle, the mosquitoes hovered around the food in droves.

Elizabeth's arm suddenly itched from wrist to elbow, and she tore back her sleeve. To her dismay, bunches of small red blisters were breaking her creamy skin.

"Oh-oh," said Suzy. "Poison ivy. Better put some of this lotion on it."

Poison ivy! So Justin had been right. Over the rim of her tin cup, she eyed him malevolently. She took the bottle Suzy offered her and began to slather the lotion on her arms.

"Why don't you put some of your cucumber mush on it?" he suggested silkily.

He wore a dark-green rain jacket, mottled like a hunter's so that, with the beard stubble and jammed-down hat, he looked as rough and untamed as a northwoods trapper. And he was spoiling for a fight.

"If I had any, I would. It's excellent for skin irritations."

"Of course. Your motives are always rooted in pure altruism."

She glared through her lashes savagely and refrained from scratching.

"I make a good product. People get their money's worth."

Justin's mouth curled into a quintessential expression of disdain. Firelight caused the raindrops on his jacket to glisten. His slight movement hinted at unleashed male energy.

"Oh, sure! And so do you. Don't get holier-than-thou, Elizabeth. We both know pure greed is what drives you, just like any other businessperson. You were quite willing to kick back profits to get Diana Daniels's services."

Suzy was still nearby, very quiet, examining with concentration her long wooden spoon. Justin and Elizabeth ignored her. It didn't seem to matter who saw them shouting; their public demeanor was blasted for good.

"Oho!" retorted Elizabeth. "Listen to this from Honest Abe. All that Archer money behind you and you would have cleaned out little kids' piggy banks if you could. I saw you try it. I should know!"

His face went so dark with angry blood that even Elizabeth was frightened of what she had said. But she had learned early never to back away from a fight. She stuck her chin out stubbornly and met his slate-cold eyes.

"Get the facts before you go making accusations you'll regret!"

"What facts!"

Justin made a half-involuntary movement forward before drawing his lips into a thin, forbidding line. In fact, he closed up like a clam, as if another word would never be pried loose.

Both of them took their plates and ate in separate silence, disdaining the orange tarp Suzy and Moose had strung up as shelter for the others. Elizabeth sat in the lee of a big old pine and listened to the almost inaudible drizzle around her. She slapped a huge mosquito away from her face and her hands. The lotion Suzy had given her was relieving the poison-ivy itch, at least.

She wolfed her food. Mixed with her anger now was the heady rush of a warrior at last allowed to draw sword and plunge openly into battle. Oh, how reckless and intoxicating it felt after so many years of tight-lipped constraint. As they cleaned their plates, she herself launched another gibe. Her blood was up, and perversely, she wanted to prod the tiger.

"Don't look so glum, Justin. I'm sure there'll be another tanker of chemicals waiting for you when you get back. I know how much you enjoy palming them off on the public."

He jammed his bowl down with a clatter and shook the water from his hands. With a tiny, forbidden thrill, Elizabeth saw she had really roused him.

"Oh, and I suppose I should have produce trucks drawing up in front of my plant the way they do at yours. With your stuff, Elizabeth, the customers aren't sure whether to put it on their faces or serve it up for lunch!"

The unheeding loudness of their voices attracted the attention of the whole camp. Faces took on expressions of half-horrified fascination as they realized they were about to witness a fight. Moose continued mopping out his bowl with his bread, showing every inclination to let them kill each other if they wished.

"It irks you like crazy, doesn't it, Justin, that I made it without a lot of high-tech folderol? When you blackballed me, I started just by working from my own kitchen. Every year I've gotten bigger. Next year my company will be zoom right past yours. Just wait till you see what I'm hitting the market with in the spring!"

Goodness, she'd almost mentioned her wonderful mousse by name! Justin drew himself up contemptuously to his full height, his hat brim throwing his face into lowering shadow.

"Oh. And what is it compounded of this time? The souls of tiny pink snowdrops gathered by hummingbirds at dawn?"

He was jeering openly at her simple, natural methods; indeed at the whole cosmetic process. This drove Elizabeth to fury. Her eyes snapped blue fire. Her hair gained body from sheer force of emotion. Her poncho swirled wetly around her.

"Don't think I don't see the contempt your kind really have for the business, Justin. You're just one more insufferable male out to make money off the female body. You...you don't know anything about it, and what's more, you don't care. Just throw any goop together and laugh when women slap it on. You haven't the slightest idea what it's like to stand for hours in front of a mirror, desperately hoping that this time...this time...you'll be pretty enough. You don't know what it's like to hobble around in high-heeled shoes and pencil-thin skirts that bind your knees, or worry all the time about the wind messing up your hair. Oh, you disgust me. You and the whole lot like you. You shouldn't be allowed to put anything on the market unless you're made to wear it six months yourself!''

It thus came out, finally, all her rage against the self-appointed male demigods of beauty and fashion who dictated all sorts of outrageous trends while they themselves remained safe in California-casual suits and untouched rugged faces. How she wanted to put the lot of them in a sack and fling them into a vat of wrinkle remover!

She was standing with her fists balled against her thighs, and her breath was coming in short bitter pants. Justin was rightly speechless. Her attack had apparently stung some male nerve, for his cheekbones stood out lividly, as did every muscle in his neck.

A loud guffaw broke out behind them.

''Hey, we'll go for the mushed cucumber every time,'' put in a breathy voice.

Both turned to find a semicircle of faces regarding them with shocked delight. Ernie was caught with his hands lifted, preparing to clown. One look at the faces of Justin and Elizabeth apparently convinced him that to continue would be more than his life was worth. Dropping his arms to his sides, he cleared his throat in a subdued ''ahem'' of mock innocence. The faces of the others conveyed the conclusion that Justin and Elizabeth were quite insane.

''Quite a performance, Elizabeth. I think I had better just leave you to your audience,'' Justin spat out. Very erect, he stalked off toward his tent.

A gust of stinging droplets assaulted Elizabeth's cheeks and caused the others to stand up. The tarp stirred overhead, crackling and rustling in the rising breeze. With murmurs, the others rose, ready to retreat to their tents. After a moment, Elizabeth followed. Once inside her tent, she peeled off the poncho and plumped herself down cross-legged on her sleeping bag.

Her mouth quivered. From indignation, she thought at first, but then she thought of Justin's livid face and burst out laughing!

CHAPTER ELEVEN

ELIZABETH PERCHED MOROSELY on a flat-topped boulder and forced herself not to scratch the poison-ivy rash, which was now trailing fiery blisters up the inside of her left arm and the back of her left thigh, where she had fallen back against the shore. The poison-ivy spots differed from her mosquito bites only in size and in intensity of itch. The deerfly bites were undoubtedly the most picturesque, each one centered with a round chomp mark, where the creatures had taken a bite out of Elizabeth's flesh. Completing the ruin of her skin were crisscrossed scratches from low brush and scrapes from scrambling up rocks and sliding down them on her behind.

The sun was not making an appearance. Mist hung over the river and advanced in a heavy smothering wall. Elizabeth had gotten up early because sleep had been impossible most of the night. If her body was being wrecked by the perilous outdoors, her psyche was being bent by Justin Archer. Even she had been shocked by the amount of vitriol that had erupted from her during their quarrel last night. She had not guessed she still harbored so much resentment toward him or such passionate philosophical feelings about the business they were in.

The drizzle had ceased, leaving a wet patina on the rocks and sogginess in the crevices. The birds were up and at it regardless, chirping optimistically in the trees. Behind Elizabeth, the sounds of breakfast preparation caused her to rouse herself at last. She had developed a voracious appetite—perhaps to prove Justin couldn't put her off her food.

She walked to the fire. Molly, official assistant to Suzy, was bouncing around getting breakfast ready. If a hurricane or a hailstorm descended, Elizabeth mused, Molly would probably be flipping pancakes and humming pop songs right in the middle of it. Her energy was the direct result of her being twenty-one years old and having overactive hormones. Others were taking down their tents and strapping up their packs. Justin could be seen outlined against the gray sky, staring grimly into the distance. Heathcliff couldn't have done better.

Ah, the injured-prince routine, thought Elizabeth disdainfully. Nevertheless, her eye slid along his tapered hips and splendidly proportioned body. His head was lifted, his profile etched sharply against the swirl of mist in the background. He looked broodingly sensitive. Elizabeth stood still for a moment and pondered all the complexities of human nature. Then, the corners of her mouth tilted down.

Humph! I wonder how many princes are really toads inside!

Breakfast was a damp affair; the mist shed silvery droplets over everything. Afterward, Suzy carefully doused the smoky fire and then piled earth on top.

"Remember, it's fire season," she said seriously. "A little rain doesn't make the least bit of difference. It would take days of downpour to wet down all these tinder-dry bushes and pine needles."

Fire season, all right, thought Elizabeth as she dragged her pack to the canoe, where Justin already waited. He took the stern today, and Elizabeth felt every vibration as he settled himself in his seat. Oh, how she wished she hadn't kissed him. Then she wouldn't have that dizzying rush of pleasure to smother each time she saw him again. Besides, she'd decided he was just as detestable as ever. The heady rush of their battle yesterday had faded, along with the brief burst of humor at the end. Today, she was scratching busily at her poison ivy and was in a very bad temper indeed—too grouchy even to worry about the Fang Spirit.

She set her shoulders and put her back into the paddling, working with strength and concentration as if she would somehow show Justin what she was made of. Her bad mood lasted through midmorning, when the mist dispersed and gusts of wind came, carrying more drizzle. Justin did not speak to her at break, and at lunchtime he took himself off to sit on a distant deadfall, leaving Elizabeth to eat her food in isolation. If it had been bad being a group outcast together with Justin, it was much worse, she discovered, being an outcast on her own. Her only consolation was the knowledge that Justin had to be as fed up as herself.

Do him good to have a bit of discomfort in that pampered life of his. I hope it keeps raining on his head!

This thought did wonders for her, and she immediately recovered from her early-morning disgruntlement. Moreover, the activity of paddling seemed to have calmed the poison-ivy itch. Now fit, she wasn't the least bit tired. In fact, a curious thing was happening to her. She had long gotten over the first shock of being kidnapped and tossed into the woods with strangers, and though she was still angry about it, her innate practicality recognized that there was no escape, and therefore no point in fuming anymore.

And though she had lately led an existence quite as cosseted as Justin's, she had a different past. She had been cold before, she had been tired before, and she knew what it was to be in a hard situation against her will. She was able to accept it without sulking; she could stand this camping trip easily if she had to.

To wrench her attention from Justin's arresting figure, Elizabeth lifted her head and surveyed her fellow campers, taking a good sharp look at them. Naturally, she couldn't help analyzing them from an aesthetic point of view.

Molly lay flat on her stomach, hanging over a ledge of rock, trying to spear a piece of waterweed with a long stick. Again, her endless energy brought a tiny smile to Elizabeth's face. Molly wore a startling deep-purple T-shirt with bright yellow shorts. *With her short blond hair and English-rose skin,* thought Elizabeth, *she really ought to wear restrained pastels instead of trying to knock everyone's eyes out.* The impulse rose in Elizabeth to tell Molly so, but she swallowed it back, knowing how hard it would be to butt heads with the natural, if misguided, exuberance of youth.

Her eyes slid to Suzy, whose mass of tawny hair was out of control, as usual, and tied back carelessly with a clip, as if hair was the last thing Suzy was interested in. *Such lovely hair,* Elizabeth thought, unwittingly echoing Justin. *What a shame.*

Behind Suzy, Elizabeth noticed Kate, sitting qui-etly—almost fading into the bushes. There was a most unusual lack of correspondence between Kate's looks and her personality, Elizabeth decided. Beneath her thick, shining black hair were ruddy cheeks and vivid violet eyes made for laughter; yet she said virtually nothing and moved with such diffidence one scarcely knew she was there. She walked with her shoulders slightly raised as if perpetually expecting someone to leap up and yell "Boo!" from behind her. She wore the faded colors that would have turned Molly into an enchanting blossom but that washed Kate out en-tirely. *Why, they ought to switch wardrobes,* Eliza-beth thought. The vividness of Kate's coloring demanded nothing less than the strongest colors in the palette.

They ought to change personalities, too, Elizabeth mused, then rejected the idea. She wouldn't change Molly's sunniness one jot. But Kate acted old before her time. If only she would smile and get rid of that lanky braid at the back, her head wouldn't look so flat on top or her features so blunt and plain.

Elizabeth sighed, then was distracted by a walking rummage sale. It was a measure of how much Justin had preoccupied her that she had missed a close ex-amination of Libby. Libby was an interesting phe-nomenon. She wore her clothes in thick layers, as if she hadn't been able to decide what to wear from her pack and so had donned everything. She was trying to tuck a sprig of goldenrod into her hair and was not getting it straight. A Swiss-army knife was attached to her belt by a string. A whistle, a compass and a ring hung on a chain from her neck. She was hauling a pie-sized stone toward her canoe. Kate, her partner, was at last stirred to life by the sight.

"Oh, no, not something else, Libby. Really!"

"But it's so pretty. Have you ever seen one like this? It's banded gneiss. I've decided to start a rock garden."

Immediately Elizabeth diagnosed Libby's problem. She was a pack rat. Pack rats were people who had great difficulty with decisions. They clung to everything they came across so that they never had to make a choice. She was glad she was not Libby's canoe mate, and she wondered what would happen when the canoe began to list groggily from sheer overload.

She examined each of the men—except Justin. Roy was exposing himself to the cold, damp air, head thrown back, eyes closed, like a warrior in the midst of some arcane initiation rite. She had since discovered that Roy disdained a tent and slept each night under a canoe propped up with forked sticks. Spence, with the air of one who had scrimped long and hard in order to save for it, was worriedly examining his camera for moisture. Moose was, as usual, sitting stoically, cross-legged on a rock. Ernie was doing something obscure with a strap of leather. Tim and Eileen stood in the shelter of a pine, hands clasped around each other's necks, foreheads together, just listening to each other breathe.

The drizzle slacked off in the afternoon, frustrating Elizabeth's plan of cracking heads with nature. By the time it was time to make camp, the sun was slanting tentatively down, striking the tree trunks in great pink blotches.

Suzy gave her customary nature lesson, the campers following after like the scattered chicks of a comfortable mother hen.

"Here," she said, breaking off the leaf of a waist-high nondescript-looking shrub, "is some sweet gale. It used to be much in demand, and the perfume made from it was very expensive. Just break off a leaf and see how it smells."

Elizabeth perked up at once; a perfume plant she hadn't heard of. People snapped off pieces and held them to their noses. A number of them shrugged. Suzy smiled, her lenses glinting wisely in the weak sun.

"You've got to be quick about it. The oil is so volatile it evaporates almost immediately."

Elizabeth managed to catch the sweet fleeting scent. Little wheels of commerce whirred in her head and were stopped. Every leaf and patch of moss and spiderweb sparkled around her, their simple beauty making her temporarily forget that she depended on these natural finds for her survival and continued success. Yet, a couple of years ago, she would have been packing sweet gale posthaste to her lab.

Maybe I've already got enough of everything!

Eileen was laughing and rubbing a crushed bit of sweet gale behind Tim's ears. Elizabeth quickly turned her eyes away. Libby, by sheer habit, was collecting handfuls of the aromatic plant for her collection.

"Probably won't last," Libby commented to the air, and kept on gathering, nevertheless.

"No, it won't," put in Elizabeth. "You should get a good flower-based perfume at home if you like this kind of thing. If you like, I can tell you a few."

Libby glanced up, faintly surprised at the friendly words and direct overture of friendship. Elizabeth waited to be snubbed. If she were, she thought, she richly deserved it. But she was suddenly tired of carrying grudges. What was the point of taking her pique out on the other campers? Besides, she felt she had to somehow make up for her embarrassingly raucous public fight with Justin last night.

"Oh, do tell me," Libby asked immediately. "I never could figure out how you were supposed to choose."

"So you chose them all." Elizabeth smiled, guessing that Libby's dresser was strewn with bottles of every conceivable scent and sort.

Libby nodded guiltily.

"Yeah. Sometimes I think I'll never use up the stuff in a dozen lifetimes, but when I see another one I like, I buy it, too. Can't seem to stop myself."

Elizabeth laughed. How often had she seen this same battle going on over and over again at the cosmetics counter? People needed some personal references to go by.

At least three others looked around at the sound of Elizabeth's laugh. And one of them was Justin, for he, too, was following Suzy's lecture. He had commented in the canoe that she should laugh more. Well, laugh she would, and let him just stick it in his craw.

That was how her tentative friendship with the campers began. It was much easier than she would have imagined back on that first day, trapped on the school bus. She took a natural delight in people. That, after all, was why she was in the business she was in. Though she was now spotted with fly bites and clad in sagging cotton, she found that it didn't seem to matter. The considerable warmth inside her suddenly flowed out via bright smiles and quick laughter and friendly, uncontrived gestures of her hands. This was when Elizabeth was at her most beautiful, though she didn't know it. Molly and Libby were immediately drawn over to talk to her.

Just as she was continually asking questions of Suzy, Libby began quizzing Elizabeth about perfumes. Libby, it turned out, was a librarian with an insatiable capacity for information. She simply looked at you round-eyed, and you ended up telling her everything you knew about centipedes, car maintenance or the Spanish royal family. Elizabeth, at first awed and bemused by Libby's intellect, soon perceived that her mind was like her pack and her canoe: overstuffed. She seemed unable to differentiate between useful facts and trivia. Her brain reeled under masses of excess information, and Elizabeth suspected she unloaded the information in bulk on unsuspecting souls who asked her questions while she was on duty at the library.

Suzy moved on to late-summer flowers, and Libby tried to fix a piece of fireweed over her other ear. It clashed with the sweet gale and drooped beside her ear.

"Here, let me show you," said Elizabeth. "It's just your color."

Quickly she tossed away the now limp sweet gale, replacing it with a shorter single sprig of scarlet fireweed. Libby tried to retrieve the discarded branch, but Elizabeth stopped her.

"No, Libby, less is more. Anything else would spoil the effect."

"But—"

"Really, it would," Elizabeth reiterated firmly. "You can only wear so many things at a time."

"Hey, that looks neat, Libby. Liz here's got a touch."

Molly was a natural enthusiast. Libby was impressed. Her intellect was suddenly turned toward the art of personal appearance, and she again began to ask questions. Elizabeth, feeling as if she had stepped in front of a giant vacuum cleaner, threw up her hands, laughing.

"Goodness, you're asking for a university course. It would take me weeks. The trick is just to pick out the stuff that is useful to you."

"But—"

"No buts. I'll try to tell you what's best for you personally, if you like."

"Oh, I couldn't...."

Libby stopped, disconcerted, and fingered the fireweed by her ear. Elizabeth recognized the expression. She had seen it a thousand times on the faces of women she dealt with—wild curiosity mixed with lack of confidence. Why, oh, why did so many perfectly attractive women suffer from this?

Her heart contracted in sympathy. This was her raison d'être, what kept her passionately driven in her own business. She wished she could help all the women in the world. By bringing out the loveliness of each woman who sought her help, Elizabeth tried to make each as strong and as confident as she had the right to be.

And damnation to a vulture like Justin for using women's fears and insecurities to line his pockets. How could he possibly understand? He was a man!

Molly, now fascinated, jumped in.

"Oh, go on, Libby. Let her tell you. She's supposed to know about stuff like this."

They were back relaxing by the fire. The sun had managed to warm the evening air and dry the rocks. Elizabeth found that her conversation with Libby had made her forget the mosquitoes and her poison ivy for minutes at a time. She had also, with the lightning professional expertise that had made her so much money, seen all of Libby's possibilities in one vivid flash. Elizabeth's kind heart wanted Libby, as she wanted all her customers, to find her personal best as soon as she could.

With the air of one who was being very brave, Libby stuck out her lip and said okay.

"You're sure now?" Elizabeth asked, the light of enthusiasm dancing in her own eyes. "I'm pretty thorough, you know."

Libby still agreed.

Elizabeth then set about giving Libby a going-over that a rich woman would fork over a fortune for. First Elizabeth removed two of Libby's extra vests, all but one of her necklaces, the knife from her belt and all of her bracelets. Over dismayed protests, she stripped Libby down to a single outfit but kept the fireweed.

"Only warm pastels for you, Libby. I can't do makeup here, but your skin has lovely peach undertones. You'll have to get rid of those fussy silver earrings. Gold only, I'm afraid. Simple styles without clutter. It's going to be hard on your jewelry collection."

Molly inveigled Libby into dumping out her pack. Sitting cross-legged around it, the three participated in a ruthless purge. The pack was as huge and crammed as Elizabeth suspected. Molly looked on, mesmerized as a kitten in a drawerful of yarn. Libby courageously restrained her dismay. Kate, all but invisible just behind them, leaned forward to see and fixed her brows in a quizzical slant.

"Okay," declared Elizabeth. "These clothes—" she patted a pile "—are good colors for you. You can wear any of them together, but don't start piling them on top of each other or you'll look like a clothesline in the wind."

Molly giggled, and Elizabeth peered quickly around, belatedly hoping she hadn't offended anyone. She wasn't, after all, here in her official capacity, and she was immensely enjoying just being friendly with these women. She was so used to awed reverence during consultations that it did her good to have to prove herself on merit alone. Here, no one was impressed with her name. Alarmed confusion struggled in Libby's face along with a newborn hope that at last she might have found someone who could forge a path, however tenuous, in her wilderness of disorganization. Relieved, Elizabeth patted a second pile of clothes.

Why, this is fun. We're just like teenage girls in a bedroom.

When she was young, Elizabeth had been too poor and too preoccupied to have this kind of party. Later, she had striven for a cool, smooth polish in her business.

"These are all the wrong colors, and you'll have to pitch them as soon as you get back. You'll have to do the same thing to the rest of your wardrobe at home. I'll come over and help you, if you like."

Elizabeth realized she had made the offer only after it was out. She surprised herself mightily; her time had become so valuable of late that it would have been inconceivable for her to march into the house of some stranger and sort out a wardrobe. And to offer to do it for free, yet!

Yet these were the people I most wanted to help. Maybe I have been getting out of touch.

"Do me, do me next," Molly begged. "What should I wear?"

Elizabeth was amused to find such interests surfacing in people she had considered, on first sight, hopeless ragbags. But she knew no one was hopeless; they just had to be coaxed a little bit.

"Tomorrow, Molly, I promise. It's getting too dark now, and I think we'll soon have to go to bed."

"Then what about my skin? Just tell me about my skin now."

Elizabeth closed an eye and gave her the professional once-over.

"Beautifully grained, pink as a petal under the tan. But there are signs of breakout. Have you been eating sugar or drinking pop and not getting your greens?"

Molly blinked; a sure giveaway.

Elizabeth shook her head. "Shame, shame. And you so young. All the makeup in the world won't do any good if your nutrition's bad. And most people don't drink enough water. They get their liquid from tea or coffee, which actually saps liquid from the body."

"Really?" exclaimed Libby, her attention fully engaged again. "Maybe you could just give us a few hints about how to eat." The intense brown eyes were fixed on Elizabeth, the impressive intellect revved up to gulp knowledge in huge chunks. Behind her, evening clouds with pewter undersides were drifting along the sky.

"You're asking for another week of my time," Elizabeth chuckled. "But I have one helpful hint I pass on to everybody. Go to the supermarket. Look at each person, then look in their cart. If you don't want to look like that person, don't buy what's in their cart. People under fifty don't count. You want a chance to see the real effects of their diet."

This idea delighted them all as encroaching darkness called them to the fire. Kate said little but remained on the sidelines, watching. Elizabeth had found out that Kate had dropped out of high school and survived on part-time work at a cardboard-box plant. She saved madly every year for this camping trip. Elizabeth eyed her keenly.

She's the one who needs this the most. She wants it, too, though she'll be a hard nut to crack.

What Elizabeth didn't notice was Justin sitting in the shadows. While appearing to stare moodily into the woods, he hadn't taken his eyes off her all evening. His brows were tilted slightly downward and his lids were half-lowered. His expression was torn between cynicism and thoughtful, somewhat uncomfortable contemplation.

The next evening, true to her word, Elizabeth worked on Molly. Since her body had now adjusted to the physical work of paddling, she realized that they were not, as she had previously imagined, covering prodigious distances each day. Instead, they were progressing in a leisurely manner down the river, with the emphasis on enjoying the outdoors. Suzy pointed out things as they went along, including an abandoned iron boiler, a beaver dam and the odd massive white pine. They always made camp in plenty of time to putter along the shores. Not knowing what the woods might hide, Elizabeth stayed safely near the camp fire with her newfound friends.

Molly did not take quietly to being separated from her beloved screaming colors. Elizabeth had to run a small demonstration, using Kate as a model, as to what the wrong color could do to an attractive face. She pointed out how it could make the skin sallow and highlight every blotch and hollow. When Molly saw how her own clothes caused Kate to light up, she did an about-face and insisted that Kate have her purple pullover, screaming-yellow shorts and her collection of vampire-black T-shirts. Though Kate could not see herself, the reflected admiration of Molly, Libby and Elizabeth communicated itself. She accepted the clothes gratefully on the condition that she could pass her own pale-pink and almost invisible-lilac clothes over to Molly. Tactfully, Elizabeth mentioned Kate's heavy braid. It took another day before Kate got up the courage to come back to the camp fire, a pair of nail scissors in hand.

"Do you think you could, um, cut it for me?" she asked in trepidation.

Elizabeth tilted her head. Vidal Sassoon she was not, but surely she could manage a straight line. Kate's courage might never be so high again.

"Sure. Sit over here."

An audience gathered and held its breath as the bulk of the braid dropped irrevocably to the ground. Kate shut her eyes as if she were about to be machine-gunned down, but she didn't move. Even Ernie kept quiet as Elizabeth fluffed the hacked ends and began her painstaking progress from one cheek, around the back to the other cheek, working mightily with the tiny scissors to get all the uneven parts straight. Then, de-

ciding with professional swiftness, she pulled the front
down and cut bangs, blunt and even, all the way
across. Molly produced a comb and ran it carefully
through Kate's shiny, utterly straight locks.

"There!" cried Elizabeth. "What do you think,
folks?" She was holding her breath as if this were her
first makeover job.

Kate still wouldn't open her eyes. But what a
change. Her heavy hair fell perfectly into the blunt cut
Elizabeth had given her, abstract and pure of line as a
piece of modern art. Kate's full, heavy features now
became grand and imposing as her freed, dense hair
sprang out to balance them. Her violet eyes, when she
finally showed them, looked huge and mysterious now
that the over-large expanse of forehead had been hidden. Molly's deep purple sweatshirt gave Kate's skin
a rich, luminous, dusky glow.

"Faaaaantastic!" croaked Spence. "She looks...
Egyptian with that Cleopatra haircut. I've got to get
a shot!"

Before Kate could even breathe, Spence's camera
was clicking, catching forever on film the young
woman's first dawning wonder that she might actually be beautiful.

In honor of Kate's transformation, the camp fire
that night acquired the atmosphere of a party. The
people were happy for Kate, as much because of her
bravery in getting the haircut as because of her
changed looks. Shy and overwhelmed at first, Kate
was soon sitting happily in the middle of the log, her
shoulders straightened and in animated conversation
with Spence. If anyone crept up behind her now to say
"Boo!" she would probably turn around and slug
them back, Elizabeth thought in amusement.

Elizabeth silently scraped out her individual pudding tin and looked on with the pride of a mother. Justin was behind her, she knew, and just to her left. As she swallowed her last spoonful, she let her eyes wander to where he sat, almost out of range of the firelight. The set of her head told him plainly that she knew very well that Kate was the kind of woman his company would never bother with—plain and poor and lacking confidence.

You can lay on the gold packaging and Maria all you like, Elizabeth taunted him silently, *but this is what it's really all about!*

Justin put down his spoon and shifted his eyes away, as if turning from her bad opinion.

CHAPTER TWELVE

"STORM'S COMING. We'll run for it to the islands over there before it blows in. Everybody clear on what to do?"

Suzy stood on a rock at the mouth of the river addressing the group. Behind her, a clump of trees was bunched against a grim horizon. In the foreground, muddy yellow waves tossed spume tearing from their tops. The campers were digesting a late lunch in preparation for the first truly open water they had encountered on the trip.

"Isn't it, ah, a little rough out there today?" inquired Elizabeth, pushing wind-whipped hair from her eyes. The sky was an ominous charcoal color, and the seagulls were taking shelter in the lee of outcroppings.

Suzy laughed.

"Hey, the waves aren't even eight feet yet, and it's time everyone had a go at them. Just keep your flotation vest on. If you get dumped, the worst that can happen is you wash up on shore back here. Somebody'll come and get you."

Icy little feet of fear trotted up and down Elizabeth's spine. There was no use in looking at Justin; he'd been remote as a sphinx these last three days.

"Yaaaay! Some tough stuff at last!" Roy did a little war dance all around his pack. He was sunburned in long lobster-red swatches, and he flaunted his prickly-ash scrapes like trophies.

Suzy went on unperturbed. "Look out for those foamy patches. They're shoals and they'll hole your canoe. I'll give a bit of rough-water demonstration before we start the fun. Get cracking or it'll be too windy to go."

Big tragedy that would be, Elizabeth thought sardonically.

Unwillingly, she lifted her pack. The canoe pranced in the water like a mustang chafing for the plain. Justin held it while she stepped in gingerly. Though their eyes didn't meet, Elizabeth knew from his hands and his body movements exactly what he was doing. Their fight lingered in the air between them, an impenetrable black cloud. Justin was still deeply disgraced, in Elizabeth's eyes, for getting smarmy with Suzy.

They remained canoe mates. Reluctant as they were to spend time with each other, they had gotten the hang of working together. Today, Justin took the stern, where the strength would be required, and settled himself on his knees to lower the center of gravity. Elizabeth kept glancing at the curling fronts of the waves and squelching her misgivings. Suzy had got them this far without serious mishap. Elizabeth supposed the woman knew what she was doing.

After Justin had boarded, the canoe settled solidly into the water. In spite of herself, Elizabeth thought of the strong barrel of his chest and his bronzed arms lightly shifting the paddle. Yes, he did have his uses. At once she felt better about facing all that water.

"Always keep the bow pointing into the waves," Suzy shouted from her bobbing craft. "Otherwise you're sure to get swamped. Don't grab onto other

canoes or both will tip. And once you get out there,"
she continued, grinning, "whatever you do, don't stop
paddling."

As soon as they left shore, the waves struck. There
was nothing to do but thrust the bow straight into the
wind and paddle for all they were worth.

Hunkering down, Elizabeth bulled into it. Part of
her was scared. Part of her was bent on putting on a
good show for Justin Archer. And part of her, the
other secret part that had raised her from poverty and
driven her all these years, began to rejoice in the hard,
concrete challenge. All her life, most of her problems
had involved her brain; her exercise classes were
merely a means of maintaining her limber body. Now
she perceived what a physical contest really meant,
and she felt her body gather and stretch to meet it.

Her arms worked with an urgent, machinelike action. The wind tore at the neck of her shirt and tossed
spray at her shoulders. An hour seemed to pass, then
another. The more they paddled, the less they seemed
to be going anywhere, though the shore was receding
slowly behind them. In the face of nature's might, the
canoe was nothing, a speck on a fluid surface capriciously skidding backward and sideways despite their
best efforts. The piston action began to slow. A challenge was a challenge, but this was ridiculous, Elizabeth thought. Halfway to their destination, she began
to tire. Others around them slowed down, too. As they
did, the waves began to grab at the bows of the canoes and tried to pull them sideways, where the break-
ers could neatly turn them over.

Up ahead, Suzy still treated the crossing as a vigorous game. Elizabeth felt her heart sink as each of the
waves lifted them up and up, then dropped them into

a trough directly in the path of another hungry roller. Her arms were straining in their sockets. The river mouth faded behind her, but the islands they were heading toward seemed only marginally closer. Despite the strong shove each time Justin's paddle dug into the water, she wasn't sure their efforts were having any effect.

The wind grabbed Elizabeth's hat and flung it into the wet bottom of the canoe. Hair whipped across her eyes and stung her cheeks. Anger began to surface. Diana Daniels had gotten her into this. Who did she think she was that she could push Elizabeth Wright around?

Elizabeth had braced herself in a kneeling position in the bow, her knees cushioned by an old sweat shirt, her weight as far down as she could get it to steady the canoe. Water splashed in over the side when she was so clumsy as to let the canoe drift sideways. The sight of a gray-backed wave rolling at her, eager to flip the boat over, made her work frantically to bring the bow around again.

Slowly, agonizingly, the islands crept nearer. Bent into the wind, Elizabeth felt her arms growing wearier and wearier until she was sure they were about ready to drop off at the joints. Twice, the canoe had close calls with shoals. Each time, the dark ridge of a half-submerged rock would appear in front of them so suddenly that Elizabeth had to frantically veer the bow. Then the canoe would dip and buck crazily in the water as the two of them struggled to slide the bottom past before it got carried up onto the waiting trap. The third time, all Elizabeth's efforts seemed fruitless as the canoe rode toward the granite spines. Without thinking, she half turned to Justin, her panic etching her face.

"Paddle!" he shouted without pausing in his motion. "Just keep paddling. We can't afford to lose control of this thing!"

Spurred, she bent to it. The stern slithered by within a few feet of the foaming rock. The action made her vividly aware of the hard-driving, methodical strength of Justin in the stern, a very large part of the power that was propelling them through this watery mass.

Doesn't he ever get tired?

No. He'd drown before admitting such a failing.

Crazy as it seemed, Elizabeth almost wished they had upended on the rock to prove a point to Justin.

The shoals increased in number as they neared the archipelago. Repeatedly threatened with disaster, Justin and Elizabeth maneuvered with such keen team unity one would never guess that on dry land they would be at each other's throats. Time and time again, Elizabeth yelled out as she spotted danger, while Justin kept them steady and drove them through the fractious waters. Finally the first sheltered channels of the islands came into view.

By now the small flotilla was widely scattered. As Elizabeth and Justin neared their goal, the wind picked up, tossing hatfuls of whitecaps into the bottom of the canoe. Elizabeth gulped back her alarm as spume struck. This was no place to lose one's cool.

Halfway across, Suzy had pointed out the large gap between two islands that was to be their rendezvous point. Now the wind gusted frighteningly, driving them away from it. Up ahead, Suzy waved her arm urgently until she was sure all of them had seen her.

The message was clear. *Run for shelter as fast as you can.*

Elizabeth and Justin needed no repetition. They plunged their paddles into the Georgian Bay water in deep, muscle-wrenching strokes. Elizabeth desperately tried to follow Suzy toward the gap, even though that meant slanting dangerously against the direction of the waves. Justin's force overrode her effort and kept them in a straight line toward the right of the gap.

"Suzy's over there!" Elizabeth tried to shout, letting go of her paddle with one hand in order to point.

Justin shook his head vehemently. "We have to keep into the waves. We'll find her when we're in the shelter of the islands!"

The bow slewed under an avalanche of foam, drenching Elizabeth's knees. She grabbed her paddle and began to work in thumping fear. The canoe straightened and drove forward, slicing the crests, rolling and plunging at twice its previous speed. Water sloshing over the gunwales served only to spur them on, as did the sight of the prow periodically plunging so far down as to be out of sight. Elizabeth paddled as if pursued by twenty demons, her protesting arms forgotten in her panic to get out of this. Instinct still tried to drive her in Suzy's direction, but Justin kept them inexorably on the line he had chosen. All the while that Elizabeth wanted to fight him, she was again conscious of the mighty forward thrust of the canoe each time Justin's paddle came down. They would make it. However bullheaded he was, Justin wouldn't let them drown!

After dragging themselves from the clutches of one last shoal, they shot suddenly into the lee of the first outlying island. The water ahead of them was choppy and blackish, but it was locked in a long channel and offered no substantial threat.

"We made it!" Elizabeth shrieked, carried away for the moment by sheer galloping relief. "Hooray!"

Twisting around, she grinned broadly at Justin, who was grinning back with exactly the same expression crinkling his face. It took a full thirty seconds for them to remember themselves and swing away.

At the same moment, their muscles realized the push was over, and they both went limp. Elizabeth found herself leaning over the bow to groan. Justin threw back his head against the leaden sky and closed his eyes, his paddle laid across the gunwales in front of him like a religious object. While the canoe rocked gently, they gave themselves up to the hard-won luxury of rest and would have forgotten where they were altogether had not Justin straightened.

"We'd better move. I can't see any of the others."

Indeed, they couldn't. Water sloshed around in the bottom of the canoe, reminding them of the melancholy prospect of damp packs.

Who cares about damp packs? Elizabeth thought. *I just want to find everybody else.*

With renewed urgency, they started down the channel, swinging left at the end of it to where they judged the rest of the scattered canoes would have come in. They could see a wide gap out to Georgian Bay again, but no people. Ahead there were more islands and more channels, giving them a choice of practically any direction. Pressing their lips together, they took a second left turn and paddled harder.

After rounding three more islands, they saw no one and not a single trace of a canoe. Elizabeth looked back at Justin wildly.

"They can't just have...vanished off the face of the earth."

"No," he replied, looking just a little nervous. "They're in here somewhere."

The question was where.

"There are dozens of these islands. A single wrong turn could have gotten us well off the trail."

They tried shouting, but the rush of wind carried the sound away. No replies would come no matter how hard they strained their ears.

They began to paddle again, this time with a tense urgency. They rounded four more islands. No members of their party came into sight. Light was fading, and off to the west, massive thunderclouds were building up. Elizabeth's shoulders twinged dreadfully. Her heart was beating loudly. She hadn't realized until now how much she'd been depending on the group.

Pulling into an arm of quiet water, they sat breathing heavily. The bullrushes nearby rustled sharply, like thin sword blades, in the rising wind.

"We can paddle till we're blue and we'll never find them," Justin muttered. "We're lost!"

Elizabeth stiffened like a stepped-on cat. Her relief at arriving evaporated as she realized they had missed the proper entrance because of Justin's intransigence. Anger at Justin and anger at herself spurted up to blot out the panic bubbling underneath. The waters looked as grim as the Arctic Ocean. She felt as though she were a thousand miles away from anywhere.

"We should have tried for that gap back when we were in the open and could see," she said, her aggrieved voice accusing Justin of bringing on this disaster. The water in the bottom of the canoe was seeping up around her knees, and her right hand had chosen this moment to inform her of a queen-size paddle blister.

Justin must have had ten blisters, from the way he bristled back at her. "Sure. And I suppose you think we could have made it going slantways through those waves to where she was pointing."

Her shrugging shoulders declared that she didn't really think so, but she certainly wasn't going to say it.

"The point is," she asked loftily, "what are we going to do about it?"

"Nothing, until you tell me whether you're implying it's my fault we got separated."

So the crossing had shaken him into a foul mood; he wasn't going to let this drop. Elizabeth responded instantly.

"Did I say that? Stop being so touchy, Justin. It won't help us now."

"Touchy!"

The canoe lurched as a result of Justin's irritated movements. At the same moment, the wind dropped into a momentary lull, causing his voice to clap back at them, loud as a dropped pan in an empty house. Before Elizabeth could reply, a renewed gust sent waves from the open bay crashing loudly against the island at their back. Inky clouds boiled up directly over the crown of pines sheltering them ahead.

"We've got to do something quick," Elizabeth breathed, ignoring his last outburst in renewed apprehension. "I read somewhere that if you get lost, you're supposed to stay put until they find you. Maybe...we better make camp right here."

Her face was half fright, half defiance. If Justin scoffed, she would strangle him. She was suddenly desperate to get dry land under her feet.

"Here?" Justin echoed, looking at the granite hulks as if they were in some nether region of the Antipodes. The pines were bunched into towers of gloom, and the sky had become a black blanket. The water stretched in all directions, a pewter wasteland. All Elizabeth wanted was her own warm bed and her Laura Ashley pillows to pile over her head.

"Yes, here. Unless you have a better idea!"

Justin wished mightily that he did. Yet they each had a full pack with a tent strapped to the top. Paddling around any more was clearly a futile activity. Suzy would make camp as soon as she could once she was near an island. In the morning, if the wind ever went down again, they could shout their heads off until they found each other.

"Okay, you win. This island beside us is as likely as any," he agreed with distaste and reluctance.

I win! raged Elizabeth inwardly as they pointed the bow of the canoe toward an indentation in the shore. *I win! Oh, Justin Archer, I hope you get soaked to the eyeballs!*

Like all the rest, the island consisted of great humps of broken rock covered with moss, underbrush and trees. The trees were denser and taller than usual, though Elizabeth was too preoccupied to consciously pick up these distinctions. She knew very well that no matter how large the island was, it wouldn't have a level spot on it to set up for the night.

They maneuvered the canoe up to a precipitous shoreline and scrambled out, wetting their feet. With their packs unloaded, they dragged the canoe far out

of the reach of the waves. The last straw would be to
wake in the morning and find it gone.

The wind was acting strangely now, dropping almost to nothing, then blasting capriciously. The air
felt damp and heavy, presaging a chilly night. Un-
speaking, the two wayfarers tramped off in different
directions to set up their tents. Justin found a deep,
moss-cushioned hollow. Elizabeth, wanting to keep
her distance, took higher ground, though it slanted
precariously under her. Against the plucking fingers
of the wind, she managed to get her tent erected,
loading it with plenty of rocks lest the nylon bubble
take to the air as soon as her back was turned. When
she had flung her pack inside, she edged back to Justin, her fingers tucked into her sleeves for warmth.

"I don't suppose you have anything to eat with
you?" she inquired, knowing very well all edibles were
in the food packs guarded by Suzy and Moose.

"If I did, I would have said so by now."

He seemed determined to irritate her. Elizabeth was
exhausted from the long crossing, starving and starting to shiver from her wet ankles up. Justin had to be
in exactly the same condition, yet there he stood,
looking out at the water with his hands clasped behind him as if he were out on a Sunday jaunt. Typi-
cal!

Well, he could freeze elegantly if he wanted, Elizabeth decided, but she was going to do something about
it: first get warm, then see if there were any blueberries in the bushes. "All right, then, we better get a fire
going," she said briskly. "Give me some matches."

Automatically, she started to gather twigs. Justin
gave up staring at the horizon and started going

through his pockets, first distractedly, then with a frown.

"I haven't got any. You'll have to look in your pack."

"There are no matches in my pack. How about yours?"

He shook his head shortly. Neither could believe they were without so simple a thing as a match. Yet after a flurried search, their eyes met in confusion. He really had no matches, and neither did she. How were they to start a fire?

Elizabeth shivered. She might manage without food, but a night in the dark without a friendly fire was unthinkable.

"Indians made fires by rubbing sticks together," Elizabeth suggested. "We'll have to try."

"I'm not in the mood for jokes, okay?"

Justin was scowling, all traces of charm long gone. Elizabeth realized he thought she was making fun.

"I'm not joking. We've got to start a fire."

"Then go right ahead. I'm not about to make such an idiot of myself."

He turned away with that imperious grinding of his heel that drove Elizabeth to madness. This was vintage Justin at his most repulsive. Elizabeth longed to sling river mud at his museum-quality profile.

"All right," she hissed venomously. "I will!"

With exaggerated care, she selected two bare sticks from the inner regions of a pine so dead and dry it looked as if a single hot breath would sent it up in smoke. Then she crumbled mossy tinder into a tiny pyramid. Sheltering it with her body, she began to rub the sticks together assiduously.

Head down, she rubbed them and rubbed them, growing redder and more furious by the minute as she felt Justin's gray eyes fixed on her back and knew they were growing steadily sharper and more sardonic. Nothing happened to the sticks except that the inner parts grew faintly warm to the touch and two whitened grooves appeared. Finally, a gust of wind reached around and blew the pieces of moss away. The first spatters of rain landed on the unfortunate sticks. Elizabeth threw them down and stood up.

"I hope you're satisfied," she said through her teeth. "It was a complete failure."

Instead of a hot retort, she found Justin tightlipped, as if he had been deeply stung. The wind flung his curls across his forehead, giving him an uncivilized Gypsy look.

"What makes you think I'd be satisfied with a failure of yours?"

"Come on, Justin, that's what you've been gunning for since I left your company. Rubbing two sticks together is as good a place as any to start."

The raindrops became thicker, leaving wet marks the size of quarters on the rocks. Half a dozen drops struck Justin in the face, but he didn't flinch even as they clogged along his lashes. His gaze remained on Elizabeth.

"Yes," he said bitingly. "Yes, that's what I *was* gunning for."

"Was?"

Elizabeth, cold, hungry and halfway to being wet, packed all her irritation and provocation into that one word. She was intensely aware of Justin standing immovable even as the forces of nature gathered behind him. *Was* echoed in her brain, filling it with unsettling implications.

"That's what I said, though perhaps the idea is beyond your powers of deduction!"

Elizabeth pretended she didn't feel her throat go rigid. Rain was laying a cold hand on the back of her neck, making her speak even more curtly.

"I deduce we are going to be soaked inside of five minutes if we stand here arguing."

Was it her imagination or did Justin's face screw tighter?

"It's off to our tents, then, isn't it?"

"Yes."

For a moment they stayed there, something stubborn and reluctant mixed with their discomfiture at being alone and stranded. Then they retreated to their respective shelters, resigned to separately enduring a long, wet night in the wilderness.

Elizabeth spread out her sleeping bag and crawled into it. Her stomach growled, and of course she had a pebble under the groundsheet. She wished she had managed to get a soft mossy base the way Justin had. She wished she had something to eat and something to read. She wished the wind didn't sound so threatening or the raindrops like stray shrapnel. She wished she had human company. She wished she could ask someone, even Justin, to share her tent.

She wished she could put her head under a towel and have a good cry.

Darkness flooded in with scary speed. As soon as it was pitch-black out, the rain broke with a vengeance, pounding Elizabeth's tent as if it meant to beat it loose from its moorings and sweep it away.

Frightened and cold, Elizabeth sat up and clutched her hands around her knees. Such torrential rain! However was the tent going to stand it? She wanted to call for Justin, but she clenched her teeth. There was no need to give in to foolhardy impulses just because she felt like the last person on earth.

Driven by the capricious wind, rain spurted, died down and spurted again. In one of the lulls, she saw a light and knew it was Justin's flashlight. He was leaving his tent. For a fluttering moment, Elizabeth willed the light her way. Instead, it receded. A call of nature, she decided bitterly. Justin would never think of coming to her for company.

She watched the light. It half descended a sharp slope, then bobbed there. And bobbed. And bobbed. Another bout of streaming rain struck, but still the light didn't move. He had to be absolutely drenched.

Forgetting that this was exactly what she had wished upon him, Elizabeth waited on tenterhooks until she saw by her luminous watch dial that over an hour had passed. What was he doing out there? What?

Finally, the rain slackened. Pulling on her poncho, Elizabeth cautiously unzipped the flap. The world was as black as the inside of a drainpipe, except for the tiny light in the distance and her own flashlight glancing off shining expanses of rock.

"Justin?" she called tentatively.

She was answered with a low growl of thunder and a flicker of lightning like the wink of a cold yellow eye. Her heart raced. No answer came to her and the light seemed very still.

What if he's hurt?

Instantly, without thinking, she sped through the brush, heedless of it tearing at her legs, and scrambled up slippery flanks of rock, scraping her palms as she tried to hang on. When she got to the light she expected to see Justin's broken body. Instead she saw Justin partway down the slope next to a skinny sapling. Save for his clothing plastered to his body, he looked perfectly all right.

"Justin, what have you been doing down there for so long?"

"Standing!"

He spoke so explosively that Elizabeth almost backed away. If this was his idea of a fun time, he was welcome to it.

"Well, come on up and go back to your tent."

He remained unmoving as if he'd grown roots.

"Justin!"

"I can't."

"Why not?"

The rain, beginning to pour down again, assaulted their faces.

"I'm stuck."

The words might have been pried out with a crowbar.

"Stuck?"

Elizabeth advanced cautiously to the edge of the slope and looked down. Her stomach plummeted as she realized that right behind Justin, a sheer drop fell away to the water, where jagged rocks glittered. As she swung her light around, she noticed that one of Justin's feet was apparently jammed into a crevice between a root and a lip of rock.

He couldn't go backward for fear of falling off the edge. He couldn't go forward because there was nothing for him to hold on to that would guarantee his passage up the slippery lichened granite.

"You mean you've been standing here all this time without opening your mouth...."

The rest sank off into incredulity. Setting the light where it would shine downward, Elizabeth grasped a stunted jack pine with one hand and eased cautiously down the slope until she had reached the limit of her arm. Stretching her other arm as far as it would go, she could just reach Justin.

"Elizabeth, be careful. I didn't ask you to—"

"I know you didn't. Just grab on. You can't stay there all night."

Something told her that he could—and would if he had to. At last she understood just how deep the core of stubbornness and determination ran inside Justin. Sort of... breathtaking, no matter how misguided.

When she was within range, Justin's hand clamped around her wrist. He stuck his flashlight, still on, into his waistband. It shone upward, bathing his wet face with a weird yellow glow.

"Are you sure you can hold me?"

He seemed quite ready to let go again, even at that point, and last out the night in the rain. Elizabeth, straining and braced awkwardly on precarious footing, spat out a small but effective curse through her incisors.

"Yes, I can hold you. Come on."

She supported his full weight for a moment as he unhooked his foot. Then, with her hands grabbing on to the quivering tree, she arched her body backward until he had skidded up the rock and stood panting on the crest beside her.

Elizabeth was terrified that he might have hurt himself... and furious that he thought so little of her that he'd rather spend the night beaten to a pulp by the rain than call out to her for help.

"So," she sputtered, the moment he was safe, "you're still playing those dumb manhood games. Like the time you almost drowned us in the rapids."

His face was as stiff as concrete as he started out toward his tent, his flashlight in his hand again. Somehow, this made Elizabeth all the more enraged. She scrambled after him, slipping and sliding on the wet moss. Fright and anger were all mixed up in the blast she fired off at him.

"You've got a head like a petrified log, Justin Archer. What if you'd broken your neck back there and I was the one who had to deal with it? You spoiled, pampered phony, strutting around and giving yourself airs. Why, you wouldn't know how to get along with another human being if your life depended on it. I should have left you there. It would have served you right!"

She had worked herself up to a high boil. She sizzled with anger—all the anger she had been storing up for so long. Anger that he had used love to take advantage of her. Anger that he wasn't the kind of human being she wanted him to be. Anger against the outdoors, where she was now trapped.

She was so taken up with her emotions that she slammed right into the back of Justin as he pulled up short before his tent. His light shone down on a dismaying sight. In his absence, the comfortable mossy hollow where he had pitched his tent had collected all the runoff and become a pool. In the midst of the pool, with about six inches of water flooding its floor, stood Justin's rain-battered tent.

Serves you right! Elizabeth was about to say again when a bolt of lightning seared above their heads, turning the landscope into a fiery white nightmare. Elizabeth gasped, the sound lost in a clap of thunder. In one instant, all her fury was transmuted to stark primeval fear.

"Come on! My tent is dry."

Justin resisted. Elizabeth grasped him by the elbow and yanked, almost tearing him off his feet.

A second bolt of lightning bisected the blackness, followed by another roar of thunder. Elizabeth and Justin almost flew through the air until they arrived at her tent. Once there, Elizabeth dived in, dragging Justin after her.

CHAPTER THIRTEEN

INSIDE OF A WINK, the pair fumbled the zipper tight, as if flimsy nylon would protect them from the wrath of the elements. Two bodies crammed into a space barely large enough for one person and a pack.

Petrified, they crouched, fully expecting a tongue of lightning to sever them in half. When only blackness and rushing wind ensued, Elizabeth became aware that her poncho was streaming water onto her warm sleeping bag and Justin was utterly drenched. Not only that; when she touched him, her hand recoiled from the deep chill of his skin.

"Why... you're shaking!"

She was dumbfounded. Dragging her flashlight from where it had been grinding into her back, she saw bedraggled hair plastered across his forehead and droplets glistening everywhere. Quickly, she pushed her pack far to the side and stuffed her dripping poncho behind it.

"Get out of those wet clothes," she ordered, rebounding from fright into a state of hyperactivity, partly due to the close contact with Justin.

"I'm all right," he grated recalcitrantly.

"No, you're not. You're shivering and you look like a drowned tomcat. In another minute you'll have my sleeping bag sopping, and it's about the last dry thing I have. I'll see if I can find you a shirt."

Wincing at the thunder, she rummaged in her pack until she came up with a garment she guessed would fit him.

"I've nothing for the bottom," she told him curtly, not daring to think what she was saying, "so you'll just have to take off those shorts and make do."

Justin failed to move. Drops fell onto Elizabeth's hand, stinging her strung-tight nerves.

"Hurry up. Nobody can see you in here! Modesty is about the last thing I'd accuse you of!"

Switching the flashlight off, she chucked a towel at him, feeling it strike his shoulder. The tent quivered as he toweled his head. Next came a pause, them some undefined contortions. Elizabeth snatched a wet wad of fabric away from him in the dark and jammed it atop her rain poncho. She handed him the shirt and watched it slide up one of his arms. He was seeking the other armhole when lightning blazed across their heads, followed by an earsplitting clap of thunder. Elizabeth jerked upward. The tent rocked violently while the flashlight jumped from her hands and rolled away under the edge of the sleeping bag. Her heart pounded against her ribs like a piston ripping free of its rods. The awful hollow sound was her breath.

"S-some storm." She did not recognize her own voice. Nothing like this ever happened back in Rosedale.

"Yeah."

"Doesn't it . . . bother you?"

"Oh . . . it's okay."

Good old Justin, still playing Iron Man. Yet he'd been glad enough to hie himself into her tent, Elizabeth thought with satisfaction.

Rain struck, pounding as if a high-pressure hose were being turned on the rock outside. The fly sheet of the tent bounced and shook under the force. Elizabeth hurried to drag her pack a few inches from the tent wall lest it start a leak.

"Gosh, sounds as if we're going to get washed into the channel. I've never heard such rain."

"Me, neither."

Now where had all Justin's belligerence gone? Though he was trying to sound casual, his voice was almost as weak as Elizabeth's and he sat as still as a jade Buddha. Feebly, he was taking up his searching motion again when the great bolt struck. This time it seared straight down out of the sky, a savage river of fire so vivid the tent might have been tissue paper. A tree not fifty yards away was electrified into a fiery torch.

Simultaneous thunder and a flattening avalanche of noise shook the rock beneath them. Elizabeth felt her eardrums shred and the plates of her skull loosen. She uttered a piercing screech and threw herself at Justin, arms milling until they lodged around his rib cage and clamped into a death grip. Every ounce of her strength went into trying to burrow against him at a point just below his collarbone.

The storm burst upon them as they clung together and crouched to the ground. Outside the tent, one lightning bolt after another shot its way downward until all the surrounding firmament was ribbed and veined with rivers of hissing fire. Thunder battered their already jolted nerves, and terrible tearing sounds shivered from horizon to horizon. The sky seemed to have virtually split down its center, and rock foundations shuddered and quivered in preparation for crumbling into the bay.

Racked with pure terror, Elizabeth emitted shriek after hoarse shriek, jamming her face into Justin's neck, squeezing her eyes uselessly against the terrifying brilliance that penetrated even the most fiercely shut lids. A nearby crash indicated that the struck tree had fallen. Elizabeth prepared for the rest of the forest to come toppling into their tent, smashing herself and Justin into nothingness.

The tent leaned and jiggled and danced around them, restrained from leaping into the air only by the weight of its inhabitants and the many rocks Elizabeth had piled around the pegs. Slowly, it stopped straining, and the whipping of the fabric began to be heard through breaks in the tumult.

In one of these lulls, Elizabeth stopped screeching, then gasped as hard as she could, desperately trying to suck air into her collapsed lungs. She was prevented by a kind of steel trap that had clamped itself around her. If she had escaped the lightning, she was about to die of suffocation. In the midst of heaving wildly, she realized that it was a pair of masculine arms that were doing their best to cave her ribs in.

She went still.

Justin!

Justin was holding her.

Justin's image blazed through her consciousness as vividly as the lightning had. Her eyes flew wide. Her heart thudded as blood rushed back to all the parts of her body that had been drained by her recent ordeal.

Justin. Gripping her like a drowning sailor clutching a barrel. As madly scared as she.

Her fear crumbled as her nostrils filled with the damp scent of him mixing with the smell of fresh cotton from the shirt she had supplied. He smelled of wood smoke and rainwater and pine, and her instincts recognized the combined scent as pure masculinity. He seemed sculpted beneath her hands. Yet Elizabeth could feel his heart pumping as violently as her own.

It took only the slightest motion of his body to make them break apart. In the utter darkness of the tent, they could tell each other's position by the warm breath sliding across their cheeks. The wind dropped as if a vent had been closed. The wild deluge of rain calmed to an uncertain, pedestrian patter. The thunder and lightning seemed to have moved several islands away.

"Well," they sputtered, both at once, sincerely surprised at still being alive.

Freed of Justin's vicelike grip, Elizabeth expanded her ribs, filling her lungs with air. An enormous bubble of relief welled up in her. Spontaneously, she giggled aloud.

"We . . . we made it!"

She was between hiccups and felt like chirping from a treetop.

"That we did. I thought we were goners for sure. Whew!"

Elizabeth didn't even recognize the novelty of such a statement from he-man Justin. She was too shaky, as if parts of her had fallen all over the place and she couldn't gather them together quite yet. "I . . . I had no idea it could be like this. I mean, storms back in the city . . ." Words were inadequate to express the experience she had just gone through. Her knees were still shaking. She seemed to have the print of Justin on her cheek and shoulder.

A brief silence reassured them that the thunder was indeed departing. The rain on the fly sheet was light, almost comforting now. Elizabeth put a hand up to push hair out of her eyes. Her elbow bumped lightly off Justin's invisible knee. She giggled again in apology, unsure where all this glee was coming from. "Sorry."

"Bit crowded in here."

"Yeah." She didn't mind a bit.

Justin arranged himself more comfortably, tucking both legs under him to give her room. The loose arm of the shirt she had lent him trailed across her thigh. She remembered that he'd had it only half on when the storm had struck.

"Too bad we can't celebrate our new lease on life with something to eat," Justin commented slowly. "I'm starved."

All the starch had been leached out of him by the storm, it seemed to Elizabeth, leaving no trace of the recalcitrant man she had dragged into her tent. Elizabeth's giddiness had perhaps infected him, too. Except for the vibrant undertones, Elizabeth might not even have recognized who was speaking.

And since he had reminded her of her stomach, Elizabeth realized she was ravenous. "Me, too. We don't even have a chocolate bar. But whoever put together my pack had a sense of humor."

"How do you mean?"

Was Justin shifting closer in the dark?

"This!"

Elizabeth plunged her hand to the bottom of her pack and came up with a round, smooth object bulg-

ing at one end. Grinning, she let Justin feel the shape
of it.

"Apricot brandy," she told him daringly. "Shall we
have a swig?"

"On empty stomachs?"

"Why not? We'll enjoy it, that's for sure."

They fumbled around until they peeled away the
silvery seal at the neck and worked off the top with
their thumbs. Immediately, the potent scent filled the
tent, mixing with the smell of rain and wet moss. Justin searched out the other arm of his shirt and
shrugged it on. He made no move to button it down
the front.

"Ladies first," he declared with exaggerated gal-
lantry. The storm must have shorted out a few of his
circuits, Elizabeth mused. He sounded perfectly
agreeable.

She took a gulp straight from the bottle. The brandy
burned down her throat but left her mouth full of a
delicious sweetness. Groping for Justin's hands, she
pressed the bottle into it. Breathlessly, she listened for
his soft swallow.

"Whooooeee! Some stuff!"

He had kept hold of her hand so that he could pass
the bottle back. Elizabeth took a second swig, recklessly larger than the first. When it was down, she
licked the fruity liquor from her lips.

Midhiccup, her hand flew to her mouth. She giggled again, very softly. The brandy was hitting her
system forcefully, shunting heat all through her veins.
When she passed the bottle back to Justin, she was
sure she could feel him smiling in the dark.

"Ah," he sighed. "We're stranded, but not totally
without comfort."

"Northern comfort," Elizabeth replied, and giggled again.

The rain fell lightly above them. The thunder, barely audible now, reminded them of what they had escaped. The outside world seemed to have totally disappeared, along with the past and the future. They might have been two aliens cast up on a deserted planet a million miles from nowhere. Growing jolly in the manner of shipwreck survivors, they passed the brandy back and forth in the dark, feeling with their hands to find each other, not always letting go when the bottle had been transferred. An apricot-colored lightness lifted them. Elizabeth realized that there was nothing like an empty stomach and a recent encounter with elemental terror to put some zip back into life.

She was entering a most peculiar state, glowing inside but so sensitive she could feel the cool dampness of the night air penetrating the tent. Items of wet clothing strewn around added to the faint chill. Peeling back the flap of her sleeping bag, she half wrapped part of it around her. On one of her journeys to hand the bottle over to Justin, her hand encountered his chest and found it cold.

"Hey, you'll get pneumonia like that. Take part of the sleeping bag."

Companionably, Justin tucked the free end of it around himself and let out a sigh of comfort. Uncharacteristically, he didn't balk at anything, but Elizabeth was floating a little too far off the ground to comment. She only shoved her pack around so that it formed a comfortable prop for her back. As she leaned against it, the sleeping bag pulled toward her. With it came Justin. Accommodatingly, Elizabeth moved over so that he, too, could stretch out his legs and share the warmth of the sleeping bag, which was three-quarters over them, coverlet fashion. It was a very good-quality sleeping bag and was making the tent quite comfortable. Hot, even. Justin's thigh gave off radiant heat of its own as it brushed against Elizabeth. During his turn at the brandy, he tilted his head back for what seemed ages, then uttered a cheerful curse. "Blast!"

"What?"

"Bottle's empty."

"No!"

It seemed they had barely tasted it. With regret, Elizabeth took it from him and stuffed it into the corner of the tent where the rest of the evening's discards had been crammed. The brandy coursed merrily through her body while Justin edged closer, as if to get warmer. His hip pressed against hers so that he, too, could lean against the pack. Heady alcoholic fumes permeated the air.

Justin burped.

Elizabeth thought this excruciatingly funny. "Gesundheit!" she cried, choking with merriment. Justin responded by chuckling deep in his throat, an easy sound Elizabeth had never heard from him before.

"You know—" she took up one of their former conversations "—I like your laugh, too. I really do."

"Hey, no kidding."

He sounded boyishly pleased and not the least bit sarcastic.

"No kidding. It always reminded me of a sinful drink. Hot chocolate, maybe. That's my secret thought for the day!" Taken with her own wit, Elizabeth snorted in the darkness. She felt on the edge of a fit of silliness. Lord, when had she last allowed herself to be silly!

The wind had now died completely, and so had the rain. The only water bouncing on the tent now fell from the trees. As Justin and Elizabeth lay listening to their own soft sounds, a gentle intimacy bloomed around them until it seemed to penetrate the very air in the tent. Elizabeth thought it was perfectly fine that she was now propped against Justin's rib cage feeling the steady thump of his heart through his loosened shirt.

"I didn't know you had secret thoughts about me," murmured Justin in a lazy, teasing voice.

"Oh, I have all kinds of secret thoughts. So must you. It's your turn to tell me a secret about you."

His breathing paused, as if he were turning selections in his mind.

"I have caps on two of my teeth," he said without warning. A few hours ago he might have allowed himself to be set adrift in a bait bucket rather than reveal such an imperfection.

Elizabeth was too far adrift herself to twit him about it. She pursed her lips and struggled to cap his confession with something equally scandalous.

"Well, I lighten my hair. No one is supposed to know."

Glee bubbled up, as if she had just played a joke on half the province. After all, it was only lemon juice, and not really a lie when she passed herself off as a natural honey blonde. Still, there were detractors who would love to get hold of this tidbit.

Justin's ribs moved rhythmically up and down, and Elizabeth thought it the most comfortable motion in the world.

"Do you worry about your hair, too?" Justin asked, not the faintest bit scandalized.

"Goodness, all the time. Everybody's always looking at it, you know."

"I know," he replied understandingly. "Just one hair out of place and, zappo, they get you for it!"

"Exactly."

Elizabeth was enjoying the very pleasant friction caused by her thigh resting against Justin's skin. The warmth from the sleeping bag was wrapping both of them around in a smooth cocoon. The fly sheet, draining itself in leisurely drips, was as good as a lullaby.

"I didn't know you had such nice curls," she continued after a moment. "You know, you should get a shorter haircut and just let them come out."

"You think so?"

"Uh-huh. You go too heavy on the sophisticated look."

Her palms developed a deep desire to run through Justin's mop to show him what she meant. She turned her head slightly and let his curls brush along her forehead. His head bent as if to accommodate her. Enjoying the sensation, Elizabeth closed her eyes.

"You know," Justin murmured after a brief silence, "at least once a week I put a mirror up to the back of my head to see if I'm losing hair there. That's where it started on my father."

"Oh, no!"

There had been a framed corporate photograph of his father in the foyer of Justin's building. He'd had rather tentative features and a pate aglow from the photographer's lights. Though Elizabeth had known who it was, she had never been able to associate him with his vital son. Now she realized that that bald head represented a genetic time bomb for Justin. Her hand found his in swift indignant sympathy for the terrible burden of being male.

Bad enough to be a dishwater blonde. How unspeakably awful to wonder when one's hair is going to fall out by the roots!

Justin's fingers squeezed back, signaling, "Message taken." Elizabeth felt she had to offer some similar torture to be even.

"I once had some hairs removed from my upper lip by electrolysis. You could hardly see them, but with all those closeup photos you can't be too careful. Hurt something terrible."

She felt him nod in fellow feeling. Her weight was leaning heavily onto his right arm, probably cutting off his circulation. He relieved it by lifting it up and tucking it snugly around her shoulders. Elizabeth's head fit very neatly in the hollow provided. The edge of his shirt ran down under her cheek so that part of her face rested on his exposed chest. His skin felt wonderfully firm and elastic. Her nostrils were filled with the comforting scent of him. Apricot heat curled all around her. She had previously thought of him in terms of metals—iron, bronze, brass. Now she couldn't remember why. She snuggled luxuriously as Justin continued to spill dark, personal information.

"Gad, the things people do to themselves! I had jug ears as a kid. They were fixed surgically before my parents would let me go out without a hat."

"Jug ears!"

This was too much. Despite her attempt at control, Elizabeth's chest heaved once, then twice, and then the two of them simultaneously broke into a paroxysm of giggles. Their bodies shook together as if caught in a single bowl of custard. Justin's arm tightened around Elizabeth to keep her from sliding sideways. His laughter, transferred through her ear against his chest, echoed deliciously inside her body.

When the giggles died away, they both released a long sigh. The silliness had passed, replaced by a closer, more speculative mood. The last droplets fell from the trees, a tiny musical interlude. The brandy had brought them to that point at which wine-soaked philosophers begin offering profundities in bars.

"Actually, we're pretty lucky people, all considered," Justin observed meditatively, "give or take a few spare hairs. Not many folks are as successful in life as we are."

"Yeah," Elizabeth agreed. She knew she should quibble about the word "lucky," for she'd slaved and sweated—yet quibbling didn't seem worth the energy. Besides, right at that moment, she felt lucky all over. So lucky that she was developing an inner desire to lay herself out for Justin like a gift.

"I wasn't always rich," she declared, delving back almost as far as her memory went.

"Oh."

"Nope. I grew up poor as a park squirrel. Just my mom and me. She worked as a waitress, and half the time we had to get welfare. I'd have scrubbed streets to get out of there."

"Hey, no baloney?"

Genuine surprise sharpened Justin's voice. And no wonder. She'd been true to her vow to forget her past. But now she was growing inexplicably sentimental about it. She was proud of how far she had come, and she wanted Justin to know it.

"No baloney!"

Without trying, she found herself describing the third-floor-tenement rooms and the roaches and her mother's swollen feet. It was like a tap opening, and she was relieved of a pressure she hadn't even known was pressing on her until she began unloading. It felt...healthy, as if she were shaking herself and old, dry masks were dropping away.

When she had finished, Justin lay in silence, his fingertips circling lightly and almost unconsciously on the softness above Elizabeth's elbow. Elizabeth savored the delicate sensation. Her mind was filled with a jumble of early memories, and now she began recalling other times with Justin. If she put her mind to it, she could remember the exact texture of the pads of his palms, and the way the large, strong veins on the backs of his hands used to fascinate her. She liked the sensation of being tucked against the firm arch of flesh between his shoulders. After a while, she felt Justin tilt his head back. Had they been outside, he might have been trying to look at the stars.

"Look, a wealthy childhood isn't all it's cracked up to be, either. I, for instance, was sent to a very private, very expensive and very exclusive boy's school. From the outside, it was posh. Inside...it was hell!"

"Hell?"

"Living hell." His voice hesitated, caught and took on a darker tone. "After all, my family made its money out of lipstick and eyeliner. Have you any idea what happens when you're eight years old and the rest of the fellows find out something like that?"

Elizabeth didn't want to guess. She suddenly had an image of the young Justin in her mind, all skinny legs and aggressive curls, his two small fists warding off the world.

"What?" she asked, holding herself in.

"Constant name calling, constant torment. The first week I was there, half my class put on lipstick and blew kisses at me. I'd find face powder dumped in my gym bag, perfume sprayed all over my locker. Once Tyler Brant filled my pencil bag with nail-polish bottles. When I opened it in class, three of them fell out and went rolling right over to the teacher. As I said, he only did that once."

Embarrassment writhed through Elizabeth as if she'd been there beside him. Life in the streets had taught her that little boys could be the nastiest creatures ever put on this green earth.

"Good heavens, what did the teacher do to him?"

"It wasn't what the teacher did, it was what I did." For the first time, the slightly boozy burr of his voice cleared and took on the steeliness Elizabeth well knew was inside him. "After school, I sent him wailing to the infirmary with a broken arm. I was nearly expelled, but it was worth every detention I got."

"Did they leave you alone after that?"

A low laugh vibrated in Justin's throat, strangely humorless.

"Oh, they kept trying, right up until I was ready for high school. They only backed off when they found out I had learned to be tougher than all of them. That was the key. To beat them in class and in the gym. If I didn't, somebody would try to give it to me. I taught them that I never forgot a nasty turn. It got rid of the lipstick jokes, all right. Did me good, I suppose. I discovered early that you have to be ruthless to survive."

Ruthless!

Even in the blackness, Elizabeth knew Justin's lips had curled back. Suddenly, she understood why he swore she would never work elsewhere if she dared leave his company.

"That's why you're so competitive," she murmured. Hazy from the apricot brandy, Elizabeth regarded all this interesting new information impartially, from a great height. Her former passionate fury seemed to have been washed away with the rains. Justin shifted as if remembering himself. Warmth on her cheek told Elizabeth his head had bent closer to hers.

"Not tonight," he whispered. "Not tonight."

The atmosphere inside the tent grew thicker and cosier by the second and buzzed with a hypnotic vibrancy. The scent of apricots was everywhere, as if Elizabeth and Justin were lying in the middle of a summer orchard. Justin's arm slowly tightened. Elizabeth shuddered pleasurably as Justin's lips nuzzled her ear. Without hesitating, she tilted her head back to give him access. In a moment, his mouth had worked its way along her cheek and found her lips. A slow gentle exhalation of his breath caused her to shiver. Her lips opened of their own accord to admit his explorations.

Silently, he pulled her closer, childhood tales forgotten. Elizabeth's lungs struggled to breathe faster but her chest felt weighted with a glorious languor. A thrilling ache sprang alive in her abdomen. Her hand flew to Justin's face and she felt the rough, suddenly unbearably exciting texture of his beard. Her other arm slid behind him. His flesh seemed hot, so very temptingly hot under her palm.

A liquid yellow gold penetrated Elizabeth, as if she were actually swimming in the brandy. The kiss lingered on and on while Justin buried his fingers in her hair and tipped her face up to his. Somehow his other hand had gotten loose and was fingering the gentle outer curve of her breast. The sleeping bag, too hot now, slid away. Their bodies, following natural inclination, slid with the sleeping bag until they were lying full-length, their heads bumping softly against the bulge of the pack.

Neither spoke. Words seemed irrelevant. Elizabeth switched away from all but the immediate present, wholly absorbed in physical sensations, drinking up the sweetness of Justin against her, his thumbs delicately tracing her nipples, his hips leaning more and more heavily against her own taut belly.

The shirt she had lent Justin was now clinging to him by only one cuff, for Elizabeth's questing hands had managed to peel the rest away. As he twisted, the towel he had dried himself with also fell away, and with a shock, Elizabeth realized he was all but naked against her.

"Oh," she cried softly. "Oh...oh."

An old emotion surged in her, lifting her toward him, carrying her home, home to his arms. Eyes shut tight, her mouth opened in a soundless laugh of happiness as Justin kissed her belly button, then the lovely hollow curving up to her hip. Oh, for how many years had she yearned to be right here, doing this, adoring him with her hands, her mouth, her body, feeling him twine around her as if he belonged exactly there?

Exquisite little starts of joy ran through her as his hands slid silkily across her skin. Laughing softly, she nuzzled him while he laid a trail of small glowing kisses down her stomach and along her thighs. Slowly, then swiftly, the delight turned into a hungry vital urge.

Her lips tasted his throat, his nape, his shoulder, the long groove that divided the wonderful hardness of his chest. *Make love to me,* her mouth said. *Make love to me now. Make love to me now and always.*

With a surge, his body answered. His weight slid over her, bringing his delicious male scent to her nostrils, and a rush of rampant desire. With a groan, he entered her. Uncontrollable forces were unleashed and carried them wildly over a sea of apricot brandy to the apex of their desire.

CHAPTER FOURTEEN

VERY SLOWLY, Elizabeth opened her eyes. Something, as usual, was sticking into her back, and her body was pointing downhill. However, this morning, all petty discomforts were overridden by her state of blissful, drifting delight.

Under the folds of the sleeping bag, she had nothing on. Why would she need clothes when she was so securely enclosed in two manly arms, which twitched periodically as if to make sure she was still there? Since the interior of the tent was a bright orange blaze, Elizabeth deduced foggily that the sun was up.

Turning sideways, she snuggled deeper into the hollow of a shoulder. Her head felt fragile, and a strange taste lingered in her mouth. Everything had to do with apricots.

The shoulder yielded to accommodate her. The hand that cradled her began to move slowly along her side until it quietly found her breast. Elizabeth released a soft sigh and nuzzled the chest under her chin. The fingers began to circle her nipple. The nipple responded, spilling a languid heat through Elizabeth's body.

Jumbled memories swam to the surface and turned over, like otters floating in the sun. She had made love last night, had at last embraced the man who had hovered in her mind whenever she had kissed someone else, laughed in a fast car or toyed with a hand by candlelight.

Justin.

The tender Justin of her secret imagination had shed his other objectionable selves and become real, as if he had been dropped by magic out of the storm. So tenderly he had clasped her. A miracle....

"Mmm, darling," murmured a husky voice at her ear. "I can't be dreaming...."

Elizabeth curled against him.

"No dream, my sweet. I—"

A twig cracked not five yards from the tent. Elizabeth and Justin went still, their attention shifting with great difficulty. Justin's hand was just sliding to the inviting hollow of Elizabeth's hip when a bush rustled sharply once, then stopped. A rapid scuffling sound and a low grunt sounded almost at their ears. Elizabeth's eyes flew wide.

"Shh!" Justin motioned when she tried to speak.

The scrabbling and scratching were like...claws on bare rock! And the scuffling surely meant that...there was a hungry beast nearby!

Elizabeth's diaphragm collapsed as the raspy breathing moved in a leisurely fashion around to her side of the tent. Reeling awake through several levels of consciousness, Elizabeth realized it was coming closer.

The Fang Spirit. Always famished. Waiting for the unwary in the bush!

She tried to sit upright, but Justin's hard arm held her still. His head was tilted in a listening attitude, his profile bold against the sunlit wall.

"What is it?" Elizabeth mouthed, her eyes wide and ringed with white.

Justin shook his head. His lips half opened. She thought she saw them form the word "Bear!"

Bear!

Her heart plunged against her rib cage, trying to flee separately while her body bunched into a single quivering muscle, ready to follow, tent or no tent. She was not waiting around to fool with any bear!

Sensing her intention, Justin's arm tightened and held her rigidly against him. Elizabeth fought her panic, turning her head upward.

"Let's get out. Cut open the back of the tent," she whispered urgently. "I saw a movie—"

Justin shook his head and indicated there was no knife close at hand. He was now all hard concentration, taut and tense as the scuffling proceeded erratically around the tent. Muscles stood out from his body. Everything about him screamed action and readiness to fight.

Silently, he slid forward, his hand feeling around for the tent zipper. In the suffused sunshine, his arms shimmered burnt orange. Each hair took a sliver of light to itself and glowed dimly.

Finding the tab, Justin pulled softly, then jerked at it. A soundless curse escaped his lips. The zipper was stuck. The scuffling came closer, the sound of claws distinct and dreadful. Justin began to struggle frantically with the zipper, working it back and forth until it burst free and whipped around its semicircle with such force that the tent rocked on its flimsy poles.

The half-moon door collapsed outward. Justin exploded through the opening, a single cannonball of motion. His arms windmilled. His monstrous bellow would have paralyzed half the bears in Ontario. He landed on his feet, legs braced apart, head thrust forward, teeth bared, fists raised for mortal combat.

He was an instant throwback to twenty thousand years ago: the primeval caveman warrior relying only on his bare hands in the desperate battle for survival. His hair stuck out wildly from his forehead. His eyes bulged with fury. His stomach was sucked hollow to protect his vitals while ropes of sinew crisscrossed his glistening brown body.

Altogether, he was a terrifying sight. Certainly too terrifying for the adolescent raccoon that had been reconnoitering the failed camp fire. The creature staggered back on its haunches, tore trenches in the moss as it reversed direction and turned into a frightened gray-brown streak careening madly into the trees. No other signs of life could be spotted save the motionless silhouettes of birds, all rendered speechless by the force of Justin's shout.

For a number of seconds, Justin stood as if cast in bronze. Slowly, muscle by snapping muscle, he released the tension holding him rigid. He caught Elizabeth on her hands and knees, gaping from the tent door. His body, from the backs of his heels to his earlobes, began to turn a violent brick red.

"If you laugh," he breathed, "I'll throw you into the bay myself—with pleasure!"

Laughing was the last thing on Elizabeth's mind. Every cell still hammered with fright. Her mouth was dry, her nerves knotted up against being eaten alive.

"I w-wasn't—"

"Well, don't!"

Justin's savage tone grated into Elizabeth's consciousness, jerking her back to the here and now. The old Justin was back, angry and rigid. Her couldn't stand being made a fool of—and he was acting as if this was all her doing!

With a couple of hiccups, she got air back into her lungs. The brilliant sunlight assaulted her eyes and a gong started pounding at the back of her head, shaking her with each brazen crash. The pit of her stomach suddenly tried to get loose while dizziness made her want to collapse back on the sleeping bag, her chin limp against the rough, cool rock. The more she blinked, the more her vision was filled with the shimmering figure of Justin. Justin without any clothes on!

"I just . . . you haven't . . . you're stark naked!"

Justin jerked back, realizing he was standing on a rise visible from umpteen directions. His hands flew down to protect himself.

"Oh, thanks!" he sputtered. "If you're so offended, I just better get myself something to wear."

Darkly, and a mite unsteadily, he strode to his own tent and managed to crawl inside despite its wet and wretched state. His bare buttocks gleamed palely in its gloom.

Simultaneously, Elizabeth realized she was in the same condition. She retreated inside. The sleeping bag was still a downy tumble heated by their bodies. Wet clothes lay in a ball atop her rain poncho and flashlight. A large, dry shirt was all jumbled up with her own shorts and underpants in a corner near the flap. Assailed by the strong conviction that she had peeled the shirt off Justin herself, Elizabeth sat down hard and lifted a hand to her mouth.

Yes, she had made love with Justin last night. She must have. Why else would they have woken up buck naked together in each other's arms!

There had been thunder and lightning and buckets of rain. She had taken Justin in. Well, *dragged* him in, if she wanted to be truthful. But there, her recollection blurred. Why would she lose her normal, utterly reliable memory? And why did she feel so bad?

Her hand moved from her mouth to her throbbing head in an attempt to muffle the din inside it. Her stomach heaved and lurched. As she twisted to get fresh air from the door, her heel dislodged a smooth, clinking object. Immediately, the tent filled up with a pungent odor of apricots.

A brandy bottle. Empty! Why... she must have gotten drunk! No wonder she felt like the underside of a warty toad. She was hung over!

For some moments, Elizabeth crouched there, bare knees lodged under her chin as she struggled to orient herself. Two impressions assaulted her simultaneously. The first was of that brief time of waking when the world had seemed compounded of pure happiness because she was in Justin's arms. The second, the one she was suffering now, was of profound dismay at what she must have done. The two impressions were forcefully bisected by the fright about the raccoon, which had turned everything into galloping confusion.

Donny Clenman had had a case of beer.

The gong inside her head stepped up to double time. Elizabeth put her hands to her forehead, but that did nothing to stifle the pounding. If she kept sitting there, she might be gonged until her head split open. There was nothing she could do but get dressed, crawl outside and get on with things. On top of everything else, she remembered that they had nothing to eat and they were lost.

Unsteadily, she reemerged with Justin's damp shirt and shorts trailing from her hand. Squinting into the sunlight, she found him moving his unpegged tent bodily up onto the bare, sun-heated rock. His pack was spilling its soaked contents out at his feet. His sleeping bag hung dejectedly over a stump to dry.

Elizabeth simply stood looking around her. From the weather, one would never have known a storm had taken place. The sun blazed merrily from a high blue bowl of a sky, and glorious light reflected off the waters of the channel. The mosses and lichens had resumed their crackly dryness, reminding Elizabeth that a single storm could hardly make a dent in the dry season. Leaves hung still on bushes where birds flicked their tails saucily. Only in the deepest hollows did jewellike traces of wetness gleam.

Thinking about shoes, Elizabeth turned. The sight of a charred, giant skeleton of a tree struck her like a blow, bringing back in full the lightning slashing through the night and the thunder jolting her bones. She tucked her elbows close to herself and let out a breath as she stared at the shocking black ruin.

That could have been me! she thought with a gulp. An image of Justin's arms grew all mixed up with the echo of thunder crashing around inside her fragile head. Why, they had cringed together like cats in a barrel. And they had lived to see the morning.

To her left, Justin was making himself very busy hanging out every piece of his wet clothing. When there was no scrap left in his gaping pack, he straightened. Eventually, he forced himself to peer at Elizabeth. His brows were knit together fearsomely.

Just looking at him made Elizabeth dizzy. She shut her eyes. Disjointed fragments of memories floated up. Not only had she slept with Justin while she was drunk; she had told him she lightened her hair!

And perhaps told him of her heart!

No, no! She had not gone that far. Surely not!

Involuntarily, she reached for the top button of her shirt, closed it tightly and caught the fabric in her fist. Justin's eyes moved to her fist, then to her face. His cheekbones stood out as though they'd been carved. His mouth became a thin line slashing across his face.

Astonished, Elizabeth watched the expression possess Justin's features and harden there. Consternation. He felt exactly the same way she did.

He's remembering all the stuff he spilled. He's wishing a thousand times over that he'd kept his mouth shut.

She tried to dredge up his revelations but was struck suddenly with the realization that she had related the tale of her poverty-stricken childhood. In fact, she'd admitted openly that she'd have done anything to get out of it. She'd more than opened herself to the razor-sharp stings of Justin's cohorts in the press and loaded Justin with piles of extra ammunition should he ever choose to use it. What's more, she'd given him one more reason to think she'd run off with the formulas for her own greedy benefit. Oh, dear, why did she have to run off at the mouth like that?

"As you can see, I'm dressed now," Justin declared in his cool boardroom voice. "Satisfied?"

His body language was anything but cool. He acted as if he'd just jumped out of a patch of nettles, causing Elizabeth to react in kind. In doing so, she brutally shoved away an image of a small boy cruelly outnumbered in the schoolyard.

"I don't care whether you have clothes on or not."

"Last night you certainly preferred them off."

So, she realized he thought she had been making fun of him back at her tent, and he was rushing to throw her off balance by attacking. Elizabeth might have protested had his tactic not smacked so much of corporate infighting. She pulled herself out of her fog long enough to grope for some familiar weapons. She had learned on the street that the only defense was a good offense.

"I did, didn't I?" she snapped back, thinking that if he started gloating, she would throttle him with her bare hands. "Of course, now in the daylight, I have to wonder what kind of fellow would take advantage of a woman when she was, er, intoxicated!"

Justin's fingers curled into fists.

"Intoxicated! You mean drunk, don't you Elizabeth? And to refresh your blotted memory, it was you who produced the bottle and you who pressed me to drink. We might just examine who was doing the seducing here!"

The gong shook loose a dim recollection of the bottle coming from Elizabeth's own pack. The vague memory was coupled with the awful suspicion that, indeed, she had been the one to initiate the drinking session. What else was there to do when they'd nearly been fried to cinders by the lightning and the nearest thing to eat was swimming half a mile under the bay?

"You were glad enough of a swig at the time," she accused. She could see that neither of them was going to admit their terror at the time. "Are you going to complain of outraged virtue now?"

Justin took a step forward. Elizabeth stood her ground though she was rattled at discovering how unhinged Justin seemed to be.

Donny Clenman had dared her to drink beer from his case! The thought came to her in an instant. They had sat in the back room of his friend Al's house and had taken swigs from the brown, foaming bottles. She had felt so tough and alluring. They had fallen, giggling, to the mattress. . . .

Emotion sizzled up inside Elizabeth, and her eyes snapped back at him, full of dangerous blue challenge. Yet the bottle had been in her pack. She had dragged it out and opened it. She had taken the first swallow.

Oh, the whole thing was ridiculous. Abruptly, Elizabeth sought the horizon with her gaze, wishing she'd never mentioned the jumbled night.

"Look, it's not doing us any good to fight," she muttered. "I'm starving and we're still lost."

That brought their situation home. Justin, as glad as she to be diverted, stopped where he stood and looked around them. In the sunshine, the islands formed a dramatic tableau against the water. Miles and miles of water stretched in every direction and twisted in tortuous ribbons among more and yet more islands. And nowhere was there the faintest hint of human occupation.

The view, picturesque as it was, sobered both of them. They knew Suzy and the others had to be around somewhere. But where? And how much effort, considering how out of favor they were with the group, would go into looking for them?

Such were the unspoken thoughts plaguing both their minds. Elizabeth swallowed. How insignificant the two of them were in this windy wilderness.

Justin grew brisk as he became a man of action trying to counteract a depressing truth.

"I say we stay put on this island. If we move, we'll only get more lost and make it harder for anyone to find us."

Elizabeth was not about to disagree. Besides, the day was going to be blistering. She could feel the parched heat already rising from the rocks. Sunlight glared off the water, hurting her eyes, and fiery rays of heat beat down on her head from above with a hot heavy fist. Her stomach, unattended to for almost twenty-four hours, echoed inside her. She needed nourishment to counteract the shocks and discoveries she had been subjected to. If she didn't get fed, she would keel over.

"But we don't have anything to eat. We'll starve," she declared plaintively, already imagining her bones decorating a shelf of rock.

Two lines bracketed Justin's mouth.

"Surely you haven't missed all those nature lessons. We'll have to live off the land until we're rescued."

"Ha! Very likely!" Now he was making fun of her.

"I couldn't agree more, but we'd better try, anyway."

"Fine, then," Elizabeth sneered. "I suppose you have some ideas."

Justin considered her words for a moment, and then his brows sprang up.

"As a matter of fact, there's some kind of manual in my pack. I'll get it and see."

To Elizabeth's surprise, he returned with a plastic oblong object, just like the one tucked into the pocket of her own pack. Seeing it didn't contain makeup, she hadn't paid attention to it. Now, Justin extracted a small book full of practical suggestions, and a sealed packet containing plastic line, fishhooks and matches.

"Hey, look! If we'd only found this last night!"

"Wouldn't have done any good. The rain would have drowned any fire, and we still don't have anything to eat."

Momentarily forgetting their feud, they pored over the pages, skipping the parts about building brush shelters and putting splints on broken legs, to get to the part about edibles. The choices were not particularly abundant.

"Well," Justin said when they got to the end, "it's either blueberries or a fish."

"Blueberries," Elizabeth said hastily.

"Okay, let's look."

Half an hour later they were back where they started, their tin cups empty. The few scrawny bushes wedged in rock crevices were practically without fruit.

"I think the trees are too big. Blueberry bushes can't grow in the shade."

"So that leaves trying to catch a fish."

Elizabeth was too hungry now to argue. Wordlessly, they picked up the manual for instructions. First off, they had to catch a minnow for bait, which Elizabeth actually succeeded in doing by blocking off a tiny pool with her hat and then trapping the almost transparent sliver of movement in her cup.

"It says we might catch a bass or a pike behind a rock face in the shade."

Blundering through the underbrush, they found a suitable-looking drop of granite. Justin tied the end of the plastic line to a stout stick, using a knot suggested in the book, and then dropped the baited hook into the water. He and Elizabeth took turns swishing it around and jiggling it up and down.

Nothing happened except that the morning progressed and they grew more quietly frantic.

"The fish are too smart for this," said Elizabeth gloomily as the dripping hook came up empty for the umpteenth time.

"Looks like it. Here, your turn."

"I don't think...aaaaaah..."

To Elizabeth's astonishment, the stick was bobbing up and down in her hands, threatening to be pulled down into the water altogether. Reacting blindly, she jerked it upward and a long yellow-green fish dropped, flapping, onto the moss at her feet. She leaped back and stared at it. Justin was just as immobilized. Neither of them had bothered to think about what they would do if they actually caught something.

"Knock it on the head!" Elizabeth shrieked. "Knock it on the head or it'll get away!"

After a scramble, Justin found a rock and dispatched the unfortunate creature. When it went still, they could see they would have a fine, fat dinner, though it was still a long way from being on their plates. Elizabeth thought of a number of restaurants that could do it up smashingly.

"We better, uh, start a fire and cook it," Justin said. He was keeping a safe distance from the catch, the same as Elizabeth.

"Yeah."

The matches, of course, were back with their packs. Faced with the problem of transporting their slippery, glistening prize, they fumbled around until Elizabeth finally got the idea of looping some fishing line around its tail and carrying it on the end of the stick. When they arrived back at the site of the previous day's camp fire attempt, Elizabeth began gathering the scattered sticks together.

"Give me one of those matches. I'll get the fire going; you clean the fish."

"Oh, no," Justin protested vigorously. "I'm not cleaning any fish!"

His free hand flattened over the matches in his breast pocket, holding them hostage against the possibility. Elizabeth slowly stood up, her stomach tightening lest she be stuck with the job.

"Well, somebody has to clean it if we're going to eat it. I know for a fact you have a pocketknife."

"So do you!"

They stood nose to nose, both almost on the verge of saying they'd go hungry rather than tackle the scaly beast. Justin thrust the fish yet farther away from himself and extracted a penny from his trousers.

"Toss you for it."

Fifty-fifty odds were better than a hundred-percent odds. Elizabeth hesitated, then nodded. Justin flipped the coin into the air. Tails! He lost, and Elizabeth burst into a huge grin. Justin backed up a step in alarm.

"Two out of three."

"Uh-uh. You lost. Take your lumps like a big boy."

"I've...never had to do anything like this before."

All the privileges of his life hung in that statement. Oddly, the statement evoked a creeping sympathy from Elizabeth—especially since, despite her background, she had never had to clean a fish, either.

"All right," she said unexpectedly. "Fair is fair. If we're both going to eat it, then we'll clean it together."

With the air of two executioners, they marched to the water's edge, where they accomplished the deed. The result was two ragged but plump white fillets. The match caught easily in the moss and dry twigs. The tiny flame wavered, then flared upward, causing Justin and Elizabeth to release enormous breaths they didn't even know they were holding.

United by the success of their efforts, they carefully threaded the fillets on thin sharp sticks and sat roasting them over the flames. A delicious scent wafted from them, finer than that of any gourmet meal. After a time, they cautiously tasted the white flesh, careful not to burn their fingers.

"My, my!" Elizabeth sat with her mouth full, excited by the clean, wild taste. Either she was unhinged by hunger, or the fish was indescribably succulent.

Justin agreed by devouring his portion ravenously. Some of the tension between them melted as they shared in the joint achievement of their meal.

"And now for our vitamin C." With an air of a magician producing a rabbit, Justin drew out one of his wet T-shirts, now stained with blue speckles.

"Blueberries!" cried Elizabeth, quite forgetting that she had tried to be stiff with him. "Where did you get them?"

"Back there, where we were fishing. There's only a handful. I thought they'd make a good dessert."

That he had saved them as a surprise moved Elizabeth. "Oh, let's eat them in the shade, then. It's getting so hot out here."

Despite the heat, they carefully stoked their now substantial fire before letting themselves leave it. Who knew how long they would be stuck there? And they had only five more matches.

They retreated into shade softened by unbelievably thick layers of rust-colored pine needles, dry and whispery beneath their feet. Though they were only a few yards in among the trees, they had the impression of being deep inside an immense forest. This was partly because of the unusual size of the island and partly because of the size of the trees. They were massive, larger than anything Elizabeth had ever seen or imagined possible. They towered far up into the sky and spread great gnarled branches far out from their heavy trunks. The atmosphere was as hushed and otherworldly as that of a cathedral. Immediately, Elizabeth felt as though she'd been transported to some faraway, tranquil region. She leaned back in the soft needles and gazed up at the green branches pierced with spears of golden light. Then she sat up excitedly, pine needles falling from her shorts.

"Hey, do you know where we are? This is the island with that stand of virgin white pine on it that Suzy was talking about. The one they're signing a petition about, trying to get made into a park. Just look at the size of those trees!"

Now that Justin and Elizabeth had food in their stomachs, they could appreciate the sight. They sat in silent awe among the great twisted roots that seemed to have been around since the days of the woolly mammoth.

"It really should be a park. Everyone should get a chance to see this!" Justin commented with a conviction completely new to him.

"Too bad that one got struck with lightning last night." The loss of one of the giant trees was doubly sad in light of their great age, Elizabeth thought. Indians had camped among them, and voyageurs had whooped past them, their canoes loaded for the fur trade. Campers a hundred years in the future might lie under them and drink in their cool, sweet shade.

Sighing, Elizabeth and Justin gave themselves up to the blueberries, enjoying them as only hungry castaways were able to. Elizabeth shut her eyes, bursting each plump fruit between her tongue and teeth and savoring the tang as she swallowed it down. Nearby, she knew that Justin was doing the same. She thought of his tongue sliding over the roundness of the berries, and a wave of sensation spread out from the pit of her stomach. Last night. Oh, what really had happened last night?

Lulled by the whispering shadows and tantalized by each other's presence, they forgot time—and also forgot the fire. The first hint that their small paradise was going awry came when they saw a gust of smoke and heard a crackling sound far beyond what their tame camp fire was capable of. As they heaved themselves up, their scalps tightened.

"Holy Toledo!"

The fire they had left unattended had somehow spread to some nearby brush and was now licking through dried moss and pine needles up the hill toward the main forest. If something wasn't done quickly, the entire island, humans included, would be incinerated.

Justin grasped Elizabeth's hand and ran with her along the blade of granite away from the fire. He stopped at the top and looked this way and that. Down at the bottom, they spotted their overturned canoe.

"We can make it into the water," he said, threads of smoke already tickling his lungs, "and get away."

However, he didn't move toward the craft but stood stock-still, as if waiting for Elizabeth to give the word. The fire was snaking out in several directions, following rock crevices filled with flammable brush and pine needles. The main tongue, hungering toward the pines, licked up a small jack pine and sprung up into a horrifying spiral of orange flame. Elizabeth stood rooted to the spot. For some reason, Suzy's calm and earnest face was printed on her mind. As she stared at the infant conflagration, a young raccoon skittered past, confused and frightened, almost at their toes. There had to be hordes of small creatures in among the trees. How would they survive if their homes went up in flames? Elizabeth wondered.

And behind her, against the horizon, towered that line of massive trees, dwarfing the vegetation of the other nearby islands. They had survived centuries of storms, loggers and freaks of nature. Were they to be laid low by a couple of inept city slickers who couldn't be trusted alone with matches?

An emotion Elizabeth did not recognize clutched at her throat. If she and Justin left, they would be responsible. The dismay she imagined in Suzy's eyes would also extend to the hundreds of their people who knew about and appreciated the trees: the people who had signed the petitions and campaigned for the preservation of the irreplaceable phenomenon. People Elizabeth had not dreamed about one week before.

"We can't just . . . let everything burn up. Not after we started the fire."

"We'll get our own tails singed but good."

"I know."

Their eyes met. The strange emotion flowed between them. Getting singed seemed of no importance at all.

Without conscious command, Elizabeth's muscles gathered for action. Something composed of courage, tenderheartedness, responsibility and a galloping need to prove herself to Justin took possession.

Justin stood regarding her intently. His face tightened as he saw she was watching to see if he'd run. He swung toward the fire.

"All right. Come on."

They flung themselves into it, stomping the small flames and flailing at the big ones. The only thing they could find to beat them out with was Justin's clothing, still wet, which they snatched from the bushes where they'd been spread to dry. The fire was not so much large as many fronted, spreading along any line of accumulated debris. No sooner had one serpentine flame been stamped out than another leaped up, as if coming from under the ground. Once again Elizabeth and Justin faced a raw force of nature and were unable to hide behind shields they were used to. The strength of the fire multiplied each time it found nourishment. It leaped at them savagely and rolled dense black smoke into their protesting lungs. Crackling and roaring, its fiery maw devoured everything before it. Green leaves twisted and blackened. Birds flew up, shrieking, into the sky.

Mindlessly, Elizabeth attacked it, stomping and flailing, heedless of burned running shoes and smoking pant legs. As the struggle intensified, Elizabeth panted and gasped and swiped at her smarting eyes.

She had a pair of Justin's jeans in her hand and she slapped them down again and again on swirling flames that spurted skyward under her blows and tried to catch at the smoldering fabric. The only thing she was acutely aware of was Justin at her side, fighting as grimly as she, somehow always between her and the worst of it.

At last, they managed to cut off all the randomly creeping threads of flame and flung themselves at the major arm of the fire. It roared hungrily over a log toward the massive pines, which were so filled with resinous oils that they would ignite like gasoline should the sparks reach them.

Justin and Elizabeth closed in, catlike, on the ravenous spiral, leaping in to slap at the root of a tree, leaping back before their hair caught fire. The jeans were now only a blackened rag swinging from Elizabeth's equally blackened hands, yet she wielded them as if they were a single broadsword against an army of blazing dragons. Burning cinders fell on her arms and shoulders. The flames got behind her and snatched at her shirt. New fires kindled with treacherous swiftness all around her feet.

Elizabeth struck back, heedless of the blistering heat and the unpredictable explosions of flying embers. Inch by inch, she and Justin fought the conflagration back, beating at its burning lip until the flames weakened and finally died among the blackened skeletons of brush already consumed.

It took a moment amidst the burgeoning coils of smoke to realize the struggle was over. Elizabeth and Justin stood panting, their knees beginning to shake from the crazed effort and the sudden release. Their pant legs were smoking, their faces streaked and smeared with grainy soot. Sparks had left scarlet welts on their arms, and their clothing was full of charred oblong holes.

When Elizabeth had finally gotten enough fresh oxygen, she dropped the jeans she'd been convulsively gripping and looked at Justin. He was a sight, his curls straight on end, tangled with twigs and burned fragments of leaves. Out of the blackness from his forehead to his jaw, his gray eyes gleamed with stirring brightness. Something had changed about him, she registered. The ramrod stiffness was gone, burned out of him by the very fierceness of the battle. The set of his head bespoke a man struck with humility at his true place in nature. At the same time, he seemed full of a new, startled pride born of this physical victory with only his bare hands and his courage as weapons. All of his limbs had loosened and grown easy, and he was full of an animal grace that was at one with the island atmosphere.

Elizabeth felt joined to him by something new and different. Her body vibrated with the physical imprint of Justin's courage, the courage he had shown just now fighting the fire, as well as back at the rapids and even that morning against an unknown threat. Each time, his courage had been spontaneous, not at all calculated. He had turned himself into this blackened, barely recognizable figure merely to save some pine trees and a few small animals, none of which could provide a profit for his company.

And in her bones, Elizabeth knew he had also done it for her. That heady intuition nearly unhinged her. Perhaps, just perhaps, there might be a real heart in Justin after all!

"Well!" Justin exclaimed, letting out a long breath. He stood just where the burned blackness ran next to the live summer greens of the rest of the island. How joyous those greens looked now beside the ruin the fire had left.

"Well!" Elizabeth echoed—a word that said it all.

She wet her parched lips and wiped at them. Justin's eyes followed the movement, then dropped to her blackened hands. Shock rippled across his face. He was midstep toward her when shouts spun them both around. Racing down the channel behind them came the campers, waving to Justin and Elizabeth as if they had found them after six months lost at sea.

"We saw the smoke," Suzy exclaimed, leaping from the bow onto the sloping rock. "We paddled like the devil. Goodness, we half expected to find you cremated."

"Oh, no. We could have taken our canoe anytime."

"But you didn't."

Suzy, her loosened hair telling the tale of her haste, surveyed the charred tip of the island and the living greenness of the rest of it just beyond the fire line, then regarded Justin and Elizabeth narrowly. The pulse in the hollow of her throat seemed to be going extraordinarily fast.

"Well, no," Elizabeth explained. "You see, we recognized those white pines you were talking about. We couldn't just . . . let them go up in smoke. Especially after it was our camp fire that started it," she added somewhat sheepishly.

On second observation, the burned area was a lot larger than Elizabeth had realized. Had she and Justin really beaten out a fire that big?

"Do you know what could have happened had it caught those pines?"

"It would have gotten away from us. We would have had to ship out," Elizabeth answered hesitantly.

"Might have exploded. Just like a bomb. Incinerated you before you could have taken three steps toward the shore."

Elizabeth and Justin paled as one. Always, at the back of their minds had been escape anytime in their waiting canoe. Sudden death hadn't figured in their calculations.

"No kidding!" Justin breathed, wide-eyed.

"No kidding." A smile broke through the sternness of Suzy's face. "But you got it out in time. I'm proud of both of you."

"So are we! Three cheers for Justin and Elizabeth! Hip, hip, hooray!" All the campers, even Moose, let out exuberant shouts of approbation.

Elizabeth felt like dancing, so filled was she with happiness and a deep sense of accomplishment. Justin looked astonished. When he saw that the cheer was meant for him, too, and that everyone was smiling at him, a flush of pleasure bloomed under the soot, and a grin, not anything like his charity-benefit smile, broke out across his face. For a moment, just for a moment, he showed his inner self, shocked with happiness at being suddenly and unexpectedly taken to the group's heart. In some indefinable way, he looked as if he'd just been handed the Nobel Prize.

Suzy stood for a very long time, just looking at the mighty pines and back to the fire line. Her face took on a complicated expression, though Elizabeth wasn't quite sure why.

"All right," said Suzy. "Let's get you two washed and fed. You deserve the best breakfast in the pack."

Escorted by their new admirers, Justin and Elizabeth went down to the shore to wash some of the black from their bodies. Though neither of them said a word, they both knew that from now on there'd be no more thoughts of running away.

CHAPTER FIFTEEN

"READY OR NOT," Justin yelled, "here I go! Race you!"

He laughed aloud, not the cultivated, lightly cynical laugh Elizabeth knew from the city, but a spontaneous belly laugh, completely of the moment.

Elizabeth's head snapped up, and she caught him poised on a spit of granite and clad only in bathing trunks. The minute her glance found him, he bounded into a breakneck gallop beside Molly and Ernie, who had had a head start, sped the length of the rock and leaped off its broken end high above the sunny waters of the bay. Instead of a finely executed swan dive, he jumped feet first, legs bicycling comically, one hand holding his nose as he went down amid shrieks of glee into a tremendous splash.

The three surfaced, gulped air and then went bottoms up, their kicking toes vanishing as their bodies scattered underwater. One by one they came up, Justin last. He shook water from his hair and triumphantly held aloft a handful of black objects retrieved from the depths.

"Whoopee! I finally found some clams!"

For the umpteenth time since the fire on the island, Elizabeth gaped. Justin Archer, the smooth tycoon *extraordinaire*, oblivious to what anyone might think, was waving his muddy prize around as if it were a handful of Spanish gold doubloons.

So many of her preconceived ideas had cracked around her lately that she had begun to feel as though she were in a fun house, watching the mirror fall to pieces. Whatever had happened to the Justin Archer she knew and detested?

The gang was making a forage meal that night—freshwater-clam-and-bullrush stew. Over to the left, deep in a thicket of reeds, were two canoes, their occupants busily pulling up tall green spears and unpeeling the succulent pale centers that were to be their vegetables. Elizabeth had volunteered to open the clams, which she did with a large blunt knife, finding the crevice and prying the shell wide against the determined resistance of the crustacean.

She could not say that she didn't understand why Justin was acting the way he did; she, too, was under the same influence. Two days ago, after the fire, when the campers had swarmed around with relief and joy at finding their lost members, her last resistance had cracked. What else was there to do when all ten people had wanted to hug her? And she couldn't forget Suzy, who'd adjusted her glasses and said little but who'd had a keen, matter-of-fact respect in her eyes that meant more to Elizabeth than all her new advertising campaigns put together.

The group had made a meal especially for Justin and Elizabeth and sat in a circle watching them eat it. Packs were turned out joyfully to find replacements for the clothing, including Justin's unfortunate jeans, that had been ruined in the fire. Their blisters and burns had all been inspected and medicated, the little red welts fitting in beautifully with Elizabeth's collec-

tion of scratches, deerfly bites and healing poison-ivy
rash. She joked about starting a new trend when she
got back: the speckled look would be "in."

I've earned my place here, Elizabeth thought, attacking another clam. She had spent so many years
alone studying, struggling to start her business, then
carefully building her image and shouldering the responsibilities of command, that she had all but forgotten what it was like to be just one of the crowd.
Here she was exactly that—and she found it an enor-
mously freeing experience.

This same feeling, she supposed, was probably what
was responsible for Justin's reverting to his second
childhood.

"Watch it, Liz!" Kate exclaimed.

Eyes upon Justin, Elizabeth had absentmindedly
opened a clam and was pressing the knife into the
muscle at the back of the shell, which threatened to
give way and let her bisect her thigh.

"Oh!"

She tossed the clam to Kate, who was scraping the
succulent pink meat from the shells and turning it into
chowder. Covertly, she followed Justin as, carefully
holding his catch, he swam toward the campsite with
a long breaststroke. Sunlight rippled across his body
which was just under the surface of the water, and
streaked his upturned face with silver.

Gliding to where Elizabeth sat, he wordlessly deposited his find on the rock beside her. She knew he
had searched the bottom for over an hour before
catching on to how to spot the inconspicuous little
creatures. Cheerfully, he had followed instructions
with no sign of his normal overriding competitiveness
and consuming desire to be the first, the best and the

fastest. Either a genuine change of character had taken place or it was a fantastic feat of control, Elizabeth thought, wishing she knew which.

Though they had exchanged only wary courtesies since their rescue, Elizabeth was overcome with the feeling that Justin was placing the clams beside her as a gift—as he had previously offered his courage and the strength of his body in beating out the fire. The gesture in its simplicity was both deeply manly and enchantingly boyish with its element of "See what I did. I did it for you."

His gray eyes swept down her bathing suit, boyishness quickly fading. Beneath the droplets caught on his lashes, a hunger flickered, then was veiled.

"You should come in," he invited.

Mutely, Elizabeth shook her head, for she still could not swim.

"Oh, go on," prodded Kate, laughing, behind her. "You haven't been in once since you came."

Under the new haircut was a new Kate: cocky, bold and unexpectedly full of mischief. She simply flicked the clam knife from Elizabeth's fingers and pushed her backward.

"Eeeiiiiiii!"

Elizabeth's shriek died in the middle as she plunged under the surface, barely managing to shut her mouth before the water surged over it. The rock dropped off straight down from where she had been sitting, so there was nothing to support her. But thanks to the frantic motions of her arms and legs, she surfaced again. Coughing and sputtering, she sought about madly for something to grab on to before she went under a second time. Water was a maddening thing, flowing through her fingers, offering not the least support for her kicking heels. She was going down again, sideways, when she encountered a shoulder. After she came up, she managed to shove her hair back from her face and open her streaming eyes. She discovered Justin beside her, eyeing her in surprise.

"I—I can't swim," she blurted, half indignant at being pushed in and half terrified she would sink again like a stone. Justin's shoulder was slippery.

Kate hung over the lip of the rock in consternation at her own misdeed. Justin's brows shot up in sudden comprehension of why Elizabeth had been avoiding all those rough-and-tumble games in the water. Elizabeth herself was shocked at how easily she had just admitted to this carefully hidden weakness.

"Can you dog-paddle?" Justin asked.

Elizabeth, torn between bolting back to the rock and staying to be supported by Justin, nodded uncertainly.

"I'll hold you while you try."

There was no hint of a sneer in his tone, only an apparently sincere desire to help. Justin slipped a hand under one of her arms. Elizabeth, after listing alarmingly, began to pedal with her hands and her feet until she found, to her amazement, that she was buoyant on her own.

With Justin hovering near enough to grab her should she sink, she labored to stay in one spot, then gained enough confidence to go a little farther out from shore to where the clam divers were at work. The expanse of water made her a little nervous, but Justin remained close by. Soon she had learned to stretch on her side and do a clumsy but effective sidestroke.

"Why don't you look at the divers?" Justin called encouragingly.

"How?"

"Just hold your breath and put your face in the water. Don't worry, you won't drown."

Pressing her lips tight, Elizabeth daringly allowed herself to tip over. When she opened her eyes she saw a startling landscape of rock and sand and silt and plants, all bathed in an aqueous light that made her feel as though she were on another planet.

So this is what I've been missing! she thought in wonder.

She suddenly realized that part of her resistance had been pure resentment of Justin's ease, as much a result of privilege as of physical skill.

She tipped back up, for one panicky moment almost losing her equilibrium. Justin surfaced some way off and looked at Elizabeth as if to read her feelings about this new world he had introduced her to.

"How do you dive?" Elizabeth asked, sputtering through the water. Now that she was wet, she decided, she might as well go whole hog.

Justin assessed her for a moment.

"Just turn upside down and kick your feet. Nothing to it."

So Elizabeth sucked in a huge lungful of air, turned her pink-clad derriere to the sky and kicked downward. She actually ran her hands over the roughness of the rock before she realized her lungs weren't getting nourishment. Panicking, she clawed her way back to the surface, coughing and sputtering, her sinuses afire from having inhaled lake water. Justin brought himself over to her side while she wheezed and choked.

"Maybe you'd better go back to shore."

"No," she declared through strings of sopping hair. "I want to find some clams."

When her head cleared she dived again, stiffly, her hair fanning out behind her. Again her hand scraped over the bottom, but she couldn't have found a clam if it had jumped up and bitten her. At least this time she managed to keep the water out of her nose. The realization came when she broke surface, and it gave her the energy to continue.

After two more tries, a dim shape glided near. A hand took hers and guided it along a rocky edge until it encountered the unmistakable oval shapes, pried them loose for her and helped her hold them as she rose to the top. The shape had been Justin.

"Thanks!" Elizabeth panted, quite delighted.

Justin closed his fingers securely over her catch, then slowly released his grip. A swift erotic message darted between them. Elizabeth's fist, holding the clams, flew to her breast. Justin ducked his head and swam away, water streaming rhythmically over his shoulders. Dog-paddling furiously, Elizabeth struggled back to shore.

The campers, going nowhere in particular, spent the day horsing around and making the stew, which had evolved into a daylong task. Elizabeth, who formerly had known only the water inside her luxurious hot tub, became fascinated with swimming. She practiced her sidestroke and stretched out her body in the clear, invigorating waters of the bay. She avidly studied the various rock shapes, the water plants and the miniature marshes. The power of nature was overwhelming her city-bred senses. The storms were so violent and the sun so strong. She could lose herself here, she realized.

Just in the week that had passed, her body had become more flexible and springy. Now she darted about the water like a newly awakened mermaid. Oh, how those Indian women must have enjoyed cavorting about in the glorious hot summer evenings of long ago.

Her skin was far browner than was good for it, but she was past caring. She had completely given up on her hair and let it fall where it would, the magical mousse but a memory. Everyone had already seen her at her worst, so what was the point of worrying? How good it felt to be free of the constant demands of appearance.

The much-labored-over stew was consumed in triumph for all its remarkably bland taste. Elizabeth, pleasantly weary from swimming, sat in a circle with Libby, Molly and Kate and chatted merrily. Justin was new pals with all the men and passed easy jokes with Ernie and Roy. Periodically, he looked over his shoulder to eye Elizabeth carefully...and she did the same to him.

This curious, wordless communication had existed between them since their rescue. They weren't at war and they weren't at peace. When Elizabeth let herself think about that long night they had spent alone together, shivers would come over her. Her dreams were haunted by the sound of driving rain and the touch of a lazy mouth wandering the secret, silken places of her throat. Lightning too, would dance across the landscape of her mind, and a queer delight would pirouette in her heart upon waking.

When darkness fell and laughter rose around the fire, Justin lost the thread of his conversation for a moment, and looked at Elizabeth. From the way he swiftly turned his head, when she caught him, she knew he was remembering, too. Yet there was no trace

of cool hostility; only an indrawn, silent contemplation that left her no clue of his feelings. Elizabeth
watched him covertly, a warm, tilting feeling in the pit
of her stomach at war with the old, ever-on-guard
distrust.

Does he have friends? she wondered suddenly. Not
people attracted to his presence and charm, but real
buddies who would stick with him through thick or
thin?

Do I?

She enumerated the people she knew. There were
some who knew much of her business, such as Elsie,
but none who could claim to be a bosom pal. She had
been too busy these past years to cultivate close
friendships. Now, in the midst of all the pleasant
joshing around the camp fire, she felt the lack acutely.
And wondered if Justin did, too.

Ah, so you're going soft about poor, lonely Justin,
jeered the rational part of her mind, *even though he
has the lovely Maria and every other female tripping
all over him, including yourself. Lonely indeed!*

A hazy memory offered her the image of Justin as
a small boy squaring off before a row of wolfish young
faces; Justin learning the hard way to come out on top.

The problem pursued Elizabeth to her tent, where
she lay listening to the crickets and thinking about
Justin's lean, compact thighs. After he had washed off
the soot of the fire, he had turned into the best sport
the campers had ever seen. Who would have believed
it. He would saw any amount of firewood. He helped
Moose stack packs. He stirred spaghetti and scrubbed
pots and even laughed at Ernie's dreadful puns.

Was he up to something? Elizabeth wondered, ab-
sently scratching her latest mosquito bite. Was this just

one more act she hadn't seen before? Or was Justin actually enjoying himself?

Never underestimating his possible deviousness, Elizabeth watched Justin a lot the next day out of the corner of her eye. He continued gathering wood and skipping pebbles off the surface of the water and lying on his stomach to watch the schools of minnows delicately grazing along the shore. He retained the animal grace that had crystallized after the fire. His gray eyes reflected the water and the sky.

"Things were never like this when I was a kid," he once quipped half-wistfully.

A picture of the private military school of Justin's childhood emerged in Elizabeth's mind. He probably never had the chance to climb trees and get dirty and act like any other little boy. Now he was getting it all out of his system.

Elizabeth pulled on a stem of foxtail grass and nibbled its tender end. She had always assumed that her problems had come as a result of being born poor and struggling. Now she realized that no matter where you got stuck in life, you had troubles.

Deep inside her, the last shred of her hunger for wealth quietly slid away.

Cloud cover drifted in that afternoon, at first no more than a white haze across the horizon, then, by suppertime, a mottled gray blanket threatening rain. In no way did this dampen spirits around the camp fire, where everyone added things to the bubbling chili pot. Elizabeth took her bowlful over to where Libby had five rock specimens lined up in a row. They were so plentiful and so tempting on these islands.

"Which one will I take home?" Libby asked, struggling mightily with the choice. She was extraordinarily drawn to rocks.

Elizabeth refused to be drawn into the battle. She merely smiled above her spoon. "Up to you," was all she said. It looked as though incurable Libby would take all five.

In fact, Libby's hand was raised to scoop them all up. Her fingers hesitated, then swooped down on the one sparkling with mica. The rest she swept away. Elizabeth burst into applause.

"Bravo, bravo! That's progress!"

Indeed, Libby was wearing only a light shirt over her tank top, and her shorts were without a collection of gadgets hooked to the belt. She grinned and pocketed the mica.

"Who knows? I might just suddenly spread my rainbow-colored wings like Kate."

They both grinned together. Kate had changed radically since her haircut. An intelligent, mature woman might remain in a shell all of her life, Elizabeth mused, yet given the right little push, she could burst out all over like a tropical flower.

Kate had lost the stoop in her walk and the hesitancy in her voice. Her laugh, when finally coaxed out of her, startled everybody, for it came out in an earthy, spine-tingling bray. Quiet Kate had suppressed it constantly. Now that she had gotten over the sound of herself, she laughed regularly, especially at jokes from Spence.

Kate was laughing now, for she was balanced precariously on a pinnacle of rock so that her Egyptian head could complement the last tangerine line of sunset and a clump of starkly outlined pines. Spence was clinging to the branches of a shaking birch directly opposite, waving his left hand, aiming the camera with his right.

"Higher," he was shouting, as if Kate were deaf. "Get your head up so it's even with the horizon."

He had been taking all kinds of pictures of Kate against dramatic backgrounds such as dawn cliff faces and foamy water. Now he fiddled with focal lengths while she stretched her neck up. It was the possibilities, Spence had explained, of the Egyptian hairdo contrasted with the white, white skin. But it was clear to everyone that it was really Kate's unfolding mind and heart that he was interested in.

"Good!" The shutter clicked and whirred, and the birch quivered with Spence's excitement.

Elizabeth stepped back to find Justin nearby, also watching the proceedings. He wore a shirt, loosely buttoned. His eyes wore their habitual expression of lively vitality.

"Poor fellow," said Elizabeth, smiling. "He's going to be a fashion photographer after all. Let's not tell him now, though."

Justin stuck his thumbs in his waistband and smiled back.

"Certainly not!" He paused. "Look," he said after a moment. "I really admire what you've done for Kate and Libby."

Elizabeth scanned Justin, swiftly wondering if she had caught a hint of his old derisive tone. However, he was merely watching Kate with a critical and approving eye.

"Is that so?" Elizabeth returned in a challenging tone. A part of her bristled, for Kate was the sort of woman Justin's company didn't bother with. He geared all his products and advertising campaigns to the well-heeled, sophisticated woman who already had a lot to work with. This side of Justin she still struggled with, the cold-eyed capitalist out to make a buck any way he could.

"I meant it," he told her, as if he had read her mind.

Elizabeth's heart jumped, and she swallowed. His praise meant so much to her. She bent her head down over her bowl of chili and saw her bare brown toes over its rim.

Justin put one foot up on a shelf of rock and leaned his elbow on his knee. Elizabeth became aware of his solid bone structure. It was so intensely physical.

"Why do you do it?" he asked, as if he was really puzzled by her motives.

Don't tell me Justin has realized there might be something beyond the monetary reasons! Elizabeth thought a trifle acidly. Yet he looked at her so soberly she was overcome with an urge to explain. Her memory went back to her mother and her young years. Something deep lurched inside her.

"Well...I don't have any great talents, really," she began slowly. "I can't do much for world peace, or cure diseases, or anything like that. But...when I was growing up I saw so many downtrodden women who looked wrecks because they thought themselves wrecks. I keep on seeing them today. I can't mend their marriages, or make their children grateful, or get them decent jobs. So I try to make them look nice so they'll feel nice—about themselves. I guess it's my way of...of reaching out and giving them all a hug."

Now, how had that all come rushing out? It was the nearest and clearest she had ever put her commercial philosophy into words, and it surprised her and moved her beyond anything she could have suspected.

And, damn it, she had exposed her naked flanks to the enemy!

Over the curious obstruction in her throat she looked at Justin cautiously to see if he was going to take advantage. His gray eyes were on her, too surprised to be other than straightforward. And in their depths a flicker of . . . could it be admiration?

No, just wonderment, probably. He seemed about to say something but couldn't quite find it inside. He looked as if he was still mentally groping about when Roy came and plunked himself down beside him.

After dinner the rain began in earnest from the leaden clouds. A cool breeze turned the drizzle icy. Soon, despite her rain poncho, Elizabeth had soaked feet and was shivering.

Suzy, undaunted, waved her arms to the people. "Come on, everyone, get under cover."

She and Moose stretched the orange plastic tarp between three trees, and the campers congregated underneath, feet squishing, rain trickling down their necks. However, the fire was near enough to reflect cheerfully under the makeshift roof, and Suzy produced a pack of cards.

"Crazy Eights! Make a circle!"

"My deal!" cried Elizabeth gleefully, jumping in, for the game was an old friend from her childhood.

The pack was in her hand and she was swiftly dealing cards around the circle before she realized what she was doing. She was squatting under a dripping piece of tarp, soaked to her knees, playing a children's game and having a terrific time. Beside her, also laughing, was Justin, raindrops studding his hair, smudges on his cheeks from helping with the fire; the new Justin, Elizabeth had seen only in the last few days. A Justin her heart stood still for. Elizabeth told herself she was feeling sentimental because she was loving the trip so much, but it was to Justin her eyes turned. . . .

CHAPTER SIXTEEN

THE STAY ON THE ISLANDS LENGTHENED. The campers lolled about as if they had turned into creatures of the woods, with nothing more important to do than forage for blueberries and float on their backs in the sun-drenched backwaters among the lily pads.

They had based themselves on a lopsided horseshoe of granite that embraced a clear lagoon in its two rugged arms. Each night, a camp fire blazed its living flag far out on one of the tips. Around it, gilded shapes lounged and laughed, clowned and gesticulated, or lay in simple contemplation of the starry night.

By now, Elizabeth was having trouble remembering how her building looked and what it was like to have to pay attention to traffic lights. The formless anxiety that always clutched her when she was away from the center of command evaporated, along with her constant fear that her success could crumble. Instead, she discovered her senses.

Until she had felt breezes sliding around her cool as silk, or had dived kicking into the sweet waters of Georgian Bay, she had not realized how dried and attenuated her senses of taste and touch and smell had become in the city. She had missed years and years of pebble searching and cloud gazing and stream wading and lying on her stomach among the ferns to watch for chipmunks. And she had to catch up on everything, absolutely everything, in the space of the few remaining days.

The greens, she thought. *If only I could just describe the greens.* Each leaf had its own variation and shone when it trembled in the sun. There were the greens reflected in the water, the green of the distant horizon against ivory clouds, the green of canoes, the pale green of dawn and the green freshness of the newfound excitement bubbling through her life.

Her nose, which had been sharpened to deal with the fragrances of her products, was now astonished by the wealth of outdoor scents: of sun-warmed rock and leaves, wet moss, goldenrod, fresh water, scrubbed cotton, hot stew, crushed pine needles . . . and Justin's hair, which always smelled of wood smoke and sunshine.

Her eyes were alive now, too. To the thousand nuances of sun-shot water as she slipped her paddle through it. To the laughter on other people's faces. To Justin, romping like a magnificent animal escaped at last to its natural habitat.

She couldn't stop watching him. He absorbed every atom of her attention, even when her back was turned and she seemed to be sleeping in the sun. And especially when she lay alone at night, consumed with the hot, blurred memory of Justin murmuring to her, kissing her, whirling her away to that star-shot place she had never been before.

Wary as a cat, she watched and watched, as if she were processing him, examining him minutely, cell by cell, struggling with all her might to get to the core of him.

To trust him.

For only now did she understand how deeply his first betrayal had torn her up. She knew of women who could survive one romantic fiasco after another and still like men. Yet, tough as she was in business, Elizabeth wasn't manproof. Two disasters had rocked her in her tracks. A third might derail her altogether.

Why, I'm thinking of getting back together with him!

Both corners of her wide mouth turned down. This is what had been in the back of her mind ever since that first kiss back when they had been stumbling to their tents in the dark. The strong sensual current ever flowing between them had surfaced violently at that moment. It had been impossible to forget it since.

Getting together takes two! she told herself firmly. And Justin hadn't exactly made any concrete offers.

She caught her breath so that her breast heaved under her bathing suit. No, he hadn't. But with the unspoken sexual tension thickening between them, he didn't have to.

Through lowered lashes, she watched Justin sprawl on the moss, his head back, the hot sun beating on his throat. Her nostrils quivered, and her blood stirred. Their strange truce, forged after the forest fire, still held. She and Justin treated each other with elaborate courtesy and stuck with the crowd. Their conversation skimmed only surfaces; their hands stayed to themselves. Yes, it was a truce, not a coming together. Yet something was brewing between them, like unpredictable weather. Breathlessly, they were waiting to see if lightning would strike.

Who knew where things would go with this Justin she never imagined could exist...a Justin at once a boy at play and the most magnificent man she had ever seen?

Must be the sun, she thought, the very same sun that turned him that toasted mocha color and melted all the hard angles off him; the sun that warmed his bones and turned flesh into relaxed, ecstatic gelatin. If anything, Justin had grown bigger, able to stretch his long form so loosely now that Elizabeth thought the ramrod figure in the pin-striped suit must be a dream. Something had snapped the wires holding him tight. The hard, controlled grace of the city had given way to a long-limbed ranginess that let him expand in all directions to his full size.

The minute he had given up on getting back to the city, worry had cleared from his face, replaced by a frank worship of sun and water and forest. When he slept on a rock, he slept the deep sleep of a basking seal. When he dived, he was as limber as an otter. When he stood among the trees, he immersed himself in the rustling greenness and stood sniffing the air in pure pleasure while the sun danced on his skin.

And a lot of the time, he watched Elizabeth, just as she watched him.

"Those up for going to the lighthouse, get in your canoes."

As an antidote to all the lying around, Suzy organized day expeditions. They had already climbed a cliff to look at an osprey nest and swum races to the opposite island. Everyone hopped up enthusiastically. Justin and Elizabeth, by means of a single glance, agreed to go. As they slid their red canoe into the water, an erotic friction passed between them.

Once out of the channel, the canoes had to buck brisk seas blowing against them. The effort shook off the lazy lethargy of the campers and stretched muscles joyously. Elizabeth was surprised to discover that a stark wooden structure painted red and white was practical and unromantic when viewed close up. It housed no lonely keeper, but only an automatic light apparatus meant to keep unwary boaters from the island shoals. She was learning more and more!

Lunch was a feast of smoked oysters from the can, crackers, fruit coils, cheese and granola bars. Fresh produce had vanished within a few days of setting out. Now they got fruit and vegetables themselves, combing the underbrush like fat bears for the ever-present riches that lay about in capricious plenty.

Justin and Elizabeth followed suit, outwardly indistinguishable from the crowd, yet linked by their own intricate web of awareness that left the others out. On the return journey, the breeze was at their backs and the bow dipped sportingly through the wave crests as if to say, "See what a team you could make."

I feel so strong and so...reckless! Elizabeth thought in wonderment. This was new for Elizabeth, this recklessness. She tried to fight it, knowing recklessness was a bad business that spelled lost profits and broken hearts. She had never forgotten the giddy daring that had come over her and driven her to give in to Donny Clenman....

Recklessness bubbled up anyway, affecting her much as those first sips of apricot brandy had during the storm. She recalled the warm, shockingly swift intoxication, the murmured confidences, the momentous lovemaking wrapped in a golden haze of passion, and the long sleep afterward. Though she knew it had all been courtesy of the bottle, Elizabeth tossed her head uncaringly. *We were drunk! So what!*

Oh, why did she have this urge to thumb her nose at common sense? She knew very well what Justin Archer was really like. A leopard might wash off his spots for a time in Georgian Bay, but he remained a leopard nevertheless. Wise people stayed clear of the claws.

Fortified by these edifying thoughts, Elizabeth swung the bow in toward the campsite and helped drag the canoe from the water. The gang was more than a little slaphappy, the full heat of August causing them to quickly seek the shade of a pretty stand of birch. Grass and moss cushioned the roots and made a sort of broad mattress on which everyone was now fond of idling. The end of the two weeks was approaching. No one mentioned it; no one gave it a thought.

Justin plopped down near Elizabeth, his brown torso naked, his strong thighs lean beneath grass-stained shorts. He had dived from the canoe halfway back for a swim, and lingering dampness touched his hair. He ruffled the back of his head meditatively and, catching Elizabeth watching him, grinned.

"Just checking for dreaded bald spots," he drawled. "If I find any, I'll have to go into seclusion for life."

Elizabeth, who had been toying with a dead leaf, let the fragments flutter to the ground. Her eyes rounded with mock shock that felt quite real underneath.

"Did I hear you talk of bald spots within the hearing of half a dozen people? Boy, somebody has really loosened up!"

Solemnly, Justin wiggled his ears, a skill Elizabeth had tried desperately to conquer at the age of ten and had failed to. She stared. A laugh, held incredulously for a moment in the back of her throat, exploded out of her. "Incurable, alas, like cellulite!"

Had she actually mentioned cellulite aloud? She had. Several pairs of eyes turned to her thighs, including Justin's. She didn't even flinch, though her thighs were deep brown, crisscrossed with scratches and sunburned above the knees.

"Oh, nay, my lady," crooned Justin in a mock-Shakespearean tone. "Fear not cellulite. Only make a pilgrimage to the sacred Exercycle. Peddle the pudding away, I say. Peddle the pudding away!"

Elizabeth burst into a giggle again, then a crazy laugh. Flopping onto her back, she made mad cycling motions with her feet. Then, just as abruptly, she shoved her elbows onto the grass and rocked herself upright again, moss clinging to her T-shirt.

"The pudding might peddle away, good sir, but leg hair! Ah, it must be shaved."

Her own legs had sprouted a delicate golden down for the first time since she was thirteen. She thought it looked very charming flecked with specks of sunlight. Justin leaned over and made a show of inspecting it.

"Downright delightful, ma'am!"

Elizabeth chortled. The sillies were upon her again. "Cellulite is only the dimples of the thigh. Just think of all those plump legs smiling at you. Eat more hot-fudge sundaes and cheesecake. Happy thighs for everyone!"

"Hear, hear!" crowed Justin. "Oh, I thigh for you!" And he collapsed into helpless mirth, waving his brown heels in the air.

In front of everyone, Elizabeth was taken with the same fit. Together, they made the nuttiest, most adolescent jokes about body hair, halitosis, ring around the collar, nose jobs and face cream, rolling about on the softness of the moss, choking and shrieking and sputtering with each new burst of humor. The climax came when Justin showed everybody the scars remaining from his altered jug ears.

Finally, when Elizabeth could catch her breath, she pushed herself up and wiped at the tears of laughter caught in her eyes. She found that Spence and Molly and Libby and Suzy and Ernie were also broken up, and even the wooden-faced Moose was smiling. Had she really done this? she thought, wide-eyed. Had she really made such fun of the business she had formerly regarded so weightily? And in front of all these people, too? Two weeks ago, she would have died of embarrassment first.

Justin, supine on the moss, rolled over on his side, his mouth still twitching, but his eyes warmed and twinkling with exactly the same thoughts as Elizabeth.

"I guess we don't take ourselves as seriously as we did before," he commented merrily.

"No. We've . . . uh, changed."

Physically, this was certainly true. When Elizabeth had finally gotten up the nerve to take a good look at herself, she had seen skin tanned more than was good for her and looking as luscious as coffee with cream. Her body had subtly changed its emphasis. Her arm muscles had grown taut and wiry from paddling, her waist and legs firm from all the swimming. Her sense of balance and sharp reflexes were as keen as those of a mountain goat from scrambling up the rocks at all hours of the day and night. She could barely remember what a flat surface felt like underfoot. This humming, vital fitness felt . . . well . . . real, as if her body had been used for the very first time as nature had intended it to be used.

The same impulse that had driven her to try to help women now directed itself toward all her fellow concrete-bound city dwellers. How could they miss this glory? And how could they be allowed to sit there oblivious while lakes were dying and trees were getting sick from acid rain?

A thoughtful, faraway sheen colored her eyes. "You want to know something funny?" she said to Justin suddenly. "I'd actually be glad to give Diana some of my profits if she intends to use them to preserve places like this!"

Justin stretched out on his stomach, his waistband riding down to reveal the tempting indentation of his lower spine. "Ditto here. Funny to find out we're born do-gooders."

His hand dropped near hers, a long, broad hand bearing as many scratches as Elizabeth's. An involuntary tremor quivered through her. How much of her unfolding, her awakening senses was due to having been touched by this man, kissed by him, held through the long night in his arms? How much of the thrill of each day came from being challenged and caressed by those mysterious gray eyes?

The shrieking, rolling laughter, the shared idiocy, the bold, shameless spoofing of themselves and their business represented the final springs let loose inside of them. The tension of years dissipated in Elizabeth, all the coiled, complicated stresses that had kept her going, kept her running, kept her fighting Justin. She was her own self here, and she had no other purpose in life than to simply *be*.

She fell silent, and she remained silent throughout dinner and the evening camp fire and through a long night filled with the songs of crickets and the cries of the acrobatic nighthawk. When, the next morning, Suzy announced they were going to pack up and cross the open water to the mouth of the tributary that would take them back to the marina, Justin and Elizabeth looked at each other without saying a word.

The crossing was an easy one, this time over a sun-dimpled expanse of smiling water that offered not the least resistance to their swift and energetic paddles. Lunch was a picnic on the other side with an unobstructed view of the vast open bay. In the afternoon, they poked about a marsh Suzy knew, looking for abandoned mallards' nests and watching the tiny green frogs diving for cover. Elizabeth, practicing her steering, took the stern this time and treated herself to an unobstructed view of Justin up ahead.

Like herself, he was now an honest brown from exposure to the Canadian sun. Already supple from indoor sports, he had become lean in some places and heavier in others. The muscles of his upper arms seemed rounder, harder and more powerful. His chest was an impressive expanse. His hips fitted snugly into the olive-green shorts the pack provided.

After Suzy had pointed out marsh marigolds, arrowhead and pickerel weed, the campers arranged themselves on a slope of granite to do away with the nuts and crackers and ever-present blueberries that made up their afternoon snack. Ignoring the invitations of others, Justin sat down close to Elizabeth. The muscles of her midriff quivered faintly.

Unable to think of anything inspired to say, Elizabeth eyed his hair.

"Your curls are great now they've grown a fraction and you've stopped trying to brush them into that city shape."

"I like your sun streaks, too." Justin bit through a cracker. "Beats lemon juice any day."

So she really had told him that. Too bad. She was unable to summon the faintest hint of dismay.

Justin grinned back, easily and spontaneously. His brows flared at the ends, giving him a calm, considering look. His mouth hadn't smirked in days. When he finished the cracker, he lay back, his hands behind his head, eyes half-hooded in somnolent ease. The soft lapping of the water and the deep penetration of the sun were the world's most powerful tranquilizer, Elizabeth had realized. She understood that she had never been truly relaxed until now—and said so to Justin.

"You know what it is?" she mused. "It's not having to worry about anything. We've been kidnapped for whatever reason, so we're not responsible. There's not a single business call we can take and not a deal to be made. I didn't realize until now what a great weight all that stuff was!"

"Me, neither," replied Justin. "I guess this is what is really meant by a holiday."

"Yeah."

The comfortable silence that fell bound them together in a bubble that enclosed them both and concentrated inside it the essence of the summer sunshine, the greenness of the trees and the brightness of the water. The air between them grew thick with anticipation and a thousand unspoken, tremulous thoughts.

For the first time since helping Elizabeth to swim, Justin touched her. His hand stole over hers, and his thumb, ever so lazily, caressed her palm. Elizabeth's stomach took an elevator ride to her toes and back again.

When they started out in their canoes once more her senses were in such a dizzying whirl she barely knew which end of the paddle to handle. Justin took the stern again, his eyes dark. Neither seemed able to speak, due to the throat-filling knowledge hovering about them. As soon as Suzy pointed out the cove that was to be their campsite, Justin's paddle blade paused, then veered the canoe sideways out of the group. Elizabeth drew a breath to question, then released it shakily. A glance at Justin's face brought the blood rushing madly through her veins.

Softly, the canoe scraped ashore on an island just out of sight of the camp. Justin leaped out, agile and barefoot, onto pink rock asparkle with flecks of mica in the sinking sun. He turned and stood with his hand out to help her disembark, his eyes glowing, his face strangely still as he waited to see what she would do. Elizabeth hesitated, then grasped his hand for balance and jumped ashore, too. Her heart was doing a tango underneath her ribs.

Wordlessly, they unloaded the canoe and turned it over so that its sleek bottom faced the sky, and then they hauled their packs to a little mossy hollow surrounded by a circle of jack pines. Finding the softest spot, Justin erected his tent. Elizabeth stood unmoving, knowing her own would never be unrolled.

Working automatically, Elizabeth started a fire, this one carefully surrounded by a rampart of rocks. Justin deposited a smaller rucksack beside it.

"This time I was smart enough to get us some food."

Why, he's been planning this. Planning, maybe, for days!

Elizabeth's blood sang like the waters of a stream over sunlit stones.

There was vegetable stew in a heatable pack, and a pot to heat it in. For dessert there were dried apples. Unsteadily, Elizabeth heated the water and Justin put the package in. When it was ready, they divided the contents into their tin bowls and ate silently. When it came time for dessert, Elizabeth could barely swallow the dried apples, while at the same time she was thinking she had never tasted anything so good.

They washed the dishes, stoked the fire and put everything in order. Then, slowly, Justin lifted Elizabeth's hand and brushed open her fingers with his lips. His kiss lingered in her palm like a gift, making her feel faint.

"You," Justin murmured, "have the loveliest palms in Ontario."

Opening it wide, she gave a half laugh. Her palm was rough with yellow calluses from the paddling, scratched from brush, smudged with black from poking at the fire and perfumed with wood smoke. Her fine nails, always buffed half moons brushed with pearlescent glow, were ragged and broken.

Justin kissed her fingers again and said in a voice she had never heard before, "Don't you think it's time we stopped our games and had a talk?"

Elizabeth nodded, her voice stuck somewhere in her throat. She could scarcely comprehend that she was hearing manly humility and tenderness in his voice.

They were sitting on a log. The headlands had turned a dark sepia against the slate of the twilit waters. A light breeze played with one tree, then moved on to another, softly ruffling the hair at Justin's brow. His face grew solemn, almost regretful.

"You know, I never quite told you the truth about the state of the company back when you were working for me," he said slowly. "It was in a desperate state, one hair from going broke. That's why I . . . wanted to develop that line of yours so badly."

This, from Justin, was a stupendous revelation. Elizabeth sat straight up. The small tree she had been leaning against whipped slightly behind her.

"I thought you were solid as Fort Knox!"

A ghost of the old sardonic smile slid across Justin's lips, tinged with wry sadness.

"Oh, that was just a front. You know as well as I do that in this business, facade is everything. Let anybody smell your wounds and they'll tear you to pieces in a minute!"

From experience, Elizabeth knew this to be more than true, but it was one of the last things she had expected pampered Justin to recognize. Now, in the gap after Justin had spoken, she suffered a stark revelatory vision of the grimness that must have underlain Justin's maddeningly debonair front. He had learned his lesson well in school, and it had been reinforced in the business world. If all this was true, it put her memories in quite a different light.

They looked at each other now, their tanned faces free of artifice. Elizabeth's shiny skin was smudged with bark dust from her search for firewood. Her softly billowing tresses got their body from the wind now instead of magic mousse. Justin had a cobweb caught in his hair, and a rough growth of beard darkened his jaw. No longer were the two adversaries searching out weak spots in each other. Kindness and warmth bound them together.

Talk about miracles, Elizabeth thought.

Justin's mouth sobered. "When I realized what a good idea you had come up with and how salable it was, I just had to have it."

Instantly, the warmth blew away like dandelion fluff. Elizabeth's heart chilled. Her habitual distrust reared up like a black sea beast. "Then...you were just using me. All that romantic come-on..."

Dark pain rent Justin's expression. He folded Elizabeth's hand tightly to his breast and turned his cheek away as if from a blow.

"No! I...cared for you the first moment I saw you. I also saw how brilliant you could be with just a little push, with someone who believed in you doing the pushing. You were like a superb racehorse, Elizabeth, who only needed to be shown the gate. I tried to do that for you."

And he had. Oh, yes, he had! She saw now it wasn't just the euphoria of love that had caused her to forge so far ahead. It was also the encouragement, the approval, the right opportunities provided, the facilities, the contact with other, more experienced minds.

The sharpness of it caught her in the heart. She had been very, very blind.

"How did the company get so broke?" she asked, confused.

A thin, acrid humor touched Justin's expression.

"Dad, naturally. Grandmother started it all and she trained Mom to run it. But Mom married foolishly, then died when I was six. My father did his best to run the company into the ground, all the while keeping up the most grandiose of appearances. That private school was part of it, I'm afraid. He trained me well to follow in his footsteps!"

Elizabeth thought of all the times she had clashed with him. She remembered the stiffened shoulders, the superior airs and the strutting that had infuriated her. Her finger traced a patch of pale-green lichen on a loose stone beside her while she waited for Justin to go on.

"I needed the loan I could have gotten on the strength of your work, Elizabeth. I needed your new line badly." After a pause, he added with a touch of bitterness, "We could have made a hell of a team back then."

A night bird skimmed the water, brown and fleeting. Elizabeth followed its flight until it vanished, while she pondered Justin's tone. If he still harbored resentment, well, so did she.

"If you'll remember, you didn't exactly offer me a piece of the action," she returned stiffly. "If you had, I might not have flown off like that. I thought you were trying to steal all my work and ideas away from me!"

"You didn't ask!"

His gray eyes narrowed slightly, hinting of the shrewd, hard-dealing businessman within. And Elizabeth had since played enough hardball to concede that he was right.

"I should have," she admitted, knowing she had failed to look out for her own interests. "But as soon as I saw how much you wanted my notes, I realized what my ideas were really worth. It was a...a huge revelation. Like a bomb bursting inside my skull. There you were, waltzing off to make a fortune, while I, like a perfect sucker, worked on a salary to make

you rich." Elizabeth's spirit flared in spite of herself.
"It was such a . . . a shock to me to finally understand
that little skinny Bessie Wright from Cabbagetown
could be a big success. At the time, I saw you as one
huge roadblock, trying to grab everything for yourself while you kept me down. In my heart I made up
my mind that nobody was going to take advantage of
me the way the whole world had taken advantage of
my mother. No way!"

"We should have talked!"

"That's the understatement of the year!" Elizabeth threw a pebble far out into the tranquil water and
watched the splash. "I should have held you up for
ransom, Justin Archer, but I was too inexperienced. I
just panicked and headed for the hills. The whole time
I was starting up my company I kept looking over my
shoulder, expecting you to steamroller me. I was so
scared and so on guard and so determined that you'd
never touch me. . . . Oh, imagine all the years I spent
thinking you were a genuine gold-plated jackass!"

Justin jerked slightly, the emitted a long, ragged
sigh.

"If I'd taken a minute to get to know you back
then, I'd have been more careful. The way I was
brought up, pride was everything. I'd rather have died
than tell you things were so desperate. When I
was . . . loving you, I was really asking you for help in
the only way I knew how."

"Oh, Justin!"

His lips twisted ironically.

"I have to admit that, much as I loved you, I
expected total cooperation. I never suspected the hard
core inside you. I was so damned arrogant about the
strength of my own charms. You seemed to have a

built-in immunity to men. After you left, I realized doubly what I had lost, and that made me all the more furious against you and against myself for muffing everything. Pounding on your company was just a hurt man's way of striking out to relieve his pain."

A pair of sparrows twittered sleepily in the growing dusk. Elizabeth knew it was time to be totally frank with Justin. The misunderstanding was as much her fault as it was his. She had so carefully kept her past to herself.

"I do have...a built-in immunity to men," she said slowly. "I got it when I was about sixteen. I thought I was pregnant, you see. And the boy skipped town as soon as he got wind of the news."

Briefly, she outlined how her mother had brought her up to be boy crazy and how she had at first fallen for it and then, after her hair-raising experience with Donny Clenman, had revolted totally, hitting the books and swearing never to be trapped in poverty and misery herself.

"But I fell off the wagon with you, Justin. You'll never know how completely. But the minute it looked as if you were trying to use me the way Donny had used me, I became frightened and took to my heels."

Justin let out an astonished little croak.

"And here I was telling myself that you were just another sharp little opportunist, after all. That you've practically stolen everything from me. That you were just a slick operator fooling a bunch of credulous women into paying good money to smear their faces with fruit pulp and vegetable juice. That's what kept my back up for so many years."

"I knew you despised my methods, Justin. Right from the start. What changed your mind?"

Elizabeth was unconsciously pulling up little blades of grass and crushing them between her fingers. Justin saw her nostrils flare and took care with his answer.

"Kate and Libby," he told her quietly. "The way they've blossomed with only a little boost from you. I'm impressed with your philosophy. You've got compassion. You really mean those ads about feeling good about yourself." Here, Justin paused, conscious of the delicate waiting lines of Elizabeth's face. "I have to admit I'm a man, and a pretty privileged one at that. You were right when you said I have no idea what it's like to be a woman and worry about what you look like all the time. I've been an arrogant bastard, as a matter of fact. I've been aiming at some mythical vision of the rich, sophisticated woman, and hoping all women wanted to be like that, without realizing that the impossibility of it all only makes them more discouraged. In a way, it's a wonder I've managed to do as well as I have. I saw you as a shark, but I didn't know you were all soft inside. Hats off to you, Elizabeth. Really!"

He leaned over and kissed her. Elizabeth sighed deeply and let him nibble her neck as her head dropped to one side.

"And what about you, Justin? Are you a shark?"

He paused in the midst of his depredations and smiled.

"I used to like to think I was."

"But now?" So much rode on his answer.

"That battle with the fire sort of shook up my self-image. What self-respecting shark would risk getting incinerated to save a bunch of trees, I ask you?"

"Right!"

288 WHAT COMES NATURALLY

Now Elizabeth was smiling. Justin, tempted beyond endurance, leaned to ravage the corner of her mouth. Elizabeth's fingers toyed with his untamed mop of hair. An enormous sigh of pleasure escaped her.

"You know," she managed, "this is great. Lately I've been wondering whether a healthy profit sheet is what life is all about."

"I suspect it isn't," Justin murmured, progressing to her earlobe. "I suspect it very strongly."

"Other people have families."

"We could, too."

He said it so casually that it took a second before Elizabeth's heart did a flip. Completely without warning, a couple of curly-haired babies materialized in her mind. Since she was sixteen, she hadn't dared even to think about such things. Now the idea was strangely appealing.

"You think so?"

Justin stopped caressing her nape and looked profoundly into her eyes.

"They claim that if two people really love each other, it has a fair chance of success."

"By the best market surveys."

"Hundreds, nay, thousands of families have so agreed. Consistently. Year after year."

Elizabeth paused. "What about Maria?"

"What about Kevin Longfield?"

"Touché."

Their eyes met. For an instant their souls stood naked and shining for each other to see. Elizabeth was moved by a surge of emotion that she no more could have stopped than she could have stopped the golden clouds from sailing across the evening sky.

"I love you, Justin Archer," she said forthrightly. "I think I'd like to add my bit to the survey."

Justin dipped his head and kissed her palm yet again, his eyes shut, his breathing ragged, like a man who had just been dragged from death in a pounding sea.

"And I love you, too, Elizabeth Wright. Shall we declare it as a possible joint project?"

"Fifty percent of all proceeds go to me?"

"Definitely. And an option on every single baby."

"Deal!"

They sealed it with a kiss; an aching, urgent, glorious kiss that bound them now and forever. Elizabeth's heart gave a mighty leap of gladness. Her hands flew to Justin's shirt, and she began to fumble with the buttons. The strong curve of his collarbone emerged, then the mat of dark hairs spread across his strong tanned chest. With a cry, Elizabeth buried her face in it.

In a moment, Justin had found her breasts, his hand sliding up under her shirt, the buttons falling open to reveal her aroused nipples to the wide twilight sky. Worshipfully, he caressed each one, playing so hungrily with his tongue that Elizabeth uttered a muffled cry and hitched herself up to press the full length of her body against his.

Justin bared her shoulders and opened her shirt to her dimple of a navel. Elizabeth shuddered and at the same time relaxed. *I am with my love, I am with my love!* her mind sang joyfully. She arched herself back so that he could lay kiss after kiss on her creamy stomach. His fingers were fumbling for the closing of her shorts when the first cloud of mosquitoes descended, attacking like spitfires. The two interrupted their lovemaking to slap furiously at themselves.

"The tent," Elizabeth gasped. "The tent!"

They fled to the haven of Justin's sleeping bag. With the entrance zipped tight, the interior of the tent was so dusky they could scarcely see each other's dim moving forms. However, they had no need of sight to know each other. Their hands and lips conveyed everything there was to learn. Elizabeth gave herself up to undreamed-of torrents of sensations. Justin trembled from head to foot as he slid over her. The relentless, driving force of their lovemaking soon whirled them somewhere far beyond the island. . . .

Afterward, they swam back to ordinary consciousness, surrounded by deep velvet blackness and lulled by the soft lapping of the water just below, where they had left their canoe. Curled together, drowsy and sated, they would have slept save for one lone intruder who had managed to get into the tent and was bent on getting her fill of love-sweetened blood. Slaps and blows did no good, for the mosquito was far too wily. Finally, they let the little beast have her meal, after which she rested, finally, in an obscure corner of the tent. In the morning, Elizabeth examined a large bite on the inside of her wrist. Not even Justin's kisses could take away the itch.

"Another joint project," she grinned, biting his neck and pretending to be a mosquito. "How about an effective brand of insect repellent instead of the one we have that just attracts them? What do you think?"

"We could make a fortune."

"And bring relief to lovers everywhere!"

Shaking on it, they crawled out into the luminescent mist of dawn, quite unselfconsciously naked.

Their fingers were intertwined. They smiled at each other, taking inventory of their bodies: the tanned parts, the strips pale from being under clothing, the assorted bites and scratches and the wildly tousled hair. Never had they looked more beautiful to each other.

"I do believe," Elizabeth grinned, "that we've melted down into real human beings after all. Lots of people would have said there wasn't any hope."

"An astonishing transformation," Justin agreed.

"Chaos has probably taken over back in our offices."

"Let it."

And the fact that they laughed over that one was the measure of how far they had entered into this new world.

CHAPTER SEVENTEEN

IT HAD TO END SOMETIME. When Justin and Elizabeth swung their canoe toward the breakfast fire, everyone was packed and ready for the final leg of the journey upriver. Nostalgia gripped the shining morning faces. The people grew slaphappy, in the manner of children squeezing the last twist of fun from summer camp. Slinging water at each other and playing quick draw with granola bars, they bore little resemblance to the responsible adults they would soon be forced to become. When they got into their canoes, they shrieked and yelped and threatened to capsize anyone within reach. Whenever they slowed, there were always a half dozen people over the sides, like eels cooling themselves in the sparkling water. They dived under the canoes, dunked each other and flicked their tanned calves at the sun. Led by Molly, they bellowed out voyageur songs.

The main casualty was Roy, struck down by a whopping summer cold, bundled up in a long-sleeved sweater while everyone else was sweating. Spence was on his last roll of film and growing maudlin. He had managed to switch canoe mates and now had a very dignified Kate in the bow. Sometime last night, Libby had effected a cleanout of her collection so that her canoe rode lightly in the water. Ernie bobbed up and down as if he were full of bedsprings. Justin and Eliz-

abeth posed for Spence, cross-eyed, tongues out saucily, not caring whether or not he would win his
contest and publish their pictures on the front pages
of twenty newspapers. Their canoe leaped along, their
paddle blades molten in the morning light. Giddy from
newfound love and the prevailing mood, they wanted
to reach their future as quickly as possible.

After about an hour, a fishing camp appeared, and
Molly pointed. "Hey, civilization."

"You kidding? It's only men," Libby huffed.

"Oh!"

Justin and Elizabeth glanced impersonally at the
motorboats tied up at a dock and fishermen lounging
with beers in front of a cabin.

"Just think," mused Elizabeth. "A little while ago
we'd have forked over three months' profits to find a
place like that."

Justin leaned back, gently swaying the canoe. He
had not taken his eyes from Elizabeth since they had
risen. He would not have been out of place in a ham-
burger joint, with teenagers who were struck with the
hot-eyed joys and torments of first love.

"Yeah. Now I'd pay the same just to stay away!"

They reached their last camp fairly early in the afternoon. They were returning via a different, much
shorter branch of the river, one that offered placid
reaches and a lazy current they wouldn't have to
struggle against. Tents popped up among the ferns. A
mighty meal finished off the food packs, with only
some oatmeal left for breakfast. Everyone stayed up
far into the night singing long camp-fire songs from a
tattered songbook Suzy had been saving for just this
moment.

Elizabeth and Justin, arms linked, joined the circle, overflowing with warmth for all the new friends they had made. At the top of their voices, they belted out the words, Justin in a vigorous baritone, Elizabeth in a strong, slightly off-key alto. Without embarrassment, they accepted the indulgent glances of the rest of the campers. Nestled in each other's arms, Tim and Eileen smiled at them knowingly. Elizabeth changed her mind about puppy love. In Tim and Eileen, she recognized the permanent thing, knowing it now so thoroughly in her own heart.

From across the channel, the full moon came up, huge and yellow in a hard, diamond-pierced sky hinting at autumn. Below it, the water shimmered with a long path of frosted light. A few yards from shore, a silver ripple followed a swimming creature gliding about in the night.

At last, the fire broke into a bed of whispering coals. The campers stood up, fondly bidding each other good-night with an emotion they knew they would not be able to express in daylight. Kate hugged Elizabeth wordlessly, but with a small sound in her throat that said it all. When she walked off, Spence joined her in the shadows.

On the way to their tent, Elizabeth and Justin walked out along a great, glacier-scored expanse and stood looking at the sweeping silhouettes of the pines.

"Know what?" murmured Elizabeth. "We don't seem to be afraid of the dark now. No more of Ernie's monsters."

"No more of our own," whispered Justin softly against her ear. "Jealousy, distrust . . . fear."

Elizabeth lifted her head and looked at him in the moonlight.

"Were you afraid, Justin?"

She had such a deep knowledge of him, and yet there was so much more to learn. All her life she would have so much to study.

His eyes glimmered. He looked quietly away. "Terrified."

"What of?"

"The word 'No.' Of asking and trying and being found wanting. You see, my mother died when I was very young. My father sent me away to that school. I'm afraid I learned a great deal about fighting and very little about love. It's always easier to attack and sneer rather than put oneself on the line."

"But you did put yourself on the line," breathed Elizabeth, filled again with a leaping, glad delight in this new Justin who would remain a continuous wonder to her.

Justin stopped at the edge of the water and folded her to him, his lips brushing her hair. Elizabeth nestled against his shirt, which was, as ever, permeated with smoke from the fire. In all her life, she knew she'd never find a perfume as tantalizing.

"I should apologize, too," she said after a moment. "All these years, I interpreted your anger at me as contempt for all women—the very women who were making you rich by buying your stuff. I had many a black thought about that, I can tell you!"

Justin's arms tightened.

"Forgiven?"

"Totally, my sweet!"

They held each other warmly for a moment. Then, grasping the mood of the evening, Justin chuckled in his throat.

"So let Ernie's friends come get us just the way we are. What a way to go!"

He tilted her head up to him and caressed each eyelid lightly. Then, he explored the delicate fold of her ear. Their bodies fit perfectly, as they already knew the shape of each other so intimately. Elizabeth trembled slightly with intense pleasure, not only of the flesh but of the mind and spirit. Her arms curled around Justin's neck. All the crickets in the underbrush chirped their approbation.

"Mmm, yes, what a way to go," Elizabeth agreed. "I'll go anywhere in your arms. Even back to our tent."

Linked together, they made a moving double shadow among the darker gloom of the trees, stopping often to meld into one, sighing softly in the faintest of breezes. Soon, they arrived at a private world....

Next morning, the campers assembled in the dew-studded stillness to head for the marina. The river narrowed, running between towering banks capped with hardy trees. The odd vacation home began to appear, snuggled into rugged hollows, making Elizabeth suspect that they might not have been so far from help that first day out as Suzy had indicated. Keeping her thoughts to herself, she paddled now with tireless strength. The fractious current that was growing stronger by the hour was nothing to her now. Soon, her own swift strokes, and those of Justin, brought her to the fateful wooden dock. A silent mood prevailed as people realized how soon they would be breaking up.

The bus, so horrific two weeks ago, now looked like a dear old friend waiting to carry them away. The leap of her heart at the sight of its shabby interior brought home to Elizabeth just how much her consciousness had evolved. The artificial shell she had erected for herself lay in pieces behind her. How narrow she had allowed herself to become in her effort to flee her own less than glamorous beginnings. From now on she would hide nothing and take pride in just how far she had come.

And from now on she would age gracefully on her labels!

Elizabeth hoisted her pack aboard while Justin helped lash down the canoes. She smiled wryly as she saw her expensive suitcase along with her purse sitting next to Justin's intimidating and elegant bag. All the props for a power play lay in those bags. Without those props, they had had to make it with just their plain, unvarnished selves. It had taken a bit of doing, learning to like what they saw. Now they were going home with a treasure far greater than any business deal.

"I wonder what Diana Daniels was really up to," Elizabeth said ruminatively as the bus coughed to life. She settled into the crook of Justin's elbow. How funny to think they had barely given Diana a thought these last several days. So much for righteous towering rage.

Justin shrugged.

"Who can guess? Maybe she thought one of us would just kill off the other and save her the trouble of choosing. It sure backfired on her. Look at us now."

They grinned, rubbing noses like lovesick Eskimos.

The bus pulled away from the marina and picked its way up the twisting dirt road. It was just turning onto the highway when Ernie lifted himself up in his seat.

"Hey, where's Suzy? She's not here."

Half a dozen voices called for the bus to stop, but Moose, who was driving, only waved one massive palm.

"She said to go on ahead. She's got her own way back."

The resultant flurry of questions only bounced off Moose's silent shrug as he nursed the vehicle into high gear and laid his huge foot on the accelerator.

Speculation occupied the better part of the drive before their first coffee stop at one of the roadside eateries scattered conveniently along the highway. People swarmed through the first building they had been inside for two weeks. They ordered everything on the menu. However, Molly and Libby and Kate, sticking to their reform, drew the line at French fries and ice cream and were rewarded with Elizabeth's much-approving wink.

The bus droned and rattled all through the afternoon, and the sun was setting when they finally entered the city. Justin and Elizabeth grew quiet and contemplative as they realized that their former lives were growing closer and closer. How would their businesses progress? How would the city look now through their much-changed eyes?

The traffic, the buildings, the speed and the noise all came as a shock to Elizabeth after the quiet of the river and the sighing piny woods.

"What a constant strain on the nerves it must be to live in this unnatural urban environment," she said suddenly to Justin. "How many people, just like ourselves, take it entirely for granted, without even a single idea of the toll?''

The wilderness had brought Elizabeth love and peace—rare gifts. Deep in her vitals, she now knew just how important it was to have the wilderness to go to, and how people had to be made to realize the importance of preserving the wilds.

Justin might have been reading her thoughts.

"Yeah. I see why Diana flies all over creation trying to raise money to save the Great Lakes. What I don't understand is why she would deliberately sabotage the opportunity you and I were giving her to promote her cause."

The bus shouldered its way through downtown and finally stopped beside the same ramshackle trailer office where the trip had begun. With many promises and much exchanging of phone numbers, the campers bid each other rather wobbly goodbyes.

With a sigh, Elizabeth and Justin watched them off. Moose had driven the bus away, leaving them standing beside an incongruous mix of classy luggage and well-used backpacks. Reluctantly, they were putting off hailing separate cabs to take them back to separate responsibilities and, however temporarily, separate lives. So much had they changed that it had not even occurred to them to phone for their drivers to meet them.

Their arms were linked. They were considering one last kiss when a gray, dark-windowed limousine pulled up. Before the two had a chance to step out of the way, the side door opened and a voice invited them in: the deep velvet tones of Diana Daniels.

Stunned, Justin and Elizabeth obeyed, seating themselves in wide seats opposite Diana. It wasn't

Diana, however, who stunned them, but Suzy, sitting at Diana's side, her hair pulled into a classic chignon and clad in a smart lilac suit—her perfect color. Smoothed down and without her glasses, she bore a striking resemblance to Diana Daniels herself.

"My sister," announced Diana in her best theatrical tones. "Susan Marshall."

After Elizabeth and Justin had recovered from their shock and had shut their gaping mouths and squelched croaks of amazement, Diana gave her famous sphinxlike smile.

"Well?" she asked. "Surprised you, didn't I?"

After another thirty seconds of muteness, Elizabeth and Justin both began speaking at once. Questions tumbled madly out. What? When? Who? *Why?*

Diana threw up her hands, an impish grin doing away with her femme-fatale mystique.

"Suzy tells me you were a bit nonplussed at my little experiment. That you swore never to let me be associated with either of your products, no matter what. Is this still true?"

"Well . . . uh . . ." Elizabeth and Justin looked helplessly at each other. Neither had imagined this possibility.

"My apologies if I've caused you some discomfort," Diana went on. "But the scheme you proposed had enormous possibilities, and I had to find out if either of you had the makings of a sincere supporter of my beliefs."

"Sincere!" Elizabeth exploded. "After all the money we promised to sink into it!"

Diana raised two expressive hands.

"Money is one thing; real concern is another. Good-hearted as you both probably were, I knew you made your offers for purely commercial reasons. There might be money for a while, but as soon as the usefulness of the gimmick was over, what was to guarantee you wouldn't pull out and leave me looking like a fool—not to mention the NatureWatch Association?''

Justin and Elizabeth looked mutually aghast.

"Oh, but we would never...I mean, we couldn't...for heaven's sakes, there'd be a contract...."

"And we all know there are a lot of ways to get out of a contract. Now I think I can rely on something stronger than contracts."

In silence, Elizabeth and Justin were forced to acknowledge to themselves that this was true. Their attitudes had undergone a radical change.

"You see—" Diana settled back to explain "—your offer was unusual, and both your companies were very attractive to me because they are each controlled by one person and not some wishy-washy board of directors. But I didn't really trust either of you, so I dropped you into the wilderness cold turkey and sent Suzy along to see what you would do. She got me into this, by the way. She's a naturalist; more properly, Dr. Susan Marshall, Ph.D., University of Toronto. And Moose is chief publicist of NatureWatch. That's why he always takes a nontalking holiday. Suzy says you behaved rather badly at the start but have come through like true nature lovers. I'm willing to lend my name now if you're not too angry to have me." The famous caramel eyes smiled from one to the other. "I'd like to lend it to both of you, and I don't know how I'd do it, considering your famous rivalry in this town."

"You would!" Justin and Elizabeth recovered their commercial wits enough to chorus excitedly, "You really would!"

Diana nodded and waited, the corners of her mouth twitching.

"Well, er, we were planning some cooperation—starting with a really effective line of insect repellent..." Justin began.

"Why don't we just bring out a joint Diana Daniels line and give all the profits to NatureWatch?" Elizabeth cried in an orgy of generosity.

"Sure, and let's get other corporations in on it. It could get really big."

Lost in the excitement of it, they planned heatedly, swiftly and professionally while Diana smiled at their fervor.

"Okay, deal," Diana said finally. "Now I have to catch a plane."

They shook hands, and then, emotion getting the better of them, the four exchanged warm embraces all around. When Elizabeth's hand was on the door handle, Diana's eyes twinkled at her. "On top of everything, I hear you two are having a romance."

Elizabeth and Justin exchanged a glance, eyes warming just from the sight of each other.

"Guess so."

"When's the wedding? Soon?"

"Well," Elizabeth drawled, "staid old folk like us can't just jump into things. We might spare a couple of months to get to know each other."

Two sets of teeth gleamed at the irony of this.

"Yeah," Justin continued gleefully. "Then we'll take out a half-page announcement in the paper. We

want to see every gossip columnist in town fall face
first into the champagne!''

Laughing, they started back to their luggage, arm in
arm, while Diana's limousine pulled away.

Once again they stood on the gravel lot. Elizabeth
spotted a lonely pay phone behind them. A huge grin,
rife with mischief, spread across her face. "Wait a
minute. I have to call my mom."

After much searching, she found a quarter. Her
mother answered on the third ring.

"Thank heaven you're back," Mrs. Wright exclaimed. "I've been trying to get you for ages. Where
on earth have you been?"

"Camping."

"What?"

"And canoeing."

"Bessie, you've never been in a canoe in your life!"

"I have now. Down one river and up another. Had
a tent on some islands in Georgian Bay."

"A tent! Bessie, don't tell me you were sleeping on
the ground! All those nasty bugs and things. Whatever possessed you? It rained cats and dogs here last
week. I hope you didn't get sick!"

All of Elizabeth's dimples appeared.

"In a manner of speaking, I guess I did. Weird
things happen in the middle of the woods, Momma.
Your head goes funny. You start seeing things."

Elizabeth could almost feel her mother puffing up
in her town house.

"Now, what did you come down with, Bess? You
get straight to the doctor and get rid of it. Then come
and get your cat. It's mad at you and chewing up my
houseplants."

Leaning back against the battered Plexiglas of the booth, Elizabeth smiled at the sky.

"Oh, it's no use going to a doctor. This thing I've got, it's incurable. It's what comes naturally in the bush, Mom. It's addled my brains so much, I think I've found the man I'm going to marry. He was sitting in the back of my canoe!"

Elizabeth winked broadly at Justin. Justin stroked his thickening beard bristles. A motorcycle roared past.

And for once, there was no answer from the other end of the line.

Harlequin Superromance

COMING NEXT MONTH

#262 TWICE SHY • Evelyn A. Crowe
Shelley Morgan is just starting to get her life under control again—then the unexpected happens. She suddenly finds herself the target of enemy agents and madly in love with her late husband's twin!

#263 YES IS FOREVER • Jane Worth Abbott
Nineteen-year-old Donna McGrath isn't lacking in career ambition—it's just that she has one brief summer to convince her best friend, immigration lawyer Bruce Fenton, that she should be his wife and the mother of his children. Her plans for coaching gymnasts can wait. Right now she's too involved in scheming to hold Bruce's interest to think of anything else....

#264 THE BEST OF YESTERDAY • Judith Bolander
Jody Jenson is as old-fashioned as the charming Minneapolis bookstore she manages. But debonaire lawyer Clif McClelland has no interest in tradition. He comes in search of a book—and finds Jody instead!

#265 AFTER MIDNIGHT • Ruth Alana Smith
Psychologist Alexandra Vaughn has her hands full dealing with Sergeant Nick Stavos. The handsome cop resists all efforts to probe his troubling nightmares, yet has the nerve to attempt seduction on her own couch!

Take 4 best-selling love stories FREE
Plus get a FREE surprise gift!

ATTRACTIVE, SPACE SAVING BOOK RACK

Display your most prized novels on this handsome and sturdy book rack. The hand-rubbed walnut finish will blend into your library decor with quiet elegance, providing a practical organizer for your favorite hard-or soft-covered books.

Only $9.95

Approximately 16" x 8" when assembled

Assembles in seconds!

To order, rush your name, address and zip code, along with a check or money order for $10.70* ($9.95 plus 75¢ postage and handling) payable to *Harlequin Reader Service*:

Harlequin Reader Service
Book Rack Offer
901 Fuhrmann Blvd.
P.O. Box 1325
Buffalo, NY 14269-1325

Offer not available in Canada.

*New York residents add appropriate sales tax.

BKR-1R